TO KISS YOU AGAIN

NICOLA LOWE

Autographed by Author

To Kelly,
All My love,
Nicola Lowe

First paperback edition November 2021

Cover design by Jacqueline Abromeit

ISBN - 9781916907997 (ebook)

ISBN - 9781916907980 (paperback)

Published by N.Lowe Publishing

www.nloweauthor.com

Dear Lily,

I don't know where to begin or end, I will try my best, from the start of us.

I tried so hard to stop myself falling in love with you, but I couldn't. You were so hurt and so vulnerable. If I had told you then I would have either alienated you, or I would have become a rebound mistake. Then we became such good friends, I have never had so much fun with someone. We'd go on a night out and I'd almost feel like we were a couple, dancing and laughing and heading home together, but it was just friendship for you. At one of those points ... that's when I should have progressed it. A night when we were in a club, pressed together and hot, I should've braved a kiss. Remember the night all the trains were off, and we stood in the pouring rain trying to get a taxi, laughing our socks off? You hugged me and looked into my eyes, so alive and beautiful - that would have been an ideal point to tell you. I remember the weekend before I went to Uganda, the chat we had about being brave. Why wasn't I brave that moment?! I thought it would be stupid to start something with you when

I wouldn't be around for a while, so the best time would be when I got back. I replay that decision so often and regret it bitterly.

I was furious at Cassie for encouraging you to meet Zack, but it wasn't her fault. She was right. You're young and beautiful and clever, why waste that time? She was trying to help you blossom. I thought you and Zack were so new, that if I told you how I felt ... I don't know ... would you abandon him and come running to me? You're too good a person for that though, and you felt loyal to him.

Yet there was something there in you, something that made you message me that night, was it the way that kiss felt on my last day? Until that point, I had concentrated on forgetting you. Instead, I now began to concentrate on keeping you in my life. I chose to come back from travel early as I couldn't wait any longer. When you came to see me, I knew there was hope there. It felt magical that we were back together, talking and laughing. You looked more beautiful than ever. More grown up, more confident, yet still my Lily-flower.

The way it felt when we did kiss, was phenomenal. I will remember it until the day I die. You tortured me though, the times you offered yourself to me. You were torn and again, I held back so I wouldn't hurt you. Maybe that was my mistake, but I can't apologise for putting you first. The time we spent together was incredible. Obviously, the physical connection between us was ... unreal ... I can't think of a word to describe an act that intense. But because of the bond and friendship we already had, everything was effortless and dreamlike. I loved knowing you would be there when I woke up, and that we would go home and cook dinner together. The time you called it home ... I so want it to be your home Lily, our home, together.

But ... It's hurting you, it's hurting Zack, it's hurting

me. I can cope with two of those, but hurting _you_ isn't an option for me. I want to hate Zack, I want to wish he never existed, but he hasn't done anything wrong has he? He fell in love with the most incredible girl in the world, how can I blame him for that? If the roles were reversed, I would insist you stopped seeing him too. I get his reasons. It was me coming back that made your life hard, that caused you pain. I know we have love and happiness, but I'm hurting you, this situation is hurting you, and I can't be that person.

Please believe me that it is shattering me to write this. I need you to understand it though, and do what I say, please. You and me, Luke and Lily, we could take on the whole world, grow old together and be as much in love the day we die as we are now. I know it. But the same could be said for you and Zack. Making this choice between us, I can see it's making you ill. You're losing the shine from your eyes, you look weary. I know your heart is going to feel broken whichever way you choose, and I know that in spite of your own hurt, you're more concerned with not hurting either me or him.

I want to ease that burden. Forget how I feel, if you're happy, that's all I need. You to be happy, safe, loved, healthy. And you will be, with Zack. He loves and adores you and he'll look after you, I am one hundred percent sure. So, you don't need to make the awful decision, I'm taking that away from you. You don't need to worry about hurting anyone, that's on me. I love you so much, more than I could ever communicate, and it's because of that I know I have to let you go. Please go and be happy and live an amazing life with him. I'm setting you free to be happy Lily.

We can't be a part of each other's lives anymore. It would be too hard. So, this has to be goodbye. The most heart-wrenching goodbye I could ever imagine, but for all the right reasons. If the universe wants it, maybe one day we'll be reunited. In our next lives Lily, it's you and me forever - don't ever forget that. I'll be searching for you, wherever and whenever that may be. For now though, live this life, be happy. I will always love you. Always.

Luke xxx

For my incredible family,
My amazing friends,
my inspirational daughters,
& the one who keeps my own romance blossoming
xxx

ONE

*W*hy had it seemed a good idea to come to the zoo on the hottest day of the year, slap bang in the middle of the school holidays? My nerves were frayed from making sure Ruby and Emilia didn't get lost or dangle over the Black Bear enclosure. Hundreds of people milled around, as if without a care in the world, oblivious to being completely in the way. I felt fidgety and annoyed at everyone. Being responsible for two children for a full weekend was far more stressful than anyone had warned me. Cassie, my best friend since high school, was far from a helicopter parent, but she seemed to take all of this in her stride.

I smiled with relief as I saw Zack head towards us with three cones, the large scoops of ice cream already dripped down the sides. I had no idea how he looked so composed, when I was a red, freckly, sweaty mess – Zack didn't even have one dark hair out of place. The girls ran to get their treats, and I pointed them towards a shady patch under a large tree. I breathed a sigh of relief that I'd remembered sunscreen, it was like the sun knew how stressed I was and wanted to add to it with August temperatures in excess of thirty degrees.

Zack took a seat on a wooden bench, carved with beautiful animal figures, just a metre away from where the girls sat, busy in comparison of whose ice cream was the biggest and which sprinkles were superior. He patted the seat next to him, and I lowered myself into it with a tired sigh. The wood felt as though it would scorch the bare part of my legs beneath my denim cut off shorts.

He held his ice cream out to me with a grin. "Want a lick?"

I surveyed it, and him, with caution. "What flavour is it?"

"Cookies and cream on top, salted caramel underneath. You can even have my flake if you like?"

The flake began to melt as I looked at it, the heat of the sun taking no prisoners today. Nausea rolled over me as I watched it drip. "It's ok, you have it. Unless they have a wine stand hidden around here, I'm fine." My eyes darted back to the girls, to make sure they hadn't moved.

Zack took my hand in his. "They're fine; they're having a great time. Everyone is having a great time. You just need to relax." He shrugged as he slurped at the ice cream, and for the first time, I found it irritating rather than endearing.

"I just want to keep them safe; it's more stressful when they're someone else's children. More pressure." I tried to explain.

"Interesting." Zack ran a cold finger down my arm. "So, if one day we come back here with our children, you might relax?"

Ruby and Emilia now had their arms linked together, like a couple with champagne at a wedding, tasting the others' ice cream. They had the same blonde, bouncy curls, and I could see sticky ice cream caught in the ends. I couldn't help but grin at them, but I think Zack thought the grin was aimed at him. I may have been doing a good job of pretending all was fine, but inside I felt far from it.

It had only been three weeks since it happened; three weeks since the email from Luke. In fact, tomorrow at about eleven forty in the morning, that would be exactly three weeks since he stepped away from my life. I felt my eyes betray me with tears even as I thought about it. *Thank God for Ray Bans hey, Lily?*

It was two weeks since I'd gone to Cassie's to collect my things, then hidden the Gucci shoe box at the back of my wardrobe. I'd sworn to myself that day that I wouldn't hurt Zack anymore. Day by day I'd been teaching myself to put all the events that had happened into a back room in my brain, a place I didn't have to go often. That way it didn't have to be a sharp, immobilising pain, more of a dull ache and sting that plagued me when I was least expecting. I could barely think Luke's name, it almost didn't feel real already.

"Lily?" Zack watched me.

"Sorry! I was in a bit of a daydream. Just wondering if we would have girls or boys." It sickened me how I lied with ease; I didn't used to lie to anyone. But I was doing it *for* him, I tried to reassure myself. If I kept carrying on like everything was fine, it would be.

Zack pulled me close to him and kissed the top of my head. "Did I tell you how much I love the zoo?" His animated smile reminded me of an excited schoolboy on a class trip.

"I think everyone here knows how much you love the zoo, Zachary…" I let his name play out on my lips longer than necessary as I slid my sunglasses up into my hair, and his deep, intense eyes met mine. I'd always loved the fact our eyes were almost the exact same shade of deep, chocolate brown. "You've been running around faster than the kids."

He whispered into my ear as I continued to watch the girls. "You know how it makes me feel when I get the full title."

"I don't know what you mean." I leant forwards on the bench and ran my hands up the salty heat on the back of my neck, up into my dark ponytail, damp with sweat against my skin.

"What time do they go to bed again?" asked Zack as he motioned towards the girls with a smile.

I stood up, my hand gently pressing his knee in a squeeze. "Come on, they want to see the sea lion show."

After being fleeced at the gift shop, we headed home and cooked pasta for everyone. Bedtime was, thankfully, brief as the girls were exhausted from the long day and the hot weather. Zack and I sank into the huge U-shaped sofa that dominated Cassie's expensive but homey living room. Two tall fans whirred; the cold air they blasted at us was a welcome relief. The August evening grew stickier and clammier by the minute.

"I love them, but they're exhausting." said Zack as his eyes closed for a moment with a flicker of those thick eyelashes.

"They definitely are." I agreed, as I took a long sip of the cold, sharp wine. Cassie had told us to take whatever we wanted from the wine fridge; my life needed a wine fridge. I made a note to myself that if Zack and I ever moved, a wine fridge was a must.

"They're asleep now, though. It's just me, you and a mini mansion. What could possibly go wrong?" Zack turned his face towards me, his eyes intense as they focused on mine. Cassie knew we called her place the mini mansion; I think she loved it secretly. The house was huge and located in an extremely posh street in the nicest part of my hometown. Cassie had used her eye for interior design and decorated with all the latest trends and her own little touches.

When Zack looked at me like that, it set off feelings and sensations that I wasn't ready for. My body always reacted to him, but my mind was a little more guarded at the moment. I thought back. This was approaching four weeks without sex now, which was unheard of for us; four nights was pretty much unheard of to be fair, until now, it hung between us like a block.

Zack and I had been 'on a break', then I was with Luke. I

just hadn't been able to face it since I got home. It was as though my body remembered that Luke was the last person who kissed it, touched it, loved it. It scared me to let Zack overwrite that. It seemed too final; I wasn't ready for Luke's touch to leave me.

Zack had tried to broach the subject a couple of nights back, and I'd just clammed up. He was incredible, and it was typical of him to be patient and understanding, to put me first and wait until I was ready, but perhaps that just meant we ignored the problem. Luke wouldn't have done that; Luke would have just grabbed me and —

"Lily?"

As I met Zack's eyes, they flicked backwards and forwards between my own, under scrunched-up eyebrows. "Sorry, sorry I feel crap from the heat. What is it with this country? Either boiling or freezing?"

Zack smiled and shuffled closer along the plush material. "I know. Guess it's too much to consider the hot tub?"

"It's way too hot. I love that tub in winter, when you have to jump out and leg it across the grass into the house before you freeze, but not in this weather." My mouth broke into a natural smile as I recalled Cassie and I doing this on many occasions, not just me and Cassie… "Maybe we could just stick our heads back in the wine fridge for half an hour?"

He took a deep breath and reached out for my hand; his fingers wrapped around mine. "I thought, maybe, we could just go to bed? Been a while since we had an early night." My eyes darted between his. I was still drawn to him; I loved Zack from the bottom of my soul. I was also going through deeper grief than I could have imagined though. I loved Luke every bit as much as I loved Zack, and he was gone. My love was gone. My best friend was gone. "We need to get back to me and you, Lily."

I pressed a soft kiss to his lips, my eyes closed, as the taste of the sharp wine mingled between our mouths. "I know."

He stood up and took my hand, pulling me up from the deep, squishy couch. "Come with me."

I grabbed our long-stemmed wine glasses. Zack smiled as he led me across the sumptuous grey carpet, up the wide staircase and into our bedroom. The spare bedroom at Cassie and Guy's felt as big as the whole downstairs of our house, with its own en-suite, super king size bed and built-in wardrobes with matching shoe racks.

Zack closed the door behind us with a soft touch, I knew he was paranoid about waking the children. The lights were out, but the August sun hadn't set yet; the room was filled with a deep orange light, which filtered through the wooden shutters. He ran his hand across the exposed skin of my stomach and around to my back, before lifting my cropped white t-shirt over my head. His mouth dipped to my neck and kissed at every crevice as his fingers deftly unfastened my bra and pulled it loose, letting it drop to the floor.

"This is a look I like on you." His eyes flashed with desire as he took a step back; they roamed up my bare legs to the cut off denim shots on my thighs, and the naked skin above. "May I?" he asked, as he reached behind me and ran his fingers amongst my long ponytail. I nodded, and he pulled the band down the length of it, his eyes never left mine. A shiver ran through me as my chestnut brown hair tickled against my back. Zack continued to watch me, and I bit my lip; my nerves were on edge, and not in a good way. My body still ached for Zack, but my mind just couldn't relax.

Zack handed me the wine that I'd put down on the bedside table. As I took a deep sip, his fingers gracefully undid the button on my shorts, teasing at the warm skin of my stomach. "You look insanely inviting, you know that?" I shrugged and tried to smile; I felt exposed and shy, rather than sexy. There was a moment of silence that lasted just a little too long. "Am I undressing myself today then?" It was an innocent enough question, but I detected a note of irritation behind it. He'd obviously sensed that I wasn't one hundred per cent with him right now. I knew it was true, but I needed to make him think we were OK. *Snap out of it, Lily!*

"Zachary…" I purred into his ear. "Are you feeling neglected? Need me to help?" I tugged his t-shirt over his head and unfastened his jeans as he picked me up and carried me to the oversized bed, my legs wrapped around him. He dropped me down onto the softness of the mattress as I heard his jeans slide to the floor. His head ducked down between my thighs, as expert fingers slid my underwear out of the way, giving him access to what he wanted.

"I need to check if… you were careful, you know, while…" He didn't need to finish the sentence.

"Yes. How about you?" My throat hurt with the pressure of held back emotions as I asked; images of how he must have been with her, flashed through my mind. *I wonder what they were like together.*

"Of course. Sorry, I just needed to check before… you know."

Could this be any more awkward? Also… that last time didn't count. I wasn't lying to him, I tried to convince myself. That last time… My eyes stung as I tried to keep the memory at bay.

I lay on the bed, staring up at Cassie's ceiling. Zack was doing everything right. He'd always turned me into a quivering wreck for him in the past, but tears ran from the corners of my eyes as I felt nothing. My mind was not going to allow me this.

I rubbed my head from side to side on the soft black sheets, letting them soak my tell-tale tears away. "Zack, sorry, it's just too hot in here. I feel gross." I pulled at him, urging his face up towards mine. His lips were pressed together as his eyes ran over my face, searching for a clue. He opened his mouth to speak, I knew I wouldn't have an answer, so I pressed my mouth over his own in distraction. I kissed him like the night we were at the wedding, when I was desperate to touch him, drowning in desire to know him. I felt his mouth against mine, trying to move and speak to me, but I didn't want him to say a word.

My fingers tangled into his dark hair as I kissed him passionately. The nails of my free hand slid down the soft, supple skin of his back with rough pressure. He tensed as I opened a small scratch below his shoulder, then he just let himself fall into the moment.

He pressed me down into the bed as our kissing continued to increase in speed and pressure. The dark, smattering of stubble from his chin scratched at mine; that little bit of physical discomfort was somehow making this easier. I needed to forget the emotions of this, everything that had happened in the past year. Zack was always so caring, thoughtful and selfless; right now, though, I just wanted him to overpower me. I needed to focus on the physical aspects of this and not the emotion; it could relieve me of this ache in my mind for a short time at least. I wanted him to go crazy, do anything and everything he wanted, like Luke would have...

Luke's face and a myriad of memories dropped into my mind in a flash. I shook my head to force those memories out but broke the kiss as I did so.

"Are you OK?" Zack's mouth was millimetres from mine as he spoke, his entire body pressed hard against me. The room was like an inferno, and as I looked at Zack, a drop of sweat fell from his forehead down onto my lip. I flicked my tongue across it and dug my nails into the skin above his hips as I nodded in reply.

"You don't always have to ask, you know?" My left hand began to play with that thick, soft hair of his; I couldn't resist it. Nausea hit me again as I thought of other girls with their hands in it. Why did I feel territorial about his hair of all things?

"What do you mean?" Zack placed a gentle kiss to the tip of my nose, and I felt the love in his action; it made my stomach twinge. I wanted to stop now, but I couldn't without upsetting him. I just had to make this different. I had to take the emotion out of it or else I wouldn't cope.

"Sometimes, maybe you should just do… whatever it is you want to do to me. Sometimes a girl wants to be loved and held and put first. Other times, perhaps she just wants you to lose yourself in her, claim whatever you want?"

"Are you this girl, or are we talking rhetorically? I'm a bit confused now. I *was* doing what I wanted, and you told me to stop?" His eyebrows knitted together in an anxious expression. "Pretty mixed signals going on here, Lily."

"I'm sorry." I let go and put my hands at my sides. "You always put me first. Maybe you should put yourself first; I guess that's all I meant. There's no need to be gentle."

"I put you first because I love you." He began to pull away, but I grabbed at his arm. The tautness of his muscle felt so strong as he held himself up above me.

"Zack. I love you. I love you so much it drives me crazy. I think me trying to act all sexy just went a bit wrong. I'm definitely not a natural." I pouted and chuckled; his face softened at my words. "I just… it's been a while. If you had certain things on your mind, just… do them. I'm all yours. I'm at your mercy. That's what I meant."

All at once, he overtook every part of me; his fingers were in my hair, his tongue was in my mouth, his body was on top of mine. It almost felt too much, almost… This was what I needed and wanted. With one hand he pinned my wrists down on my stomach as he returned to where he had wanted to begin all along. This time I just went with it. I didn't think about where I was or who I was with, I just lived in the moment, and, conversely, that gave him what he wanted too.

Zack stopped and pulled me onto him. We were both covered in sweat and the smell of each other now, as he pushed into me with roughness. His hands held my shoulders down as his teeth bit into my shoulder. I couldn't think; this was heaven for my troubled mind, which just never shut off at the moment. "Please don't stop." I whispered, knowing he never would.

TWO

We hadn't thought to close the window shutters last night and were consequently awoken by blinding rays of sunlight, which penetrated the room not long after five a.m. As I opened my eyes and squinted against the glare, I realised my head was on Zack's chest, our arms around each other, our legs tangled up together. We seemed to have woken with a void between us lately; this felt much better.

"Why is it so bright?" Zack groaned, his voice deep and half asleep.

I pressed a quick kiss to his lips. "I'll sort it, stay there."

I forced myself out of the bed and opened the large window to let a breath of air into the stuffy room. As I altered the angle of the shutters, they blocked the strong rays of morning sun.

"That's better, but I was enjoying the view," said Zack. I turned around and saw him roll over onto his side.

"No, don't move, I had a perfect little spot there." I complained as I scooted back under the covers and tried to roll him onto his back again. I, of course, had no chance.

"Am I just here as a cushion to help you sleep?"

"It was nice waking up like that, I missed it." I confessed.

"So, you want me to be nice again now?" Zack asked with a definite tone of annoyance.

"Zack—" I began.

"Look, if you just fancied spicing this up a bit, that's fine. Never going to complain. But if there's something wrong, you need to tell me. You can't keep stuff bottled up and expect me to keep up with you swinging between emotions. Yes, I've been desperate to get back to how we were, but I don't just want you physically, it's not all about sex. I want that connection back, that emotion. I don't want to be with someone who seems like their mind is elsewhere."

I lay my head back down on his smooth chest; his heartbeat sounded faster than normal. He wrapped his arm around me, and I knew I had to try and explain.

"My emotions are still a little beaten up; I'm sure yours are too. From the first time that you and I were together, at the wedding, it's always been full of feeling, and love. Do you know what I mean?"

Zack kissed the top of my head. "I do, it's one of the ways I've always known we're right together."

"I was petrified, to be honest, that the feeling might be gone. Or it would be so strong I would be a sobbing wreck, and you'd think there was something wrong with me. It was easier to keep putting it off, but I knew that was stressing you out too."

"Are you having doubts?" Zack gulped as he asked me the question.

"No." I kissed the hot skin of his chest. "No doubts. I love you."

"You can just talk to me, you know? You don't have to keep these worries in."

"I want us to look forwards and not back." I replied, not wanting to acknowledge the fact that it was just too painful to talk about.

"Me too. But I know there's stuff for us to work through, ignoring the issues won't help in the long term." Zack pulled me up onto him as he spoke, our chests pressed together under the thin summer sheet on the bed. I ran my hand up through his messy and dishevelled hair as I nodded in agreement with him. "You only want me for hair, don't you?" A dimple appeared in his left cheek as he gave me his cheekiest grin.

His smile lit me up and infected me with happiness as I found myself smiling back. "Is it a problem?" I kissed him, and his breath shifted as my naked body pressed tighter against his.

"Never..."

This was a million miles away from last night; feathery touches and soft kisses, whisperings of love and adoration. Our eyes took each other in as we synchronised together in a perfect mix. Everything in the universe felt healed and perfect for those moments. I couldn't remember what I'd been afraid of.

We knew each other inside out; our bodies instinctively moved to please the other. The sun was already blistering hot, and Zack's finger squeaked against the sweat on my back as he ran it up and down my spine. My hair stuck to his damp shoulder as I pressed my face against his neck. I struggled under hot breaths as the sensations overtook me. Zack joined me, squeezing my body with slightly too much force, that twinge of pain that I needed.

As we recovered, I lay on top of him and pressed kiss after kiss to his mouth, his cheeks, his neck. He wiped away the steady flow of tears that fell from my eyes with a gentle touch, the tears I'd been scared of. Tears of love, hope, regret, grief... all mingled into a mess that I couldn't cope with.

"It's OK, Lily," he said as he pulled me tighter against him and hugged me with such care. "We're OK, everything's going to be fine."

Then we heard the thunder that was the footsteps of two small children as they ran down the hallway and began to bang on our door. Zack pulled on shorts and a t-shirt, kissing me before he spoke. "I'll take them downstairs; you get a shower or more sleep if you want." I smiled to myself as I heard him pick them up and spin them around. The two of them laughed with joy before I heard them badgering him to make pancakes for breakfast. I lay back on the pillows and felt content. It was six thirty now... I'd gone a whole hour and a half without thinking about Luke.

I was tired, and it was early, but after such an amazing start to the day, I couldn't go back to sleep. I jumped into a cool shower and threw on a dark blue sundress, leaving my hair to dry naturally. As I padded down the stairs, I could hear more laughter from the kitchen. I was greeted by the sight of two small girls with Nutella smeared across their faces and half a jug of pancake mix spilt all over the worktop. Zack was by the hob. He held one of Cassie's favourite Le Creuset frying pans as he flipped a pancake into the air. I could see the last attempt on the floor next to him, which had, no doubt, caused the hysterical laughter. I was taken aback for a moment by how good he looked; it was as though I hadn't properly looked at him these last few weeks. Mr tall, dark and handsome was looking hot, his skin lightly tanned, his defined biceps visible through his t-shirt. He'd definitely awoken my sex drive this morning.

I ruffled the girls' soft, baby hair as I walked past them. Heading to Zack, my arms wrapped around him with love as he put the pan down. "I thought you might've wanted a lie in?" he asked.

"Beautiful day like this, and I get to spend it with you. Why would I waste a minute?" I smiled, and we locked eyes, zoned out in each other. We weren't fixed, but that had been a good step closer.

"What time's Mummy home?" asked Ruby with a toothy, chocolatey smile.

"Later this afternoon, sweetheart," I replied. "Are you missing her?"

She shrugged. "A little. I just think she'll go mad that you're letting Emilia lick Nutella straight out of the jar." She pointed at her little sister.

I whizzed around and plucked the now almost empty glass jar from her warm, pudgy hands. *Please don't let her throw up after all that!* "Well, I guess we better go to the shops and buy a new one, hey?" I said, as I tossed it into the recycling bin.

The day was just as hot as the preceding ones, but we were sheltered in the shadows of the large oak trees that lined both sides of Cassie's road. There was a soft breeze, and Zack and I held hands as we walked. I smiled at the little blonde girls who skipped a couple of steps ahead of us. They held hands as they sang. I grabbed my phone to snap a picture, and sent it off to Cassie.

Lily: Proof of life
Cassie: Haha! Are they behaving?
Lily: They're angels! I mean they get up ridiculously early and they never stop moving and they eat enough for four adults, but apart from that, angels!
Cassie: Everything OK with Zack? Progress?

Cassie knew things hadn't exactly been back to normal in the bedroom. I glanced up at Zack before I replied to the message with one hand, whilst he squeezed my other.

Lily: The Eagle has landed... twice
Cassie: About bloody time too! More of a sparrow here but never mind!

I spluttered with laughter, and Zack looked down at me with a quizzical smile. "I guess that's Cassie then? Should I even ask what she just said?"

I shook my head, still grinning as I slid the phone back into my bag. "Best not."

Once in the supermarket, I was happy to let the girls take all the time in the world to choose an ice lolly. It was so cold here in the freezer aisle, I lingered as long as possible.

"We've given them way too much sugar." I said to Zack, as a guilty frown worked its way onto my forehead.

"Just one weekend, they'll be back on couscous tomorrow." He winked at me, which brought an instant smile to my lips. "God, it's cold here; it's amazing."

"You're amazing." I smiled coyly as our arms swung backwards and forwards in a slow arc.

"Nope, you are." He grinned and gave me a quick kiss. This felt like third or fourth date territory again; this felt incredible.

"Is it still OK to go see my mum and dad before we set off home?" I asked. My eyes flicked between him and the girls. "I'll buy some ingredients now and bake them a carrot cake; my dad's obsessed with it."

"Of course, be rude to be this close and not say hi. Plus, I love your carrot cake too." Zack responded, which set off another twinge of guilt as I thought back to all the time I'd spent in my old hometown with Luke and never visited them once. Never even told them I was here, in fact; it would've been too complicated.

As we queued at the checkout, Zack's phone rang; he headed outside to answer. Ruby and Emilia held onto me patiently, then when it was our turn, they rushed to grab a bag each, ready to pack. I looked down into my handbag, searching for my purse, which always ended up buried under a mountain of stuff. I felt eyes on me.

Goosebumps began to pop up along my arms. I shivered

as a chill ran through me and looked around. The automatic doors at the front of the shop had just closed; I couldn't see anyone watching me. I took a deep breath, and, then, my olfactory senses went into overdrive. My mind was assaulted with images – breathing in the smell of Luke's pillow, being nuzzled into his neck, the smell of his t-shirt as I wore it around the house after a lazy, sexy morning.

My hand shook as I paid the bill. Had he been in the shop? Why else would I be breathing in his smell? I knew it was a risk being in my old town, so close to him, but Cassie had told him she'd be away, there was no risk of him popping around. Besides, I couldn't avoid the place where my best friend and my parents lived forever. My best friend, singular, that still felt strange.

I surveyed the street as we walked outside, the heat oppressive already. Zack laughed loudly down the phone; he obviously hadn't seen anyone, or it would be a very different scene out here now. I unwrapped the fruity ice lollies the girls had chosen; the wrappers stuck to my fingers as I tried to drop them in the bin, still looking around me.

"That was Hannah," Zack explained. "She was quizzing me about you, think she wants to arrange a night out." Hannah was one of Zack's older sisters; she was brilliant fun. I loved his whole family, though. From the first time I met them, they had welcomed me wholeheartedly.

Whatever or whoever I'd smelled was gone now. I smiled at Zack and tried to get the idiotic idea out of my head. Of course Luke hadn't been in the shop. "I'd love that, I'll message her tonight." He rubbed his fingers up my arm in a playful manner before Ruby and Emilia launched themselves at him, wanting a hand each. "I guess I'll have to get in line to hold your hand, hey?"

"I don't know what to say. When two gorgeous blondes demand me, what can I do?" He winked as we started to walk back towards the house. For me, though, a joke about two blondes was just a little too soon.

As late afternoon arrived, with no let up to the temperature, we heard the rumble of a car pull up the wide driveway. Ruby and Emilia ran to the front door and jumped on Cassie and Guy with giddy squeals as they walked inside; both were smiling and looked relaxed. Then the girls ran straight back to Zack; he was like a child magnet.

"Welcome home! You two have a great time?" I asked.

"It was amazing." Cassie pulled me into a hug. "Thank you so much for babysitting." Her blonde bob was shining in the sunlight, and, as always, her smile was infectious. Her and Guy both looked relaxed and rested.

"It's been great fun, never a problem." We looked over to the kitchen where Zack and the girls were still playing.

"He's so broody, you know." Cassie said. She dug her elbow into my side with a wink.

"Erm, I don't think so!" I replied.

"He is."

"What are we talking about?" asked Guy as he reached down and brushed a friendly kiss across my cheek, before placing a large holdall down beside the door. Guy was so tall and Cassie so short, it always amused me. I was glad Zack was only a couple of inches bigger than me, I could make that up with my many pairs of heels.

"Zack being broody." Cassie's voice was louder this time. I kicked her foot and glared, seeing Zack look over to us and listen intently.

"It's because he has that special birthday coming up," teased Guy, even louder. "He's probably feeling old." Zack would be turning thirty in the new year, and it wasn't a milestone he was particularly enamoured with. I was sure I'd be the same when it was my turn; I was glad Zack was a little older than me.

Zack wandered over to us with Emilia sat on his shoulders and Ruby holding his hand like they were best friends for life. "Why are we talking about something that's ages away?" he asked with a raised eyebrow.

"Blame these two!" I exclaimed. "I'm just going to get our stuff from upstairs."

I'd left the carrier bag from the supermarket on our bed earlier. I grabbed it to put in the bin, when a piece of paper fluttered out and landed on the carpet. I reached for it, assuming it was a receipt, but could see longer words printed on it. I sat down on the bed, wiped the back of my neck, which was clammy from the heat, and began to read.

It was almost beautiful fate
but we were in the wrong place,
the wrong time, the wrong state
Nevertheless
My soul knows yours
on this, I'm steadfast
Our connection wasn't forced
My heart misses yours
I need belief
that next time around
We... can be us...

I read it through again, my eyes watered up as I did. That was beautiful. I wondered if someone had mislaid it at the shop? Or was it a promotional flyer? There wasn't anything else on the paper. I wondered if I should take it back to the shop, but there were hundreds of people in and out, it could belong to anyone.

It was way too beautiful to throw away. I tucked it into my handbag with a smile. It made me happy to know people loved with that passion and intensity.

Half an hour later, we drove the short distance to my mum and dad's house. I reached over to stroke Zack's hand as he held the leather-covered steering wheel.

"Ruby and Emilia are besotted with you." I teased.

"All the girls are." he shrugged. "Why does this surprise you?"

"Cassie reckons you're super broody and want to impregnate me as soon as possible." I said it casually, but I did want to know his actual opinion on this. We'd skirted around the issue before things had… changed.

"And what do you think?"

"I don't know. For someone I know so well, you're still a bit of a mystery at times." I admitted.

Zack glanced over at me as we sat a busy set of traffic lights, waiting for the colour to change. "I'm a mystery?" he laughed. "You want to try figuring you out. Gives me a headache most days."

As the cars began to move again, I was fully aware that the question hadn't been answered. He parked the car on my parent's driveway, took my hand and placed a single, soft kiss on my lips.

"Right, let me get every issue that's floating around this car addressed before we go inside. Yes, turning thirty sounds hideous and old but… I'm with you, so I don't care. Wouldn't care how old I was as long as you were with me." He stroked my cheek. "As for babies… you know I want us to have babies. Not right now though; right now I need to concentrate on making sure you're OK. We'll know when the time is right."

"I love you. Thank you." I smiled as my fingers ran through that luscious hair. They seemed to just travel there of their own accord.

"Anytime, but we better go in because your dad's

watching us through the window, and he always get twitchy when I kiss you." Zack's eyes flashed dark with mischief. "And I really, really want to kiss you."

"Ha! You'll be the same with your baby girls if boys try to kiss them." I teased as we headed to the front door, hand in hand.

Mum had cooked beautiful roast beef for us but in an absolute disaster, with the potential to destroy a perfectly happy Sunday, she had no gravy! Zack and my dad were engrossed in conversation. I hadn't been paying attention to what they were discussing. I offered to nip out and solve the great gravy crisis. I knew what I was going to do as soon as I offered. I knew it was stupid, but I was doing it anyway. Since when had stupidity stopped me?

After I bought the gravy and a bunch of flowers to say thank you for the meal, I drove a different route back. I parked the car, Zack's car, on the opposite side of the road, further back from Luke's house and turned the engine off. I felt like an absolute stalker. I just wanted to see it, his home. Luke's car wasn't even there; he wasn't in, not that I would have gone near him if he had have been, for his sake as much as mine. I knew that house as if it were my own, and now, I'd never go back inside it. *This is ridiculous, Lily.* I rubbed my hands over my face, closed my eyes for a second, then started the engine and headed back to Zack and my parents, a dull ache in the pit of my stomach.

When Zack and I finally walked into our own house later that evening, it felt as if we'd been gone for weeks, rather than since Friday.

"I can't believe it's work tomorrow; I'm worn out." I flopped my head down onto Zack's chest.

"I think next weekend we should just hibernate in here

together. We need a bit of quiet time." He kissed the top of my head.

"That's the best plan I've heard in ages. Do you mind if I go straight up to bed now, though?"

"Do you mind if I come with you?" he asked, his voice low with enquiry.

"I was counting on it…"

THREE

I wouldn't say I came to terms with how it had ended with Luke, but I did begin to work out how to live my normal life around it.

Zack and I settled back into our normal day to day routine, and I remembered how much I loved it. Every morning, we'd awaken snarled up in each other's bodies from the night before. We ate breakfast together; we stood side by side at the large bathroom mirror as we did our hair and grinned at each other like love struck teenagers. At work, it was rare to have anything to do with each other, but there would be heart-warming smiles and glances if we passed each other in the large office building. Then it was back home to cook tea, curl up together on the couch and then, invariably, one of us would make a move to lure the other into bed. Thankfully, things felt a lot more natural there also.

On Thursday afternoon, I was tucked away in an upstairs meeting room as I looked at office rotas for the next month. The heatwave hadn't broken yet. Nobody seemed able to work to their full capability as we all felt the toll of the relentless sun. Warmth that was glorious if you were in a beer garden or relaxing at the beach, but that was smothering when you were in a busy office full of worried clients and overworked solicitors. My phone pinged, and I was glad of the distraction as I pulled it from my bag, smiling at the gorgeous photo on the lock screen, which showed Zack and I beaming into a selfie outside of the elephant enclosure at the zoo.

Zack: How many brownie points do I have at the moment for being an amazing boyfriend? x
Lily: Erm, about four million! Why? What are you after? If it's that thing you brought up last night in bed, I said I'd think about it! x
Zack: Where are you? Keep talking like that and I'll have to come find you x
Lily: Save that thought for later x
Zack: I know we said we'd hibernate together this weekend. But is it OK if I go out Friday night and then I promise I'm all yours the rest of the weekend?
Lily: You don't have to ask permission, of course it's OK. Just don't throw up when you get home. x
Zack: Definitely won't. Will have plans for you x
Lily: What has got into you? x
Zack: Mostly the idea of getting into you to be honest. Are you complaining? x
Lily: Never. Meeting Room D x
Zack: Be there in two minutes! X

Knowing that Zack would be out on Friday night, it seemed a good opportunity to catch up with Hannah. She'd confessed to me that it was actually Zack's thirtieth birthday she wanted to discuss, hence trying to get me alone.

Hannah arrived just as Zack was preparing to leave. "You look nice," she said as she ruffled his hair, interrupting his rummage through the sideboard for his house keys. "Where are you off to?"

"You know that new bar, where they make the cocktails in potion bottles?" He frowned and fixed his hair back into place as he spoke.

As she shook her head, her dark brown, bobbed hair bounced. "Zack, I have two children, I don't get to run around nice cocktail bars on Friday nights. Luckily, I prefer hanging out here with your lovely girlfriend, so off you go."

They always teased each other, all five of the siblings, but it was with love. They all had the same gorgeous dark hair and eyes, despite their differing heights and builds. Hannah and Zack were closest in age with only twelve months between them, and they were so similar - the shape of their noses, the way they held their heads when they spoke. It was something I'd never experienced as an only child, and it enforced the thought that I wanted more than one child when the time came.

A car pulled up outside as Zack's phone beeped with the Uber notification. He turned to me and kissed me, his lips soft and slow against my own. "I love you."

"Love you too, stay safe." I smiled as our fingers trailed away from each other, then watched Zack climb into the waiting car. I closed the front door as the car drove away, still feeling warm from the kiss.

I turned around to find Hannah with two large glasses of wine ready. "How do you two always look devastated to be apart?" she asked. "I've been counting down the days to get out of the house and away from Andy."

"Things are just..." I paused; I couldn't conjure up a word for how happy we made each other. I still managed to keep my thoughts of Luke locked away for the majority of the time. "Blissful. I know it sounds sickening; I can't think of a better word. Absolutely crazy about your brother, sorry!"

She smiled. "I was worried a few weeks back, he seemed worried, anxious. He wouldn't open up about it to me."

"Nothing to worry about, just a blip," I said as I underplayed it. "I baked your favourite brownies."

"Amazing," she grabbed one from the coffee table. "I'm glad things are OK, I'm not having anyone else as my sister-in-law!"

"Oh, I don't think we're quite at that point." I insisted.

"He's never ever been like this about anyone. I wouldn't be so sure," she said as she took a gulp of wine. "About his birthday. The only boy of the family turning thirty has to be celebrated. I might be biting off more than I can chew, but I thought we could book a huge villa in Spain or France. By the time we split it between all of us, it wouldn't cost much."

I totted up the numbers in my head. "That would be, what, fourteen of us?"

"Yeah, I think so. Wait until you see some of these places; they have pools and steam rooms and even little play areas for the kids. It would be incredible."

"Zack would love it," I agreed. "He loves to have family around him. Could I invite Cassie too?"

"Definitely! She's pretty much family, and the more kids the better! Do you think you could tell Zack it's just the two of you, though? Then when everyone else arrives it'd be a massive surprise?" she asked, as her eyes sparkled with excitement.

"Yes, that'd be amazing. He'd adore it! If Cassie says yes, that will make eighteen."

Hannah squealed and hugged me, before showing me the amazing places that she'd already been Googling. "I thought if we started to plan now, it gives us loads of time before next year."

"It's a brilliant idea, Hannah, I'm excited already!"

Later in the evening, I waved goodnight as Hannah

climbed into a taxi, remembering not to put the chain on as I had done in the past and left Zack unable to get in.

I slid between the soft sheets of our bed, a corny smile on my lips as I thought of Zack; it still left me stunned at times how I felt about him. As much as I adored him, though, it was nice to get into an empty bed for once. Warm and fuzzy from the wine, I curled up with a book I'd wanted to finish for ages.

Maybe Luke had done the right thing… the stabbing pain shot through my stomach in a flash. How could it be right to be without him, though? I tried to set my mind to something else. My brain focused on the complexities of getting eighteen people on one holiday as I fell asleep, ignoring the ache in my heart, the missing piece of me.

I could feel hot breath against me, hot breath that smelled like whiskey and orange peel. I opened one eye and became aware of Zack's face close up against mine, a wide, tipsy grin on it.

"Are you awake?" he asked. The mattress bounced slightly as he moved around.

"I am now." I stretched and yawned; I knew he'd wake me up. I pretended to be annoyed every time, but I loved it, to be honest, he was even lovelier when he was drunk and so cuddly.

"I missed you." He kissed me. I could taste the whiskey sours he'd been drinking; I sucked on his bottom lip, enjoying the taste. I was getting involved in the moment when he pulled away, utterly frustrating me. "I want to talk to you."

"Can't you talk to me after?" I was awake and frisky now, I tried to pull him back to me.

"You know I was with the guys from Astfangin tonight, yeah?"

I nodded as I sat up and began to unfasten his shirt buttons. I flicked my hair behind me and tried to get his attention back. "I don't know how you say that drunk, never mind sober. I've not been able to say it since they started working with us."

"They offered me a job," he said, unable to hide the pride in his voice.

"In Iceland?" I spluttered. My fingers stopped on his bottom button.

"No," he said as he pressed his fingers onto mine, encouraging me to continue with the buttons. "In their office, here, as their in-house legal counsel. Please don't stop what you're doing, by the way."

"Seriously? That's huge! They asked you out of the whole team they've worked with?" I ran my fingers through his hair as I smiled.

"They're emailing me the offer to look at over the weekend."

"You're so in demand. Also, you taste incredible right now, Zachary."

"I know you love it when I'm drunk, you always take advantage of me." He slid his hands up my sides which caused me to suck my breath in; they felt powerful as he climbed over me. His stubble tickled me, as he kissed the hot skin on my stomach. "I love summer," he said with a satisfied sigh. "Love you feeling all hot like this."

"Maybe don't go to Iceland then?" I grinned and tried to wriggle down the bed, but he stopped me, a sexy smile on his face as he shed the rest of his clothes.

"Don't worry, we'll find a way to warm it up." Then his mouth was on mine as we became a hot, clammy mess of skin and fingers and lips. I burrowed my mouth into his neck as the frantic exchange peaked, caressing the skin of his back with soft strokes as he ran kisses over my face, telling me over and over how much he loved me. We eventually fell fast asleep- bodies hot, minds happy, hearts full.

―――――

At around ten, I slid out of the bed and tiptoed out of the room, deciding to make breakfast and let Zack sleep in as late as he wanted. We were now officially hibernating until Monday morning. I messaged Cassie as I cooked.

Lily: Morning trouble x
Cassie: I was going to call you later, you ok? x
Lily: Yep, really good, things have felt great this week. Odd moments you know but it feels like progress
Cassie: Good. Girls are still going on about last weekend, they loved it x
Lily: I'm glad x How is he?
Cassie: Which 'he' are we referring to?
Lily: You know...
Cassie: You have to let this go
Lily: I am! I just want to know if he's ok
Cassie: He's coming round tonight, I'll call you tomorrow ok? But promise me you will stop, just concentrate on Zack. I'm not finding you another one!!!
Lily: Ok, sorry. Speak soon. Love you x

I sighed at myself, frustrated at my moment of weakness. It was ridiculous, but I was jealous of Cassie that she got to see Luke tonight and I didn't. As I heard Zack's footsteps head to the bathroom, I slid the phone to silent and put it in my back pocket, plating up a huge breakfast for him as I ignored the negative feelings that ran through my mind.

"What did I do to deserve you?" he asked as he kissed the top of my head and sat down opposite me. He surveyed my lonely poached egg on toast compared to his full English. "You didn't have to go to all that effort just for me, you know?"

"Well, if you have international companies headhunting you now, I figured I better step my game up in case you start expecting a girlfriend upgrade too."

"I should have let you sleep, sorry, was just excited," he said as he began to eat. I watched him, all scruffy hair and stubbly chin. We'd been together almost eighteen months now, but I still couldn't stop admiring that handsome face, all chiselled, dark and brooding.

"Well, yeah, I hate it when I get woken up by a gorgeous man who has good news, and then wants to have super intense, hot sex. Worst Friday night ever," I teased. "Have they emailed you yet?"

He slid his phone across the table, an open email on display. There were multiple attachments, but the body of the message had the main points of the contract in a bullet list. I glanced down them, and my eyes widened in shock. "How much money? That can't be the right salary, can it?" I asked.

He nodded, unable to disguise the look of glee on his face. "Look at the number underneath. They're offering a signing bonus."

"Oh my God! I don't know what to say! That's, like, twenty thousand a year more than you get now? And you get the other twenty thousand for just accepting the job? That's insane."

"I'd have to go to Iceland once a month though, be weird to be away from you. It's such a good job, but it takes me out of that law firm career path, I guess," he pondered. His mouth pulled away to one side as it always did when he was thoughtful.

"It does, but you always knew that was just one path. Depends on what you want. Where you are now, you just get given the clients and cases and don't have any say. I can tell you enjoy working with these guys, and they obviously think a lot of you to offer this. Worst case scenario, if you hated it, is just apply back to legal firms, right?"

"True," he replied. "But I'd worry about being away from you."

"Looking at this, it's, five days each month? That's not so bad. It's only a short flight. I could sneak away with you; you could lock me in your hotel room like a dirty secret, they wouldn't know."

Zack laughed. "That does sound pretty appealing. I just worry that maybe now isn't the right time. I would worry about you and your..." He chewed his lip before he continued. "Mindset if I was away."

I let out a slow breath; I felt like the worst person in the world. "Zack, please, don't let what we did affect your choice here. You're who I want. I understand if you don't trust me right now, but honestly, if you went away, you wouldn't need to worry about me. It's done, that whole... episode is done."

"I hate that I have to say this. But I'd worry that it would be an opportunity for you to see him." Zack put his knife and fork down, his eyes sharp and focused as he paid complete attention to me.

"And you don't think I'd be worried about you staying in that hotel again? Going to that bar again? We have to trust each other." I reached for his hand and stroked across it, back and forth. "I wouldn't see him. When I came back here, to you, I swore to myself I wasn't ever going to hurt you again. I understand why you feel reticent. Please believe me, though, I don't ever intend to see him again. You're it for me. I love you."

He placed his hand on top of mine and held it still. "Ninety per cent of the time, I feel that, Lily, but every now and then you just look like you're somewhere else; you look sad. In those times, I feel like you regret it. Part of me wants to know how you decided to come back to me, part of me is petrified to know."

I walked around the small table to Zack as I slid sideways onto his knee with my arms wrapped around his neck. He held me against him and brushed soft kisses against my cheek. "Yes, there are moments I feel sad, not going to deny it. Putting everything else aside, I lost a best friend who had been through traumatic times with me." I looked into those deep, brown eyes as I spoke, the beautiful swirls of chocolate and caramel within the iris, under thick eyelashes. "For each sad moment though, I have a thousand others where I'm happy. Happy because I'm with you. Beyond happy. I love you; I love our life. That weekend was painful. I don't dwell on it for that reason, but if you want to know details, I will tell you. We can't keep revisiting it though, I want us to move forwards, not backwards."

"Has he been in touch with you at all? Would you tell me if he was?" Zack asked.

"No, he hasn't. The last time I spoke to him, we agreed it was clear we couldn't carry on our friendship. I removed his number from my phone. I went to look at his socials before I set off home, more to check he was OK than anything else, and he'd already blocked me. We aren't in touch in any way and don't plan to be. I don't expect to ever hear from him again, but if I did, I promise I would tell you. I wouldn't risk what we have."

"You know that phone call we had while you were away?" Zack asked, his eyebrows knitted together in that tell-tale sign of tension that he had. He continued as I nodded in acknowledgement. "Did you do that with him too?"

"No, Zack. I can say, with all honesty, I've never done that with him or with anyone else but you. That always seemed a natural occurrence between us, much to my embarrassment in the early days." I smiled at him, thinking back to those memories. "That's purely a, you and me, thing."

He kissed the tip of my nose. "Is there anything else you think I should know? I don't want us to bring it up again. If there is- say it now."

I thought for a moment, at a high level, not wanting to feel the soul-sucking emotion of it all over again. "No, the only thing that matters is that I'm back here and with you."

"Subject done then?" asked Zack with a hopeful smile.

"You won't stay in that hotel, will you?" I asked, somewhat scared of the answer.

"Never. I don't want to. I wouldn't."

"Subject is done then." I confirmed with a kiss. "So, Iceland?"

"I think I want to do it." Zack grinned. He looked pleased with himself, and who could blame him? He worked hard and was so good at his job, seems the charms that had got me that day in the coffee shop worked wonders on his clients too. "Plus, if we put that signing bonus in with the money we already saved up, we could buy a house now, wouldn't have to wait."

I swung round so my legs straddled him and the back of the dining chair, our eyes still focused on each other. "I want to buy a house with you." Zack reached up and ran his fingers down the length of my hair.

"Let's do it then. The job, the house, us, the full package. You're my everything, Lily." He pulled me into a deep and delicious kiss; the wooden chair creaked ominously as our bodies pressed against it.

"Your breakfast's getting cold," I whispered.

"I don't care…"

FOUR

*T*hrowing myself into life seemed the best way past this, and, to be fair, with Zack's enthusiasm, it wasn't always that difficult. Three months later, Zack's last day at work was imminent, and it was my last birthday in my twenties.

"Happy birthday, perfect girl," Zack said as soon as my eyes began to open. I could tell he'd been waiting for me to wake up, like that excited child again.

I wrapped my arms around him, all sleepy and warm. "It's Saturday, let's stay here," I said as I kissed his chest.

"But I've got surprises. Wake up." He placed a delicious and soft kiss to my lips; he'd already been and brushed his teeth *and* done his hair, I noticed.

"Your hair looks sexy," I said as I cuddled up closer.

"You're going to leave me if I go bald, aren't you?" he teased with one of his mischievous smiles.

"No comment." I ran my hands down his side.

"Twenty-nine, hey? Getting on a bit." He poked me in the side.

I sighed and rolled over, my back turned to him now. "So rude, Zachary."

He cuddled up close to me and kissed my neck. "Come on, don't you want to get up and do nice things?"

"Can we do nice things here instead?" I snuggled further under the covers, still sleepy. "Twenty-nine isn't a big deal, I mean, if it was thirty, then that would be a whole other ball game. That's really, really old."

"I wouldn't know." He bit my neck and made me gasp. "Good job I'm not there yet, hey? Might not have the stamina for this…"

An hour later, we sat at the breakfast bar and grinned at each other. "What shall we do today?" I asked. "Or are we just gonna repeat that? Because I'm good with that as a plan."

The doorbell rang, and Zack jumped up from the bar stool. "I'll get it!" He was off before I could speak. Thank goodness he'd put shorts and a t-shirt on before we came downstairs.

I swiped through my phone and laughed at a daft birthday picture Cassie had sent me. Something smelled delicious, like caramel and coffee and—

"Ta-da!" said Zack with a huge grin. "Birthday breakfast for my special girl. I arranged for them to deliver it just for you." He placed a venti-sized coffee cup in front of me, along with a breakfast sandwich, a croissant *and* a blueberry muffin. "Wasn't sure what you'd be in the mood for, so I got them all."

I leant across and kissed him. "Did I mention that I love you? Thank you." I took the lid off the coffee and let the glorious, rich scent waft into my nose. "That smells amazing; that's the sexiest present you could've given me."

He took a sip of his own coffee and stroked my hand. "Just want you to have a perfect day. Erm… sorry, the coffee is the sexiest present I could give you?" he said with mock hurt on his face.

I grinned and took far too large a bite of the sandwich; the morning activities had made me ravenous. There were loads of birthday cards to open. I wasn't used to this; it was exciting. Some had been delivered by the postman, some given to me earlier and saved for this morning. I laughed as I read a cheeky, dirty joke from Cassie. Zack's mum and dad had written a beautiful message. There was even a hand-drawn one from Zack's nephews, which was the cutest.

I opened a dove grey envelope; the card was pretty. Sketches of Lilies in all different colours- so thoughtful.

> If this precise moment
> Was frozen in time
> I'd love the world to see
> How I made you mine

I had no idea who it was from, but it was super sweet; highly romantic, though, and maybe a bit inappropriate from anyone other than Zack. I wondered for a moment if... *No, stop being stupid, Lily. It'll be an old friend making a joke, that's all.*

Zack smiled at me as the doorbell went again. "You can answer this time."

I put the cards down and inched the door open, trying to stay to the side as I was only in short pyjamas myself. As it turned out, the man who had rung the bell couldn't even see me through the massive bouquet he held.

The beauty of these flowers was hard to even describe. They were long-stemmed, rose-shaped blooms, but not like any rose I had seen before. The heads were large with a few pointed buds yet to open. Their colour was the prettiest I'd ever seen, a cross between lavender, grey and blue. They smelled like lazy sunshine as you lay in a field of crops, the

scent of pollen carried by the bees- one more smell…
nutmeg! It reminded me of a being a little girl baking cakes
with my mum.

I opened up the card as I headed back towards Zack.

My perfect girl needs perfect flowers
Happy Birthday
Zack xxx

I placed them down on the table and wrapped my arms
around Zack's waist, my head fell onto his chest.

"I love you. I've never even seen roses like these, they're
gorgeous."

"They're nothing compared to you. They're called blue
moon roses and took me ages to find." He tilted my face up
to his and kissed me; his mouth tasted like coffee, and it was
delicious. I slid closer. I wanted more.

"Is it too early to go back to bed?" I asked. "I would slide
onto your knee now, but I'm not sure how strong the bar
stools are."

"Nope. No bed yet. You haven't opened presents."

"I've had sex and coffee and flowers, there's more?"

"There's so much more." Zack grinned, a devilish look of
excitement on his face. "I couldn't decide what to buy you; I
decided instead to work my way through the alphabet."

I continued to press kisses to his face. "I'm a long way
from S then?"

"A long way." He stood up and took my hand. "A is in the
living room."

I skipped through, giddy, and saw a present wrapped in
beautiful dusky pink paper on the couch. "Aww, I love that
colour!"

"I know you do. I pay attention."

I threw myself down on the couch, Zack snuggled up
close. The present was wrapped haphazardly with loads of

tape, but I didn't care. I opened it up and pulled out a pair of gorgeous skinny jeans and a slinky off-the-shoulder top.

"A is for Abercrombie & Fitch. Also, it's for arse. Because your arse will look incredible in those."

I giggled, giddy with all the treats, and slapped him on the arm. "Can I go put them on now? They're lovely. I love this birthday!"

I headed to the stairs but saw another present on the bottom step. "B?" I asked.

Zack nodded as I sat on the bottom step and began to open it up. I saw a name on top of the box under the paper – Badgley Mischka. "No way…" I looked at Zack.

He nodded and smiled. "You know I don't get the shoe obsession, but Cassie said this would be a perfect B."

I opened the box and gasped at the sexy nude heels inside, crystals embellished across the heel. "They're amazing!" I grabbed him into another hug.

"Again, maybe an ulterior motive because your legs will look amazing. I've ended up out of order, though, because the C was your coffee delivery."

"That's good, that means we are up to D." I grinned as I pulled Zack upstairs. It didn't take much to convince him to go with this. I pushed him down onto the bed, the covers still all over the place from the morning, then climbed on top and threw my t-shirt to the side of the bed.

"I'm quite liking it too." Zack smiled and tried to flip positions, but I stopped him. "It's my birthday, isn't it? I want to stay up here."

He traced his fingers down the front of my thighs, his touch light and full of tease. "How about," he tilted his head to the side as he spoke and grabbed my waist. "You stay on top of me, but you move up this way…"

He tugged at me, his hands forceful as he pulled me up and over his mouth. I gasped and bit my lip hard enough to draw a spot of blood as he shocked me, his mouth instantly upon me.

His fingers dug into my hips just hard enough to hurt as he held me there and gave me what was definitely my best present thus far. Was I the luckiest girl in the world that he wanted to do this at every opportunity?

As soon as he'd achieved what he set out to, he sat up and slid me down, straight onto him as our mouths met again. My arms wrapped around him as I whispered into his ear.

"Was that a second C present?"

A soft, deep laugh escaped his lips as he moved deeper inside me, drawing a loud, satisfied sigh from my mouth.

"It wasn't part of my plan, but we can class that as a second C I guess."

"I'm really enjoying D," I said as my lips stuck to his for a moment in between words.

"When did you get this filthy? Is this what twenty-nine is going to be like?" he asked, as he tilted his head back; my mouth instantly sought out the smooth skin of his neck.

"This is what the rest of our lives are going to be like." My moan was muffled against him as he held us together, and we moved in perfect synchronisation. The rest of the world simply faded away.

We cuddled up in the bed again afterwards. This was the best Saturday ever, regardless of whether it was my birthday or not.

"That wasn't the D present by the way," Zack said as he took a deep breath; his heart thumped away against me. "I was going to take you out for lunch too, if you can keep your hands off me?"

"Sounds perfect!"

Zack pulled me tighter against him and ran a finger down my cheek as he smiled, his face soft and full of wonder. "I never get over how beautiful you are," he said. "Oh, and you are definitely not baking your own birthday cake this year. Time you got spoiled."

"I wonder what I did to deserve you," I said as I placed a soft kiss to his lips. "Everything you've done today is beyond romantic."

"I hope you still think that by the end of the day," he laughed; a slight tremor in his voice.

"S isn't for stripper is it?" I asked.

Zack laughed. "Nope! But I think it's time for the actual D."

I giggled like a silly girl.

"Stop it! Did you take something? Insatiable woman!" He pulled me up and slapped me hard on the arse. It just made me grin more as he twisted me around to face the dressing table.

I noticed a present on it that hadn't been there earlier. I sat down on the plush cream coloured stool. "Can I?"

Zack nodded. "Of course."

The present was chunky and heavy as I unwrapped it. Underneath the paper – it was like Dior heaven. An eyeshadow palette, a lipstick selection, perfume, skin care. If Dior made it, it was in there.

"Oh my God, Zack! You spent way, way too much. We're meant to be saving for the house; this on top of the shoes and everything else?"

He kissed the top of my head. "I might have negotiated the signing bonus higher. And there is nothing in the world I'd rather spend it on than you."

I sighed deeply. "Zack…" I was lost for words as he pulled me to him, his mouth sweet and tender on mine.

"I love you, Lily. Get dressed, I'm taking you somewhere fancy."

"Are you sure you just want to go home?" Zack asked later that afternoon.

"Yep. Lunch was beautiful, but I ate too much, I'm tired. Let's just go home. I want to spend the rest of my birthday snuggled up with you."

"OK. Just give me two minutes, work issue."

I sat on a bench in the street, happy as I watched the world go by. I was tipsy, smiling and full of fresh pasta. This was the best day ever. I didn't mind that Zack had to deal with a 'work issue'; he'd been busy finalising everything since he handed his notice in. He was so excited about the new job; our lives were taking off. Just like Luke had wanted...

I shook my head. *FFS Lily, stop it!*

"Train or Uber?" Zack asked as he slipped his phone into his pocket.

"Can we Uber?" I asked as my mouth brushed his neck. "Really want to get home and slob."

Zack pulled his phone back out and opened the app. I casually rubbed at his shoulders as he seemed to have raised them up, a certain sign he was stressed.

A short time later, we walked up our gravel driveway, holding hands as we wobbled slightly, thanks to the lunchtime wine. Zack unlocked the door and pulled me to him, before pressing me up against it as he kissed me. "You have no idea how much I love you."

"I think I do because I love you just the same." I slid my hand inside the back of his well fitted jeans, but he stopped me.

"Shh. Don't." He smiled as he pressed a quick kiss to the tip of my nose. "You want your next present?"

I nodded. "You've set quite a precedent today, you know, Zachary."

He pushed me against the door once more and kissed me with rough, fierce passion; I could feel how much he wanted me. "Stop it, Lily. You're going to ruin the next present." He took my hand and led me into the living room.

The sight took my breath away. The heavy curtains were drawn, casting the room into darkness even though it was only late afternoon. My beautiful roses were centre stage on the coffee table, and the candles lit around the room created a soft, flickering glow as they spread the aroma of vanilla pods and caramel. Next to the roses stood a bottle of champagne; condensation dripped seductively down onto the two crystal glasses at its side.

"How did you do this?" I asked.

Zack smiled and sat me down on the couch, so I faced him. "I'm going to ruin the alphabet now, Lily."

I smiled and ran my hand through his mane of sexy hair. "Nothing could ruin today, it's incredible."

"That's good because I love you." He placed a single kiss to my lips. "I struggled with E. I thought about earrings. Eggplant, maybe, if I felt American, I know you and Cassie use that emoji a lot." I laughed and returned his kiss.

He took a deep breath. "In the end, though, there was only one thing it could be." He reached into his pocket; his hand shook as he did. "And it means ending the birthday alphabet here because this... this is everything, and I hope that no amount of gifts or shoes or cakes could ever compare." Zack held a small velvet box in front of me. My hand flew to my chest, my breath caught up there in a tornado.

He pressed his finger onto the lid, and the box sprang open; it seemed like slow motion. My eyes focused in on a stunning, perfect ring. A large, halo-cut diamond sparkled atop a gold band. I looked up into Zack's eyes, lost in the moment.

"Lily... from the first day I met you, that magical coffee, I knew that you'd be the last girl I ever wanted, the last girl I ever loved. I think that most days I tell you that you're my everything, I mean it. I mean every word. The words 'I love you' don't even come close to what you mean to me." Zack gulped with emotion, and I felt my eyes fill up with tears. "Lily Forshaw… will you marry me?" He pulled the ring out of the box and held it against the tip of my ring finger. I hadn't even noticed he had got down on one knee until now.

My own eyes met those swirling pools of chocolate brown, and I smiled as I felt a tear fall down my cheek. "Yes." I said it too quietly. I nodded and moved in to kiss him, wanting to affirm it. "Yes, Zack. Yes."

He pushed the ring down my finger and smiled happily as he wiped a tear from my cheek. I touched the sparkling diamond, involuntarily taking a deep, shuddering breath as I looked down at him. "You don't have to stay on your knee," I laughed as I pulled him up next to me on the couch. "This ring is perfect."

He shook his head as he pulled me close, our faces pressed into each other's necks. "No, you're perfect."

I looked at the ring again and smiled, pulling him to me and kissing him deeply. "I love you so much."

"You don't mind that there isn't an F, G…"

"I love that you stopped the alphabet at E." I held his gaze for a moment before I squeezed him in a tight hug.

"Does it fit?" Zack asked. He held my hand up to the light and admired the beautiful stone.

"Perfectly. How did you arrange all this?" I gestured around the romantic room.

Zack nodded with a smile. "Samantha from next door came and lit all the candles and stuff. That's why I was on the phone before."

"I can't believe you did all this." We lay back on the couch together, both looking at my hand (which seemed a hundred times prettier with a huge diamond on it!), lost in the moment.

"We should take pictures," said Zack.

"We should, yes, but I don't want to move from here. This feels perfect."

"It's not too soon, is it?" Zack asked, his eyebrows scrunched up in a little worry; it was adorable.

I shook my head, "It's absolutely right."

"I love you, fiancée." Zack grinned at me.

"Ahh, how mad does that sound?! You'll be a great Mr Forshaw," I teased as I threw my arms around him.

"Yeah, we'll talk about that one later." He checked his watch. "So, you look perfect. But if, hypothetically, people were going to turn up here later, would you want a bit of notice to get ready?"

"You know I would." I raised my eyebrow at him.

"Sixty-minute warning then, gorgeous."

I tried to jump up, but Zack pulled me back down and covered me in kisses. "I don't know what I would've done if you'd said no."

"There wasn't a chance I was going to say no." I held my face against his and sighed- tired, tipsy but blissful. "What's the sixty-minute warning then? What have you arranged?"

"Well, thinking about it now, I would've looked a right idiot if you'd said no. I invited a few people for your birthday and thought we could announce it when they're all here?"

"Sounds perfect. Just give me fifty-nine minutes to get ready." I grinned and wriggled out of his arms before I headed upstairs, a ginormous smile on my face.

I changed into a gorgeous, floaty Whistles dress with a floral pattern and kept my pretty new shoes on. I sat on the side of the bath and took a deep breath as I looked at myself in the mirror.

Today had been a lot. I twisted the ring around on my finger. There was no denying it was stunning. I dreaded to think what it had cost- so eye-catching. Was it too soon though? I didn't know.

There was one thing that unsettled me about it, and I

didn't want to let it in my mind, but it was inching the door open, and no way was it going to leave me alone. How would Luke feel when he found out?

He'd told me to go be happy, he'd let me go. I was doing what he wanted. *Then why does it feel wrong?* I rubbed my hands over my face and felt the cool metal of the ring against my skin. The ring looked perfect, it really did. *It'll break his heart all over again.*

Ugh, I hated my mind sometimes. Zack knocked on the door. "Can I come in?"

"Yep." I smiled and stood up as I saw him look at me with concern.

"Were you crying?" I hadn't realised I had been, but, yes, there were tears on my face.

I held my hand up again. "Was just checking it out from every angle. It's been the best day."

Zack wrapped his arms around me as we swayed together. "Just enjoy tonight."

The doorbell rang and Zack placed one of his softest, sweetest kisses to my lips, before he bounded down the stairs to answer.

Within seconds, I could hear Zack and Cassie begin to laugh. Music started to play, then the doorbell went once again. It sounded like Adam. I didn't really know who Zack had invited. For some reason, I felt stuck to the side of the bath, not quite ready to make this real. I jumped as a firm knock sounded on the bathroom door.

"What are you doing in there, birthday girl? If you've got drugs, I want in on that." I laughed and opened the door as I recognised Cassie's voice.

She pulled me into a tight hug before she stood back and looked me up and down. "Why are you up here when it's your party?"

"It's not my birthday party."

"It is… I'm pretty sure. How much drink have you had? I was only joking about the drugs."

I held my left hand out to her and bit my lip.

She screamed in my face, causing me to wince.

"Oh my God! That's incredible, mine looks like plastic next to it." She held my hands and did her little excited jig up and down. "Hang on, why do you not look happy?"

"I am happy. I'll tell you later about today, it's been the best. It just struck me that when everyone finds out… you know, *everyone* finds out."

Cassie smiled, that kind smile I knew so well, and tucked a strand of hair behind my ear. "Listen, you're doing great, he's doing great. It's all fine. Jesus, Lily, there's a ridiculously hot man who just got a massive pay rise and buys you mahoosive diamonds waiting to show you off downstairs. Just enjoy it. Or… do one right now, and I'll have him."

We headed downstairs together with our arms linked, and Zack pulled me into the kitchen, pressing his lips to mine in a deep kiss. His mouth was cold and tasted like beer. "You OK?"

I nodded and wrapped my arms around Zack's middle. Cassie was right, as always.

"We don't have to tell people if you don't want to yet?"

"Erm… of course I want to. Not hiding this baby!" I grinned as I waved my hand in front of him.

"I did already ask your dad's permission." Zack blushed.

"Aww, you! That's sweet. How do you do cute *and* devastatingly sexy at the same time?"

Zack pulled me towards the dining table, which, I noticed, was full of presents and cards now. He tapped a knife against a champagne flute to get everyone's attention before he passed the drink to me. I gladly gulped at it as Cassie turned the music down.

"Thank you all for coming to celebrate Lily's birthday." There were cheers, and I knew I was as red as a beetroot. I wasn't used to being the centre of attention. "There is more than one celebration today, however." Zack sounded authoritative and confident when he spoke; I didn't like public speaking at all. "You all know I've been besotted with this amazing girl since the day I met her…"

"You're welcome!" shouted Cassie. Everyone laughed, and I saw Guy roll his eyes at her, fondly.

"Cheers Cass," Zack chuckled and raised his own champagne glass towards her. "So, today, I asked her to marry me." His beautiful eyes were just on me now, and I couldn't stop smiling at him. "And I'm thrilled to say that she said yes. The future Mrs Beaumont." He pulled me into a beautiful kiss, which I was glad hid my ever-reddening face.

Then everyone was hugging and kissing us, taking pictures, looking at the ring. I took deep breaths to try and ground myself as I felt Zack squeeze my fingers in reassurance. Cassie asked for my phone and took more beautiful pictures of us. As she handed the phone back, she topped my glass up with more champagne.

"You want some fresh air for a minute? You look hot."

I fanned myself with a magazine from the bookshelf. "Yep, I'll just be a minute. Zack's gone off with Adam. I won't be long."

I sat on the bench in the back garden and rubbed my arms in the cold November evening, even though my face was still burning hot. There were a couple of stray fireworks going off down the street; Bonfire Night seemed to spread further and further out each year.

I swiped through the pictures that Cassie had just taken and smiled, they were gorgeous. I sent the best one to my mum and dad with a message.

Lily: I have a sneaky suspicion you knew anyway! Will come and show the ring off xx

It could easily have all been different. Yet, if it had have been, I might have been sat on a wall somewhere else, thinking about Zack. I held my hand up in front of my face again, the ring even sparkled out here in the dark. It was stunning.

I heard Zack's laughter from inside and as I looked through the kitchen window, I could see so many happy faces, there to celebrate with us. I wanted nothing more than to be in his arms again.

I shivered one last time in the cold air before I headed inside, back to my fiancé.

FIVE

I sat back in the uncomfortable airport seat as Zack kissed me for the hundredth time. "Are you sure you're going to be OK?" he asked.

"I'm not the one off to Iceland to start a big new job. I'll be fine. Just you wait, I'll have found us a perfect house before you get back." Zack smiled at me and rubbed his nose against mine as I spoke. "I'm going to miss you; call me every night?"

"Of course. I miss you already," Zack sighed, a sadness behind it. "I'd better go, all the security stuff takes ages."

I kissed him on the lips once more. "You're amazing, and they know it; that's why they picked you for this job. Have a great first week. I love you so much."

"I love you more." He stroked my cheek, his touch tender. "Wedding plans when I get back, yeah?"

I nodded as I smiled and watched him make his way through the security gate before I headed home, paying the extortionate car park fees on my way. It was Sunday afternoon, and I was on my own; this felt weird. Yet not along ago, it would've been expected. Zack wouldn't be back until next Saturday. *What to do!?*

I messaged Zack's mum, Lydia, to see if she wanted to come and peruse estate agent windows with me, which, of course, she did. I heard so many horror stories about mother-in-laws, but Lydia was fantastic! With five kids and four grandchildren, she managed to still look much younger than her fifty-eight years. Her dark eyes were like Zack's, and although her brown hair may now be coloured, the whole family had a dark-haired, attractive theme going on.

I earned a lot more since I'd moved to Caddel & Boone, plus Zack's salary was frankly ridiculous now, although he worked like crazy for every penny, so I knew we were lucky with the budget we had for our first house.

Lydia and I sat down in a local coffee shop with stacks of house booklets from all the estate agents in the town centre.

"Let me see that ring again," she said with a cheeky smile. I held my hand out towards her, and she stroked a finger over the diamond. "It's beautiful. Mine was nothing like that, and then we pawned it when the kids were small, we needed the money," she admitted with a regretful tone.

"Oh no. Maybe you should ask for a new one?" I suggested.

"Ahh, I'd rather get a new kitchen to be honest," she said with a giggle. "You've always felt like part of the family anyway, but I'm glad it's official now." She patted my hand, her affection clear, before picking her coffee mug up and inhaling the scent of the bitter brew.

I spread all the house booklets out on the table. "Ugh, going to have to narrow these down to ones we want to view. Is it too much to ask to be close enough to the airport, both our jobs *and* a nice area?"

"Have you asked about buying your place from the landlord? That fits all those boxes, doesn't it?"

I blushed, my cheeks burning, I couldn't help myself. "Erm, yeah, let's just say Zack feels we need a lot more than two bedrooms." Lydia raised an eyebrow at me and looked at my stomach. "No! No, no, no. Not yet," I laughed. "He definitely has plans though."

"Just him?"

"No, not just him. I feel like buying a house and planning a wedding is enough for now though. Plus, with Zack's new job, he's going to be busy while he settles in."

"I won't start knitting just yet, then," she replied as she cut a huge slice of Victoria Sponge cake in half for us to share. "Hannah mentioned the surprise trip for Zack's thirtieth?"

I nodded enthusiastically as I reached for my half of the fresh cake. "Yes. I'm going to get my planning head on this week while he's away. It will be good if we can pull it off."

"He'd love it. You know, with four daughters, I thought they'd be the soppy ones, but that award goes to Zack. He loves having his family around him. Feels like I've got five daughters now anyway." Her eyes were full of fondness as she spoke.

"Aww. See, it's you he gets it from," I grinned. "Thanks, Lydia, I couldn't have imagined a nicer family to be marrying into."

"Do you know what sort of wedding you want?" she asked. "By the way, this cake isn't as good as yours."

"No, I've never thought about it," I shrugged. "I guess we need somewhere with a lot of space. I know I want peonies, but that's it. Oh, and a band! Maybe fireworks. If my cake is better, maybe I could bake the wedding cake!"

She laughed at my response. "Sounds like you might have thought about it a little bit. You're welcome over for dinner any night while he's away, don't feel lonely in the house on your own."

"Thank you, I'll let you know. I'm not sure if I'll get chance to be lonely with all this to plan. I know how lucky we are to have each other and the money to do what we want."

She nodded. "I think the two of you would be as happy in

a cheap caravan as you would be in a big house. That's what matters, being there for each other through everything, good and bad. Not running out on each other, no matter how hard life gets."

I nodded as I took a long slurp of my coffee; worry scratched at my mind. Did that really describe us? Hadn't we run out on each other not long ago?

A couple of hours later, I flopped onto the couch and threw down a pile of house pamphlets, a stack of wedding magazines, and a few travel brochures just for good measure. I poured a large glass of wine, knowing that before I began on those, there was something I'd been meaning to look up for a while now.

Egg Donation.

Cassie and I hadn't discussed it in a while, she'd not wanted to put any pressure on me. I hadn't mentioned it to Zack yet because I wanted to get all the facts myself. There just hadn't been time. So, off to Dr. Google I went.

The medical side of how they got the eggs didn't bother me, the potential side effects seemed rare, and, let's face it, everything has potential side effects. I fit all the criteria- I didn't smoke, I was the right age... Would it be too weird, though? That's what I needed to think about. I wanted to make Cassie's dream come true but not if it would ruin our friendship through awkwardness.

I filled up my wine glass as I face timed Cassie.

"Hello, future Mrs Beaumont." Her face beamed down the phone as she answered, the novelty of the engagement still excited her. It looked as though she was in another soft play centre.

"Are you busy?" I asked.

"Nope, just at another party. Not even a hot dad to sit

close to." She rolled her eyes comedically. "Zack get away OK?"

"Yep. On my lonesome until Saturday now." I pulled a sad face.

"Hmm." She had a mum look on her face. "No funny business. You're an engaged lady now."

"Cassie, I'm surrounded by house brochures, wedding magazines and holiday plans. I'm like the best-behaved fiancée in the world, trust me."

"God, that's a lot of planning. Shall I come over one night?"

"Definitely! I wanted to talk to you. I wondered if you and Guy had discussed the egg donation? It's the first time I've felt I had space and energy to think about it."

"We did," she said. "He'd rather go anonymous, if at all. He's also happy to stick to two kids." She ran her hand over her forehead. "But I explained I don't want some random weirdo."

"Cassie, they're not weirdo's, I'm sure," I replied. Her eyes flit towards my wine glass.

"Why are you drinking already?"

"I'm looking at wedding magazines, I'm allowed to drink. It's bridal."

"Have you talked it through with Zack?"

"I plan to when he's back. The mechanics of it don't bother me. The thought it might make things weird between us does though. I don't want anything to come between us, but I also want to help you," I attempted to explain.

"Well, see what Zack says, and then we'll take it from there. I wouldn't hold it against you if you didn't, you know that, don't you?" she asked.

"I know. But I do want to help you, lovely."

Her eyes flicked to the right and flashed darkly. "Agh, better go, I think Emilia just slapped a little boy. Bloody kids. I'll call you soon." Then she was gone.

I flopped back on the couch. I was fed up already, and Zack's plane would only just be landing. How on earth did I used to love living alone? All of a sudden, I didn't know what to do with myself.

I put loud music on, stuff that Zack would've complained was too girly, and spread all the house information out on the floor. Then I organised them into yes, no, and maybe piles.

Next came wedding lists. What type of dress? Flowers? Bands? Venues? Bridesmaids? Budget? We hadn't even discussed a budget. Number of guests... I only had a small family, but Zack would need big numbers. I felt a headache brew just thinking about it. By the time a couple of hours had passed, and all the wine had settled on me, my mind slipped into a devious mode, and I had to ring Cassie back.

"You again? What's up?" she joked as she answered.

"If I ask you a question, don't shout at me. Promise?"

I heard her let out a long sigh. "Go on..."

"Does he know?" I asked, as I bit my lip.

"Yes."

There was silence- frustrating, awkward silence.

"And?" I asked, my voice high pitched.

"And nothing. Just stop, Lily. You have to stop," Cassie sounded exasperated.

"I miss him so much." I was in total self-pity zone now as I sobbed down the phone.

"Lily, you're just emotional because Zack's away, and all the wedding stuff. You and Luke... it's in the past. You just need time and to focus on the future."

I nodded, even though she couldn't see me and wiped my wet cheeks. "Is he OK though? I just want to know if he's doing well."

"He is. Him and Guy go out all the time; he's doing great at work. Please don't worry," she tried to reassure me.

"Does he ask about me?" I was scared of the answer.

"I'm changing the subject now, Lily. What was that message the other day about Zack's birthday?"

I knew there was no point trying to get her back to my question, she was a stubborn woman. Part of me also knew that she was right, and I needed to stop it. "We want to surprise him for his thirtieth, get a huge villa and have all his family there as a surprise. All his sisters and the kids. Do you guys want to come along?"

"That sounds amazing. He'll love it. When's his birthday again?"

"Not until February. Shall I add you to the list, then?" I warmed at the thought of us all there together.

"Yes, sounds perfect. Now, are you going to snap out of it?" Her voice was firm but kind.

"Yes," I sniffed away the last few tears.

"You're the luckiest girl in the world to have Zack. You just need a bit more time. You aren't having second thoughts about the wedding, are you?"

"No," I said. "I love him. I just can't get rid of this ache about Luke." The pain hit again as I said his name.

"It just takes time. Are you going to be OK tonight? I can try and sort a babysitter and come over?" she offered.

"I'll be fine, promise. I'll put the wine down and get an early night."

"Good plan. Call me tomorrow, OK?" It was more of an order than a request.

"Will do. Night bestie."

"Night lovely."

SIX

*Z*ack and I had never spent much time together at work, but it still felt a little odd him not being there. Anna strutted around like the cat that got the cream since she'd moved into his office, which was one of the bigger ones. Other than that, everything was normal. The fuss had died down about the engagement now, and, in all honesty, I missed people asking to see the ring. I often found myself in a daydream as I gazed at it, my manicures had never been so up to date.

Margaret stopped at my desk. I think I was just about forgiven for the 'emergency leave' episode earlier in the year. Her face was ageless, but I don't think it was due to botox, or any other surgical enhancement, more likely due to the fact that she never showed any emotion. No danger of laughter lines on this woman. Her black hair was cut in a sharp bob, and she always dressed conservatively. If I had to hazard a guess at her age, I'd say…. late fifties, but it was impossible to tell.

"Lily, can you come to the boardroom in ten minutes please?" she asked in her usual abrupt fashion. Maybe I wasn't forgiven after all.

"Of course." She stomped away. This would be a long ten minutes while I stressed on what she wanted.

I straightened my dress, flicked my hair back and knocked on the boardroom door. "Come in," I heard Margaret say, her voice devoid of emotion as ever.

I gulped as I looked around the room. I'd always found this place intimidating. It was old school. Bookshelves full of old legal tomes lined the walls; an imposing oak table took pride of place in the middle of the lushly carpeted room and was surrounded by high-backed luxury office chairs. The chairs we had for our desks were not that fancy, or comfortable. Margaret sat at the head of the desk, flanked by Peter – our senior family law solicitor. A man not far off retirement with a genuine, friendly face and outlook. On the other side of her sat Gavin, who headed up PR and Marketing. He was your atypical hipster and had a stunning yoga teacher, named Sienna, for a wife, who wowed at all the staff parties. I wondered what I could have done wrong to need all three of them to speak to me in such a formal fashion. Pretty sure I hadn't brought the firm into disrepute on social media or anything that would need this meeting. I'd brought a lot of cakes in recently, maybe they wanted me to stop?

"Sit down," Gavin smiled. "Don't worry, you look like we're about to fire you." They all laughed. Funny how Margaret could crack a smile suddenly. I laughed along, but it came out high pitched, like a silly little girl.

Peter coughed and took a drink from a porcelain teacup that was much too dainty for him. "We've been instructed to act on a high-profile case. I can't say too much at the moment. There's an application going through for this to be kept out of the press, but I don't think it's set to succeed."

I nodded at him and continued to listen.

"Our client will generate an unprecedented amount of media interest. Perhaps I could mention he likes to kick a ball about at weekends for a local, world-class club. He received correspondence from a legal firm yesterday, I can't recall the name, but I've never heard of them. This documentation informed him of legal action with regards to a child, whom he didn't know was his. Obviously, the first step will be to verify it is, indeed, his child." He waved his arms around with an air of courtroom drama. "Sorry, I digress."

I poured a glass of water from the chilled, expensive bottle in front of me, it was usually only for clients. Margaret began to speak.

"Peter will be the lead on this case, and he'll need someone full time to support him. It would be a huge opportunity, Lily, hard work, but you're just the person for it, particularly with your family law experience. I need you to be dedicated to it though, not distracted." She glanced at my ring finger, and I immediately felt protective. Was she implying being engaged would affect my quality of work?

"Absolutely. I'd be more than happy to help." I was excited that Zack wasn't the only one with good career news and determined to prove to Margaret that I could do this.

"Your normal duties would be shared out between the others, and we'd put you up to the salary of Peter's personal PA for the time the case takes. As we said, it's certain to be high profile and could last a long time. Think about it, and let us know on Monday, if that's acceptable?"

I nodded. "Of course, thank you for considering me," I smiled at Margaret. Nobody said a word, and an awkward silence settled; I guessed that was my cue to leave.

Back at my desk two minutes later, I sent a message to Zack.

Lily: You aren't the only one with exciting job news. Hope it's going well, and you aren't frozen yet xx

I knew he'd call me as soon as he got back to the hotel, like he had every night, and then again at bedtime. We always spoke just before we fell asleep. I twisted my engagement ring around on my finger again and smiled. I heard an angry sigh as Anna walked by, obviously she wanted to be noticed, that woman thrived on attention. It only made me smile wider, anything to annoy her. She stopped and stepped back towards the desk.

"I hear you might be coming in on this case?" Anna said.

"The new one? Yeah, possibly. Why?"

"I'm working with Peter, used to doing damage limitation. So, if you're on it too, you'll need to be on your toes to keep up with both of us." Her tinkling laugh echoed around reception, bright, breezy and utterly insincere. I knew there was no friendship in her. "How's Zack?"

"He's fine, he's in Iceland at the moment," I replied.

"Coming for a drink after work then?" Anna asked. This was weird.

"Erm, sure, OK."

Anna flounced away, her blonde extensions bounced over her shoulders as she went. Maybe she wanted to start afresh if we were going to work together? Hmm, I wasn't convinced.

By five thirty, I was squashed into a booth at the bar around the corner from the office with Anna, Amira, and Jake, who were all from corporate law, and one of their secretaries, Ella, who had only started work in the last couple of weeks.

This bar was a regular for the whole office. It was stylish, modern, and utterly insta worthy with perfect little booths for selfies and the biggest cocktail menu I'd ever seen.

Jake emptied a bottle of prosecco between our glasses and waved to the waiter for a replacement before we'd even had a sip. "Made any wedding plans yet, Lily?" he asked. Jake had worked in corporate law with Zack for the last couple of years and seemed to be a nice guy. I knew they'd hung out now and then outside of work.

"No, not had chance yet with Zack's new job. He's away until Saturday, and we're house hunting. It's all happening at once." I explained.

Anna snorted with a laugh as she put her glass down. "We all know he loves Iceland."

Be the bigger person, Lily. I didn't even let my eyes flick her way as I sipped at my drink, the cold bubbles delicious as I drank. I spotted Jake grimace at her comment.

"There's a distinct lack of male company in the department at the moment," Jake winked towards my direction. "Hopefully, Zack's replacement will be starting soon. Especially if Anna's going off on this other case."

"You know who it is, don't you?" Anna asked. Her eyes lit up at the fact she had something to gossip about.

I shook my head and waited for her to continue.

She glanced around, as if in a movie, and leaned in across the table, looking around before she spoke. "Kye Maloney."

"I don't think we should talk about it in here." I felt uncomfortable as the next bottle of prosecco was placed on the table, and Jake began to top glasses up that didn't need it.

Anna sighed again. "You are so boring. What does he see in you? He used to be the life and soul until he met you."

"Who are we talking about?" Ella asked. A look of confusion passed over her face. Amira was glued to her phone and barely listening.

"Lily's *fiancé,*" said Anna with a smirk. "He used to be great fun."

"He still is great fun," I was pretty pissed off and wondering why I'd accepted this invitation.

"Ohhh Zack?" Ella seemed to catch up with the conversation. "The gorgeous one?"

"Well, he was a lot more fun before," Anna said with a smile that didn't reach her eyes as she looked up to the ceiling, reliving a memory. "He was a total womaniser you know? Different girl every week."

Could I work with this woman on a case? She was driving me mad already. I had to remind myself it was just jealousy – I had what she wanted, and Zack had rejected Anna a long time before he met me. "That was just because he hadn't found me, Anna," I smiled sweetly at her as I spoke.

"Well, I bet he'll miss that life one day, and you'll be stuck at home all frumpy." She picked up her phone and took a selfie. There was nothing that woman loved more than her own face, and she spent enough on it, between the fillers, dermaplaning, Russian lashes and designer makeup. I had a feeling she was naturally pretty, but nobody would ever get to see. I decided to ignore her and turned to Ella as I continued to drink.

"You enjoying the job so far, Ella?"

"Love it," she said with exuberance. Ella was in her early twenties, fresh faced with stunning auburn hair and an innocence about her. "Did you meet Zack when you started your job?" Her green eyes flashed with excitement as she spoke.

"No, we were already together before I got the job. Why?" I asked. This whole evening was just annoying me now.

"Just wondered. I guess we all want to bag ourselves a Zack, don't we?" she giggled and drank her prosecco.

"What?"

"You know, hot lawyer sugar daddy scenario." She was wide-eyed and innocent, completely fine with what she was saying.

"That's not what me and Zack are," I said.

"I know!" she continued to laugh. "You're, like, as old as him. I meant if it was me and him, or someone else. I'd be quite happy."

"Riiiiight." I pressed my lips together before I finished my drink. I was about to stop Jake from filling the glass, yet again, when my phone rang with a video call. Not the most ideal time, but I didn't want to miss Zack.

"Hey beautiful." He grinned into the camera as he spoke.

"Where are you?" Zack's face made me feel lonely; I missed that face. Not just his face...

Before I could speak, Jake grabbed the phone off me. "Zack!" he yelled into the phone. "Bad news, buddy, I stole your fiancée."

I grabbed the phone back off him. "Ignore Jake, the prosecco went straight to his head. Just a few of us having a drink. I'm actually about to head home. How's today been?"

"Amazing." He looked relaxed, no worry lines on that forehead. "Miss you like mad though." Anna pretended to gag, and I glared at her.

"Miss you too. Shall I call you when I'm home?"

"We're going out for dinner in a few minutes, but I'll call you when I'm back at the hotel tonight?"

"You better had," I said, as I flashed my best smile. "I love you."

"Love you too." He blew me a kiss before he ended the call.

"Aww," squealed Ella. "Yep, I need to get me one of those."

I blew out a frustrated breath. "Amira, you OK? You've barely spoken."

She looked up as she pushed her glasses up her nose. "Yeah, I was just looking into this firm, they seem to be brand new. I can't see this case taking long."

"Right, well, I'm off. See you all at work tomorrow." I ignored all protests and jumped into an Uber, glad to be out of there but sad that I was heading home to an empty house. I really could have done with Zack's arms wrapped around me tonight.

Zack and I continued our old tradition of steamy and delicious bedtime video calls. I missed him like crazy. We briefly discussed the work situation and he agreed it was a good opportunity to take. I'd decided to speak to him when he returned about the egg donation idea. Everything finally felt like it was falling into place. We could do this; we could really do this.

Luke's absence from my life still struck me unexpectedly, at the strangest of times, but I was better prepared for it now, more able to cope with it. I wondered what he was doing, who he was with, but I knew I needed to stay away for both of our sanities.

Sometimes, though, I swear my brain went into overdrive and began to conjure him up in front of me. As I got off the tram that Friday morning, I headed to the coffee cart; it was a regular stop for me. My phone betrayed me by playing an old song, very special to Luke and I, into my ear buds- The Scientist by Coldplay. There was a point I would've had to skip it, but today, I just listened to it and smiled at the memory. Remembering us side by side, singing along. It hurt me. I felt like an ice-cold blade pierced my stomach, but I didn't want to lose those happy memories that the song pushed into my mind.

A long shiver ran down my spine; I shook my head from side to side to try and disperse it, my ponytail flicking across my shoulders as I did so. But goosebumps crawled up my arms; something was having a huge effect on me. I pulled out the ear buds and looked around me, suddenly feeling exposed. But everything was normal, nothing was amiss. It must've been the song playing tricks on my mind.

I had just over fifteen minutes to get into work. With a final shiver as I paid for my coffee, I sighed and walked away from the station. My mind thinking about what might have been, what so nearly was. The empty ache in my body from missing him didn't seem to be healing at all.

ou'd think Zack had been gone for about a year if you saw us together at the airport. He scooped me up into his arms and pressed his soft lips all over my face before planting one long, intense kiss onto my lips.

"Longest week ever," he said as he stroked my cheek. He picked my hand up and smiled at the ring on my engagement finger. "Glad to see it's still on."

I slapped the top of his arm, playfully. "Of course it's still on, cheeky." He wrapped his arms around me.

"Can I drag you home now because a girl has needs, and you left me all alone, Zachary. All alone with nothing to think about but houses and weddings and things that get me all excited about you. Plus, I baked you a chocolate fudge cake…"

Zack grinned. One of the hands that was wrapped around me slid slowly down and squeezed my bottom. "Car. Now."

A couple of hours later, we dragged ourselves from the sanctuary of our bed, reunited in every sense of the word. Despite the cold weather outside, the house felt toasty warm as heat surged from the radiators. We snuggled up on the couch with our favourite wine, Zack just in shorts and me in one of his t-shirts. I knew my long hair was wild and messy, but it fitted the moment. I ran my fingers through Zack's thick, dark hair as we talked, trying to get it back into his usual style. I may have been a little overzealous with my treatment of it while we were in bed.

"Did you miss me or my hair?"

"I missed all of you. Felt like a long week, *but* it sounds like you loved it. So excited for you that the job's going well."

"Not just mine. You looking forward to being on this case you told me about?"

I nodded as I placed my wine glass down and snuggled my head against the warm, smooth skin of his chest. "It all sounds quite exciting. Definitely more stimulating than office rotas and dictation. I just wish Anna wasn't on the case too, but apart from that, yeah, I'm eager to learn more."

"Don't let her put you off, she's more interested in herself than anyone else. Was surprised you were in a bar with her, to be honest."

"Ha! Me too. She caught me at a weak moment. She was going on about what a womaniser you used to be and how I made you dull." I made the comment light heartedly, but I secretly hoped for information. Was he the type of guy who had a different girl every week before me? I couldn't imagine it; all he'd ever wanted was to settle down since the day we'd met.

"She doesn't know what she's talking about. I wouldn't worry. She's only happy when she's looking at herself or gossiping about someone," he said.

"Hmm, I suppose. I booked us three house appointments for tomorrow, you want to see where?"

"No, I trust you to have picked the good ones." He placed a kiss to the top of my head. "You think about wedding stuff at all?"

"A little. I spent quite a bit of time with your mum, and Hannah nipped in too."

He squeezed me tighter. "Makes me happy that you guys all spend time together."

"They're all so lovely. I see where you get it from. What do you think about wedding plans?" I asked.

"I'd go with any plan as long as you were there; I love you."

"I love you too," I grinned and kissed him; I meant every word. "I wanted to talk about something, though." Zack's body went rigid for a moment.

"Lily, please don't say this is something awful again."

"What? No," I laughed and kissed around Zack's neck. "You know the problems Cassie is having?"

Zack nodded as he squeezed my waist and held me tight against him.

"Well, she asked me about egg donation."

"OK, I don't understand the whole situation, but I guess that could work for them?"

"Specifically my eggs, Zack."

He drew in a breath. "Well… yours are spoken for, aren't they? I assume you told her that?"

"No, I told her we'd talk about it; it's a fairly simple procedure."

"Why would she want your eggs? I don't get that, it's weird."

I sighed as I spoke. "I felt the same, initially, but she doesn't want a random person doing it for money or whatever. And she likes my DNA."

"Again, we have plans for your DNA, my darling." Zack snuggled up close and pulled my thigh over his own. "As soon as possible, I think."

"There's no reason I couldn't do both," I suggested.

Zack pulled his head back and looked at me, a sudden tension in the air. "You're serious, aren't you?"

I nodded. "She's heartbroken, Zack. If you could fix that for your best friend, you would."

"That depends. She'd have your baby? It would be running around with all your genes and stuff; you'd be ok with that?"

"For a start, babies don't run…"

"You know what I mean. It'd be yours and Guy's baby; that's not going to be normal, is it?"

"It would be Guy and Cassie's baby," I said.

"But it wouldn't be, Lily. We'd all know. You'd end up not friends, I'm sure. She can get an egg donor, it's not up to you to fix this. She's already got two kids anyway."

"I know it's not, but she's my best friend, and if I can find a solution to something for her—" I began to say.

"Do you not think we've had enough best friend trauma?" Zack's eyebrows were bundled up together above darkened eyes.

"Zack… please don't." I sat up and grabbed my drink from the table. "It's not a bad thing to want to help my friend."

He sat up behind me and wrapped his arms around me as he pressed his face to my hair. "I know. You just want to be lovely. But I thought we said we were going to focus on us?"

"I do want to focus on us." My voice shook as I spoke; I couldn't stop it.

"I want us to move into our new house, get married, have babies, be happy ever after. Wasn't planning on a half-sibling running around too."

"It wouldn't be like that…"

He stroked his hands down my arms. "Come on, first night back together, let's not spend it talking about this. We've got plans to make."

I leaned back against his warm chest as he slid his hands

inside my t-shirt, and I felt his fingers trace over the curve of my hips. He obviously felt like working the tension off.

"So, I know we said house first," Zack began. "But what kind of wedding do you want?"

I twisted around and placed a gentle kiss on his chest. "I don't know. I guess girls are meant to plan it out from the age of seven or whatever, but I never did."

"Let's start with the basics then. Church?"

"Hmm, I'd rather not," I said.

"Here or abroad?"

"Here, or else we couldn't invite everyone."

"A big wedding then?" Zack asked.

"Yeah, how could we not?" I grinned with pure excitement, but my mind was still on Cassie. "Maybe not as big as that castle, but there's a lot of people to invite."

"We'll have to make a list."

"It doesn't seem fair to Cassie, though," I sighed again as I returned to the previous conversation, unable to stop myself.

Zack pulled his arms away from me and pinched at the bridge of his nose.

"You know, sometimes it feels like you just don't want us to move forwards. There's always an excuse."

"What do you mean?"

"I'm doing everything I can to try and build our future here, and at the point I'm thinking it would be right to try for a baby, you want to put that at risk by going through a procedure you don't need to make someone else happy. Even though she has other ways to solve it."

"Zack, that's horrible." I clambered off him, furious.

"No, it's just true," he muttered as he took a drink. "Maybe I should've stayed at work…"

"What the… I can't speak to you when you're like this."

He shrugged, in a petulant mood now as he reached for the remote and flicked between channels. "It's a decision we should make together; I wouldn't go and be a sperm donor without checking with you."

"Cassie is heartbroken about this. If it was donating blood, or something like that, you wouldn't mind."

"It's a bit different, Lily, you know that."

I slouched out of the room and headed up to bed, wondering if he'd stop me – he didn't.

I sat on the bed and got my phone out to message Cassie, then realised I couldn't. I couldn't tell her we'd fallen out about this. I scrolled through my contacts- apart from family and work colleagues, it was, sadly, bare. A friend to talk this through with would be lovely. A friend, who, if he was in this position with me, would put other people first before his own desires.

"I miss you so much." I whispered the words into the air around me, as if by chance a breeze might catch them and carry them to him.

I straightened the sheets that were strewn all over the bed from earlier and pictured Luke as I did so. His beautiful face, his vivid blue eyes, that blonde hair that suited him whether tidy for work, or messy at weekends. His body- I'd never touched a body so fit, so muscular, before. Zack wasn't exactly a slob, but Luke was in a different league, and I knew from experience the yoga positions he could stretch into. I realised I spent too much time forcing myself not to think of him. I needed to stop that before I couldn't conjure these images anymore. I felt afraid at the idea of not being able to picture him.

I watched myself in the mirror as I brushed my teeth and imagined Luke stood next to me brushing his as we'd done so many times. I changed into pyjamas and slid under the covers. The television downstairs was noisy, but I blanked it out. Wrapping my arms around my pillow, I cuddled it close to me. Pressing my face into it, I imagined I was pressed against Luke as my tears soaked into the soft material.

I knew I couldn't be with him but just to have him back as my friend would be enough. This hole in me wasn't healing, no matter how much time passed; that thought terrified me.

EIGHT

Zack was still deep in a dream when I woke up the next day. His face looked serene, totally opposed to what I'd seen last night. I loved to watch his face while he slept. It had been a habit since day one, but today, I felt sad as I took him in. I knew his points were valid; I got his worries, but he didn't see Cassie heartbroken the way I did.

I wrapped an arm around him and lay my head against his chest, listening to his heart thump as he slept. His skin smelled clean and warm, very inviting actually. I began to press soft kisses around his collar bone and up to his neck. I wanted to make up and not start the day on a bad note.

He stretched, and his arms instantly sought me out. "It's good to wake up with you again. I didn't like waking up alone."

I wriggled up his body and felt his response as I pressed my lips to his. "I'm sorry about last night."

"Me too." He pulled me closer as he kissed me deeper. "Tell me more about the work thing; that sounded like good news."

"Are you serious?" I grinned at him. "Get me all involved in your nakedness and then want to talk about work?"

"You're not that far off naked yourself," he teased as he pulled at my light pyjamas.

"Well, I missed you pretty bad, I mean… those phone calls were nice but not quite up to the real deal." I ran my fingers through his hair and kissed his neck. "And you did buy me this beautiful ring- gives me ideas about you every time I look at it."

He took hold of my hands. "Stop trying to distract me, and tell me about work."

I sighed and rolled to the side of him. "You know, there was a time you were desperate to get me like this."

"I'll deal with you in five minutes, I just want to know about how amazing my fiancée is doing at work." He wrapped his arms around me once again; his hand rubbed in slow circles across my bottom as he spoke. "The quicker you tell me, the quicker my hands move."

I sucked a deep breath in. "It's top secret, you get that, yeah?"

"Erm, you remember what my job is, Lily?"

I slapped him across the arm, playfully. "You've heard of Kye Maloney?"

"Is that a serious question? Top goal scorer last season."

"Sorry, football geek." I wriggled up, forcing his hand lower, but he moved it straight away. "Didn't know he had a kid with this woman, court papers land on his doorstep about child maintenance, and she wants a *lot*. They're trying to get it kept out of the press, but Peter doesn't think they will." I ran my hand further down and teased my fingers along his hip.

He grabbed my hand and kissed the tip of my nose. "Rest of the story. Control yourself, woman."

I sighed with frustration. "Peter's leading the case, and they want me to be full time on it, with Anna, of course. I get extra money, and they'll get other people to cover my normal duties. You think I should do it?"

"You should definitely do it, it's an amazing opportunity. Which firm are they up against? Have they had DNA tests done?"

"Stop trying to talk dirty to me with the DNA." I flicked my tongue against his skin, which was warm against me. "It's a new firm that nobody has heard of. DNA tests should be back Monday. Kye wants to countersue, for custody, and there's some stuff about having had his child kept from him. Are we done with the work chat?"

Zack flipped me over and pressed his whole body against mine as he kissed me; his tongue rolled over mine for a moment. "I love you; we're so done with the work chat."

———

Monday morning rolled around too quickly as always. I headed to Margaret's office as soon as I'd finished absorbing that first, hallowed coffee.

She looked up as I entered. Was there almost a smile there? Impossible to tell with Margaret's unmoving face.

"Have you got five minutes?" I asked.

"Literally, five. Have you made a decision?"

"Yes, I'm in. I'd love to work on the case." I smiled as I spoke, but she didn't seem to particularly appreciate it.

"Brilliant. Take an early lunch. We're meeting at one, and it's likely to be for the rest of the day." She shuffled paperwork around and picked up her phone; I was obviously dismissed.

I messaged Zack to let him know the deal was sealed but didn't expect to hear back as it was his first day in the city centre office of his new job. My phone did beep with a message as I looked at it, however.

Cassie: Hello. You feel better now you're reunited?!
Lily: What is the fascination with my sex life?
Cassie: Hah! You just sounded glum last week.
Lily: He's definitely un-glummed me
Cassie: That sounds gross. I know it's short notice but fancy a resurrection of our Monday night tradition? I'll drive over to you?
Lily: Sounds perfect, miss you. Come to the house around seven thirty?
Cassie: It's a date, you better put out woman

At exactly one o'clock, I stepped into the intimidating board-room, which had been taken over as the headquarters for this case. A lot had happened since last week. The DNA test had confirmed this was, in fact, Kye's child, the media block had been refused, and the case was expected to become common knowledge in the evening news.

There was an air of anticipation in the room, an electric feeling as documents were handed to me to be copied for everyone. Paper and digital versions of every item for each of us, which seemed wasteful. I knew what the paperwork for a case like this would be like.

As I waited for the computer to spring to life, I glanced over the outline. Listening to all the legal jargon and knowing what the eye-watering bill would be, it was easy to forget that at the centre of this was an innocent child.

It seemed the mum was a part-time shop worker, juggling single parenting with everything else. Not a WAG or a celebrity like I'd expected. She'd fallen pregnant after a one-night stand three years ago, before Kye was famous. He'd never known, until now. The cynical side of me wondered if she was only coming forwards now because he was a millionaire – but her version was that she just couldn't manage financially anymore and needed support.

Now, though, a whole other barrel of worms had been opened up as Kye was taking action over being kept in the dark about his child. Kye had millions, literal millions, to pay us to represent him. The mother, Holly, would not have matching resources. It saddened me, but I knew how these cases went- money talked in law.

I flicked through the rest of the paperwork absentmindedly until I froze on the original documentation sent by the other side. The logo was new. The name was new. The address wasn't new.

Adamson Hughes Family Law.

I grabbed my keyboard and Googled it. *Crap! Seriously? Of all the firms.*

It wasn't a new firm at all. It was an old firm with a change of partner. A very familiar firm. Mr Draper must've finally retired, and that meant... Luke would be as surprised as me. When the paperwork was sent to Kye, they wouldn't have known he would instruct this firm to represent him.

"Lily!" Anna's voice screeched across the office. "What are you doing? We need more coffee."

I grimaced. I wanted to slap her already. Nobody else spoke to the secretarial staff like she did, and she saved the worst for me, every time.

My fingers trembled as I made the drinks. It wasn't a total disaster, it could be Hughes rather than Adamson representing, and I wouldn't see them anyway, I was just admin and support. Luke wouldn't even see my name on any documents, most likely. I wasn't important enough to be named. I would need to speak to the secretary on their side fairly often... *Why did this have to happen now?*

I sighed as I looked up to the ceiling. Zack would flip. Between this and the egg donation issue, he would not be a happy fiancé. In some ways, the last six months had been incredible for us, but it worried me how he acted at times, like I had to do what he said. It wasn't often though, the rest of the time he was an absolute sweetheart, and I guess it wasn't that weird to not want me to have an unnecessary medical procedure.

I carried the drinks through in a daze, wondering the whole time- should I even tell Zack? I couldn't get out of this work now. To tell him would stress him out for no reason. No reason at all. Except... if he found out later, he'd think I hid it on purpose.

Ugh, why was nothing ever straightforward?!

And now, I was thinking about Luke... I wasn't meant to think about him. *So pretty though.*

The afternoon dragged in a steady flow of admin tasks. Just as I was about to leave the office and head home, Anna shouted to me.

"Lily, can you be in half an hour early tomorrow?" There was a distinct lack of please in that sentence.

"Of course." I forced a sweet smile as I spoke, my jaw too rigid. She was going to make this whole case difficult, I could tell.

Cassie enveloped me in a loving hug as soon as I opened the door that evening.

"I haven't seen you in forever!" she exclaimed.

"Or, alternatively, a couple of weeks?" I said, raising an eyebrow with a laugh.

"I'm starved," she said. "Shall I just say hi to Zack, and we'll go straight out?"

"Oh, he's on the phone, new job and all that," I shrugged as I grabbed my bag and keys. He was on the phone, but he would have given her a wave. I just didn't want any awkwardness.

Half an hour later, we were sat in the window of a gorgeous

little Italian place as we split a pizza with the thinnest, crispiest base. I had a beautiful, Italian white wine; Cassie had to make do with lime and soda before her drive home.

I felt like I couldn't quite keep up with my own breaths, they were so fast with nerves. Cassie and I caught up on news about jobs and houses and kids and everything under the sun like we normally did. But I needed to tell her about Zack's reaction, and I also wondered if I should I tell her about this case?

"So, you know I said I'd speak to Zack about the egg donation idea?"

Cassie nodded, unable to hide the fact that her eyes lit up in anticipation.

"He's really not a fan…"

She reached across the table and took hold of my hand. "It's OK, I get it. I don't want to cause issues between you two."

"It's not OK though, Cassie. He's doing that thing again where he acts like he owns me. I want to help you, and he should support that," I sighed and knocked back a glug of wine.

"What reasons did he have?" Her voice had a tiny shake to it as she asked the question.

"That he wants us to try for a baby soon and is worried about the procedure and any potential impact it could have. He also thinks knowing it was half my child would cause problems with our friendship." I pointed between Cassie and myself. "I said I wouldn't be thinking of it as half my child, but he had his mind made up."

"I'll just look into the anonymous donors again. There'll be other places I can look into, try and figure what I'm getting. It's an egg, at the end of the day, I'm not going to have the family round for tea. Thank you for even considering it."

"Look into it, Cass, but as far as I'm concerned, this isn't over. He can't just tell me what I can and can't do."

"It sounds like he's thinking of your future."

"Pretty sure he's thinking of *his* future…" I said with a sigh.

"Lily, the last thing I want is to cause a rift between you two when you're back on track."

"It's him causing a rift, not you. Anyway, how are things back at home? Much changed in town?"

She chewed on her lip as she looked at me. "Such as? There's a new corner shop. Couple more coffee shops. You after some specific information here?"

"Erm. No. Just… wondered."

She wiped her mouth and threw the cloth napkin onto her plate. "They made him a partner. There was a huge debate about the name because it should, technically, be Hughes & Adamson, but everyone thought Adamson Hughes sounded better. He's doing really well, and that's all you're getting from me."

I raised a hand and gestured to my glass as the waiter spotted me. I needed another wine, a big one.

"Lily, how long are you going to do this for?" Cassie asked. "You're getting married, you're buying a house, you're both doing amazing at work. You and Zack have a life that people would kill for."

"I can just be asking after an old friend, you know."

"But I can see in your eyes that you're not."

"Six months isn't long, Cassie, I'm getting there."

"Are you having doubts?" she asked.

I shook my head slowly. "I still feel like I'd be too scared to be with Luke. He was right; this is the best way."

"Let's talk about wedding dresses then!" she said, with a smile as wide as they come. "You're going to be stunning."

"I need to tell you something first…" My voice wasn't far above a whisper.

She narrowed her eyes, almost imperceptibly, as she waited for me to continue.

"You know this big case I'm on... Well... The other side is Adamson Hughes."

Her mouth opened in shock. "And Zack's alright with that?"

"I haven't told him. I only found out today, and I'd already agreed to work on it." I grabbed my second wine from the waiter before he could even place it down on the table. "It's not like I'll have anything to do with Luke. He might not even know I'm working on it, there are loads of secretaries at our place."

"You have to tell Zack." Cassie had her stern face on. "If he finds out another way, what's he going to think?"

"He's so busy with his job, and when we're home, it's all houses and weddings. Don't worry about it, OK? I'll sort it." She tilted her head to the side and chewed on her lip. Her silence made me nervous. I just kept talking. "You're definitely on for this trip for Zack then? I'm going to book it next week."

She nodded; her smile returned. "Just me and the kids. Guy won't be able to get away from work. It's going to be amazeballs."

"I know! Just remember it's a secret. I know you get all giddy and flirty around him," I said.

"Frankly, I don't know how you *don't* get all giddy and flirty around him, not like you used to anyway."

"Cassie, stop worrying. Everything's fine. Nothing's going to go wrong," I said, wishing I truly believed my own words.

NINE

*B*y the time I got home, I was too tired to discuss the case with Zack. It was late, and we both had early starts. Plus, I always said too much after wine.

Zack was hyped up with the excitement of his new job, and I didn't want to bring bad news into the house. Well, I didn't fully class it as bad news, but... it was certainly going to raise some interesting conversations.

As Anna had asked, I made sure I was in work and ready for the day, prior to eight thirty, but I found myself alone in the boardroom. Had she got me in early just to be mean?

I threw myself into a seat in frustration- why was Anna such a bitch? Was this really still because of Zack? Between the tension at home and her non-stop whining, I could do with a break.

I pulled my hair up into a messy bun. It annoyed me at times, flopping around my face when I already felt angsty. Thank God I'd stopped for a Starbucks... at least that was one place that didn't let me down.

I'd grabbed a copy of The Metro while I was there. With the hours I'd put in lately, I deserved ten minutes to read this and caffeinate myself. Especially as I'd got to work early for absolutely no reason. I inhaled the smell of the caramel macchiato as I lifted the lid. Was this better than sex? It was the closest I was getting for now, anyway. Actually, to be fair, of all the things I had to complain about, that wasn't one of them.

The first couple of pages of news were just depressing; I needed happy. I remembered an easier life at Draper & Hughes, when we'd pore over the rush-hour crush page every day. None of us ever featured in it, that we knew of, but it was just so damned cute. I flipped straight to the page.

'To the girl on the early train to Lancaster, carriage B. We were the only ones in the carriage. I was desperate to say hi, but I missed my chance. I'd love another.'

'I see you every morning, in that red woollen coat. Would you sit with me on the train?'

I was such a sucker for romance. These always made me smile. I'd love to be someone's rush-hour crush! There were a couple more badly worded entries, then I noticed a longer message towards the bottom of the page. It stood out from all of the others.

> The scent of you close
> So near, yet so far
> A simple memory, almost a ghost
> I envy the darkness of the coffee
> As it passes by your lips
> The memory of your kisses
> still burning at my skin

I read it for a second time with my mouth agape. That was not normal rush-hour crush quality, it was beautiful.

I blew a long, slow breath out. Lucky person to have that written about them. Imagine passing by an old flame like that and never knowing. So close but so far.

I smiled as I read through the other pages; the coffee buzz

soaked into me along with the warm feeling from those words. I wanted to keep hold of the paper for times when I needed an emotional lift, so stashed it in my desk drawer as I turned my mind to the day ahead.

By the time we got to mid-afternoon, I was convinced that it didn't matter which firm represented the other side. Paperwork was just paperwork. It's not like I'd have anything to do with Luke; I kept telling myself that. I may speak to a secretary over there every now and then, but that would be the height of my involvement. I was purely here to support Peter and Anna and deal with invoices and all those aspects. I was absolutely sure… one hundred percent… honestly.

"Lily!" Anna screeched across the room at me, breaking me out of a trance. She hadn't even mentioned the fact I'd got there early for no reason. "Isn't this where you used to work?"

Fantastic…

"Yes, new partner now, though, a lot of new staff probably. Why?"

"Just wondered. No reason." She studied her long, deep red nails. "Can I have more coffee please?"

Everyone else who worked here was capable of making their own coffee except for Anna. I stood in the kitchen, again, and messaged Zack while I waited for the coffee machine to kick in. At least she'd said please this time.

Lily: Hey you. Good day? xx
Zack: Great day. How about you? Miss you x
Lily: You'll see me soon silly. It's an OK day x
Zack: Want to go out for dinner? You can tell me why it's only OK? x
Lily: Sounds great. Want to pick me up from here when you're done? x
Zack: It's a date date x

I smiled at our little, private joke; it felt old now, but so us. Coffee made, I plastered on a smile and got on with the work. Anna seemed almost bearable for the rest of the afternoon, and although it was strange at times, seeing his name on this paperwork, there was nothing particularly 'Luke' about it, it could've been from anywhere.

I rushed out of the door when Zack messaged to say he was outside. He looked especially sexy today in a dark blue suit. He thought his hair needed a cut, but to me, it was perfect. As he scooped me into a hug, I kissed him and took the excuse to run my fingers through it.

"See, you missed me too, I knew it." Zack smiled as he spoke and grabbed hold of my hand.

"Ugh, some things don't change," Anna's snidey voice rang out as she approached us. "How's the job going?"

I zoned out as they talked about something corporate that I wasn't interested in. Zack's fingers stroked mine in reassurance as I leant my head against him. I was just in a lovely daydream about where we should go to eat when I felt Zack bristle next to me.

"Did Lily not tell you?" Anna asked in an innocent voice, always the actress.

"No," said Zack as he let go of my hand. I saw Anna smirk as she noticed his movement.

"Sorry!" She bit her lip coyly as she walked away. Zack seemed oblivious to her as he focused his eyes on me.

"Why would you not tell me?" His voice was deadpan. I hadn't heard the conversation, but I knew exactly what this was.

"Well, I only found out yesterday, and then I was with Cassie, and this is the first time I've seen you properly and—"

"Lily, stop," he sighed, and I noticed his fingers were clenched into a fist, his face focused on remaining calm.

"Let's just go get a drink. I don't want to talk about it out here."

I almost had to jog to keep up with him. Why did I always feel like I was in trouble at the moment? He marched into a pub around the corner, making a vague effort to hold the door open for me. I sat at a small table by the window as he stood at the bar, his shoulders raised. It was a dimly lit pub. It felt almost as if the nicotine smoke cloud of years ago still remained.

His lips were pursed tightly together as he sat down and pushed a miserable looking glass of wine towards me over the sticky, wooden table. He drank from a whisky glass, and everything about his posture screamed of tension. I swallowed, not knowing what to say.

"So?" Zack glared at me as he spoke.

"There's not a lot to say. I found out yesterday. I'd already said yes to the role. It's not like he'll be around the office."

"You'll be thinking about him all the time again."

"Zack, if I wanted to think about him I would. It's not like a horrible child custody case is going to make me want him back," I said. "If I say I don't want to do this now, I'll look a total idiot at work."

"See, again you're putting other stuff ahead of me. Work, Cassie, him, everything comes before me," Zack's voice was eerily calm.

"That is not true! I wouldn't ask you to put yourself into an awkward position at work. It's not fair. If I was going to be sat in a room with him for the next six months, I could, maybe, see your point, but I won't even see him."

"Then why didn't you mention it?" asked Zack, his tone still calm.

"Because this is the first chance I've had. I found out yesterday and then I went out with Cassie. I already explained this. I was out telling her that you don't want me to help her. There doesn't seem to be much you *do* want me to do at the moment." I sat back and looked out of the window as I chewed on my lip in a sulk.

"Don't try and make me feel bad for trying to build something special here. If it was up to me, this time next year we'd be living in our house, married, and having a baby. If I leave it up to you, you'd be running around after him, still, and letting Cassie have your baby instead of us."

"It's not a her or us scenario, both could happen, you know." I couldn't help but raise my voice, and I could see it made him mad.

"I want you to tell Margaret you changed your mind about working on the case." His eyes bore into my own as he spoke, waiting to judge my reaction.

"They already sorted all my work out, did all the paperwork- I can't."

"Of course you can. Plans change all the time."

It felt like the two of us played a dangerous game of chicken as we both watched each other. Neither one of us wanted to fold.

"You know I don't like it when you tell me what to do."

"You know I don't like it when you put me at the bottom of your priorities. Look, forget it. I'll go stay at mum and dad's tonight. You just do your little figuring out what you want act. Again." He stood up, downed his whisky, and without a glance back at me, he left.

My heart pumped furiously with anger; I didn't know what was up with him these past few weeks. He literally just wanted me to sit around the house, have babies and not see anyone else. I hadn't done anything to make him that insecure.

Bloody Anna. If she'd kept her mouth shut, I could've explained it all on my own terms, but now he thought I'd hidden it. Which, to be honest, I had...

I trudged to the train station, utterly deflated. My mood didn't improve upon arriving home alone to find the table still full of wedding magazines, plus a list of house viewings that Zack had booked for the weekend.

I called Cassie for a whinge, and it turned out Guy was in the doghouse too. She announced she was coming over and bringing gin.

"He is such an arse!" Cassie exclaimed as she walked in, thrusting a bottle towards me. "He promised me he wouldn't miss parents evening again."

"To be fair, he was working, and she's only in year one. You wouldn't have been discussing exam results." Cassie shot me a death glare, and I immediately closed my mouth.

"Sod him, anyway. Sod them all! I brought pyjama's; let him sort the school run out in the morning."

I smiled to myself as I poured our drinks in the kitchen. Whenever Cassie and Guy fought, it was over within twenty-four hours; I knew this wasn't serious. Wasn't so sure about Zack, however.

I could see Cassie nodding off as I began to tell her the tale. She wasn't sleeping well at the moment, she'd confessed to me weeks ago. A long day with the girls plus a drive over here had obviously been too much. This was her opportunity for a night of peaceful rest, without Guy or the kids. "Come on, Mrs," I said as I pulled her up from the couch. "Off to bed, you're exhausted."

"But you were telling me about Zack…" she objected.

"And that can wait, you need sleep."

Ten minutes later, after hugs and goodnights, I wandered back downstairs and poured myself another gin. A phone began to ring, but it wasn't mine. I listened for the noise, which, weirdly, seemed to be coming from inside the couch. As I slipped my hand between the cushions, I felt the smooth, cold surface of a phone and pulled it out, instantly recognising it as Cassie's.

My heart skipped a beat as I saw the caller ID – Luke Adamson.

A battle raged within my mind, a full-on war that flashed by in an instant as I swiped to answer and held the phone to my ear.

"Hey, you ok? Sorry I couldn't make it over last night, work is insane," Luke's voice travelled down the phone to me in a perfect melody of sound.

I couldn't form words. I was frozen, one hand still down between the couch cushions.

"Cassie, you there?" Luke sounded confused.

"Erm... Cassie's asleep. She left her phone," I said quietly, petrified of what his voice was setting off within me.

"Lily..." It wasn't even a question; he knew it was me.

"Hi," I laughed nervously as I spoke.

"Is Cassie at yours?" Luke questioned.

"Yeah, but she was worn out, I sent her to bed. Then I heard her phone ringing. I should go, I just... it seemed rude not to answer."

"Please don't go, Lily," Luke's voice pleaded with me.

"We're not supposed to talk."

"Just once, it's so good to hear your voice. Is Zack there? I don't want to cause any trouble."

"He isn't here. It's crazy good to hear your voice too." I lay down on the couch; Cassie's phone pressed against my ear. "How are things?"

I heard him take a deep breath in before he answered. "Not bad, how about you?"

"Yeah, all fine..." The silence felt awkward. I didn't know what was safe to dicsuss anymore, but I also didn't want him to go. "I'm so happy you're a partner now."

"The timing all worked out well. Everyone still misses you, I mean everyone, Lily."

I smiled, knowing full well what he meant. "I miss everyone too. I think about them a lot, more than I should. Caddel & Boone are lovely, but it doesn't stop me thinking about the old days."

"I think about those days too. It feels like life will never be that good again."

"It's just different…" My voice faded out as I tried not to cry. Luke, emphatic as ever, changed the subject.

"Hey, you know the student union? They got rid of the plastic booths, I was incensed!"

I burst into laughter, remembering so many nights when our skin stuck to the clammy, dirty booths, and we belted out karaoke tunes together. "God, I loved those nights so much."

Luke joined in the laughter. "If only I'd told you how I felt."

The silence hit again, although, internally, my heart sounded like a marching band.

"Are you happy, Lily?" he asked.

"Yes, in a way, in the only way I can be."

"I need to go," Luke sounded choked up. "I… It was… I'm happy I spoke to you. Just… keep looking after yourself."

"You too, Luke. I worry about you.

"No need. Big enough to look after myself." I knew he was trying to reassure me, but he sounded broken.

"Let's think about a happy memory before you go," I suggested, hoping to try and heal him in some way.

"What do you have in mind?" Luke's voice was rich with intrigue.

A thousand memories flashed through my mind as I sipped at my gin. I felt mischievous. "Do you remember that night in the tepee? Do you remember what you did to me?" I spoke quietly, unsure if I was managing to pull off sultry.

I heard Luke take a sharp breath before he answered. "I remember every moment. It seemed pretty obvious you loved what I was doing to you."

I wriggled further down the couch, letting my jeans ride up and rub against me. Luke's voice was seriously turning me on right now.

"I think about all the things you did to me, more than I

should. I think we should make a deal."

"What sort of deal?" He swallowed deeply.

"I'm going to go and run a bath, and then I'm going to remember that night in vivid detail. Everywhere your hands went, mine are going to go as I think about you."

"Fucking hell…" he whispered, breathless.

"I think, you should go up to bed and do the same thing. And while my hands are busy, I'll think about your hands being busy."

"Deal. I miss your hands."

"I miss everything about you," I confessed, as the gin made me brave.

"Night, Lily."

"Night, Luke."

I filled the bath with water as hot as I could stand; my breath caught in a gasp as I sank into it. I had focused for a long time now on not letting myself do this, but maybe, maybe just for one night, a little think about Luke wouldn't be a bad thing? A girl had to have something happy to dream about, right? I smiled as I slid deeper into the steamy, bubbly water. My mind travelled to a much happier place- a tepee full of fairy lights and the hottest sex ever.

Yet the next morning, guilt fell on me heavily. I knew Zack was only trying to do what was right for us. I twisted my engagement ring around on my finger as I thought. Zack just got into this sulky childlike mood so easily lately. I was trying to do my best for everyone, why couldn't he see that? He didn't even know that on top of work, friends, weddings and houses, I was arranging a huge surprise holiday for his birthday. There was even more pressure to make those birthday plans perfect after mine had been so special.

The phone call- it had been a mistake- but it reminded me of the ache in me that wouldn't settle. I needed to fill that ache, and I would do so with Zack. Just how Luke had wanted but wow… how I missed him.

TEN

I sighed at the message that had just appeared on my phone as I sat in the boardroom, surrounded by paperwork again.

Zack: I love you, I missed you last night. Do you want to go see a house together after work? I'll send you the link, looks perfect, let's not wait until weekend x

Maybe we just had to agree to disagree about this. It felt weird him not being at home last night. The link flashed up for the house; it did look perfect. He hadn't said sorry though, I noted.

The house bordered south Manchester and Cheshire – easy to get to the office, close enough to the airport but also all that luscious Cheshire countryside on the doorstep. It had four bedrooms and a beautiful, established garden. Definitely top end of budget, but it had only come on the market today and did look like a place that would get snapped up.

Lily: I missed you too. Yes to the house, can you book it? x
Zack: Already done x Pick you up outside work later x

I couldn't stay mad at him even if I wanted to.

By lunchtime, I was flicking through a legal magazine that had been lying around the waiting room when something caught my eye. It was a charity ball that took place annually to raise money for a children's hospice. I smiled as I thought it would be exactly the type of event that Luke would support and then… there he was.

Nausea bubbled up in my stomach. I didn't want to look at his face, but I couldn't look away. I'd resisted the urge to look at any pictures of Luke this entire time; my only glances of his face had been from my memories. The photographer had taken a shot of him with his stunning smile and his arm around a beautiful girl.

I shoved the magazine in my handbag and rushed into the loos, locking myself in a cubicle. As my fingers trembled, I opened up the page again, ignoring the girl for now and looking only at Luke. *Still so pretty.*

I hardly ever let myself think about him, it just opened up a chasm in me that I couldn't fill. It scared me how torn between things I was. Zack and I… it didn't feel like it should, something wasn't quite right. Yet the thought of leaving him still petrified me; I didn't think I would be able to. I wanted that happy ever after with him.

But Luke…

I wiped tears from my cheeks as I looked at the girl. She was petite and cute with a little pixie cut hairstyle, totally who I would've imagined him with. It was good he had someone, he deserved to be happy. It hurt, though, a physical ache that dragged me down.

I needed to stop falling out with Zack and just move on, starting with this house and finalising our wedding plans.

I took one last look at Luke's beautiful face and put the magazine into the bin- out of reach, out of temptation. Just one more goodbye between the two of us. We had had too many already.

Zack reached over and kissed me as I got into his car after work. "I'm sorry." He stroked a hand down my cheek as he spoke.

"I'm sorry too," I said. "I wasn't trying to mislead you."

"I know. I shouldn't have asked you to give up like that. I know what these cases are like, it doesn't matter who the other side is. Just... please promise me you'll speak to me if anything is wrong?" Zack asked, his eyes soft.

"I promise. Same for you." I wanted him to feel the trust between us. "This house looks amazing; I'm very excited!"

He grinned at me. "I've got a good feeling about this one. Let's go."

Half an hour later, we stood in the amazing open plan kitchen, looking up at the skylights which glided open when the wall switch was pressed. The estate agent had slunk away to let us talk and look around alone.

I wrapped my arms around Zack's waist. "It's scarily perfect."

"I agree." He kissed the top of my head.

"This could be our forever home."

"Are you ready for a forever Lily? I still feel a bit lost here."

I placed a kiss on Zack's lips. "Trust me to work on this case Zack. I know my job isn't as big as yours, but it means a lot to me. Trust me on this, and I'll tell Cassie the egg donation is a no. Then as soon as we're married, those eggs are all yours, I promise. If that doesn't sound gross?" I giggled with nerves.

Zack smiled at me; his face relaxed again. "Well, if we bought this house, we don't need to view all those others at the weekend, which, means we could concentrate on wedding plans."

I closed my eyes as I rested my head against him. "Definitely. Let's do it."

Zack lifted me up and kissed my neck, making me laugh. "I'll go find the agent."

I wandered around the house while they talked, taking it all in. It was perfect, Edwardian, and beautifully maintained. The four bedrooms were all bright and airy, and it would be a perfect place for entertaining family and friends. I smiled to myself as I imagined a large Christmas tree in the wide hall, real of course, spreading the smell of pine throughout the downstairs. The kitchen was huge and had a double oven. I imagined myself baking bigger and better cakes, double batches of brownies, rocky road...

We could definitely do forever here.

After negotiation back and forth, our offer was accepted; totally at the top end of our budget, but we knew this was a place we could stay forever. Well, for three kids at least!

I knew Zack was desperate to go to the football with his dad on Saturday, which made this a good time to go and talk to Cassie. I was, however, dreading hurting her with the finality of this decision. Although she already knew it was more than likely a no, this was the final no.

She kissed me on the lips when she opened her front door, taking me by complete surprise as I burst into laughter. "Your house is gorgeous," she screeched. "I can't wait to come round."

"It'll take a couple of months, but yeah, it's incredible." I handed her the wine I'd brought with me. "I need to drive back, it's all yours."

"Have one with me then I'll make you all the coffee you desire." I followed her through to the garden, and we sat down in the sunshine.

"Where's Guy and the kids?" I asked.

"They'll be back soon, gone to visit his mum. I was far more interested in seeing you." She moved forwards in her seat, and I knew what she wanted to discuss.

"Why didn't you tell me Luke had a girlfriend?" I blurted it out without warning. That wasn't even what I'd intended to say next.

"How do you… Doesn't matter. I just didn't think you'd want to know. Not the kind of news I'm going to ring and tell you while you're eating lunch with Zack, is it? I don't know if she's his girlfriend, he just needed a plus one and… no, I'm not going into all this. Are you OK?"

I shrugged. "Yes. No. I want him to be happy, so it's good news, I guess…"

Cassie took hold of my hand. "Sweetheart, you've got the fanciest engagement ring I ever saw, you're buying an amazing house, and Zack literally worships you. Just enjoy it. Don't waste all this happiness."

"I'm not. Some times are just harder than others. There's something I need to tell you."

Cassie swallowed back her emotions. "I'm expecting it, don't worry."

"He just… He doesn't get it, and I need to respect what he wants. If I was the only option in the world, it might be different, but there's lots of places to try. And I'll help you every step of the way."

Cassie burst into tears, and I pulled her into a tight hug. I felt like the worst friend in the world. "I'm sorry, Cassie," I said, as I kissed the top of her head. Her fine, blonde hair tickled at my face.

"It's fine. It was a big ask. We'll figure it out. Just give me a minute, I'll be right back."

Cassie took herself inside as she wiped her cheeks. I gulped a mouthful of wine down quicker than I should have and strolled around the garden. As soon as I saw the granny flat, waves of happy memories flooded into my mind. I walked over and peeked through the window, that last night Luke and I were together so vivid in my mind. That completely unforgettable night, before my heart was torn out.

Something flapped against my foot. I looked down and saw a piece of paper sticking out from under a rock. Had the girls been hiding pictures? I picked it up with a smile, expecting to see their scrawly handwriting, but instead found printed words.

> Our smiles, merged into a kiss
> Eyes dark to the world
> You pulled me close
> Not knowing I was already
> A fragment of your soul
> Our double heartbeat
> That tandem beating
> Is it any wonder I lost myself?

I sank down onto the grass, leaning back against the building as I read the words again. This had to be him, why else would it be here?

But then… why would he? He had someone else. Or did he? Cassie hadn't told me the full story.

This was too hard for my mind; I couldn't think rationally. I jumped as Cassie came back out through the patio doors and instinctively scrunched the paper up into my pocket, cursing myself as I creased the beautiful words.

"What are you doing over there?" she asked.

"Just remembering," I tried to smile, but I knew my sad eyes would betray me.

"It's not too late, you know, Lily. You look torn."

"It *is* too late. Luke made the decision a long time ago now. We were both too late. Are you OK?" I asked, noting the redness around her pale, blue eyes.

She nodded. "We'll both be fine. Come on, let's raid the kid's chocolate drawer."

ELEVEN

All too soon, another month had passed, and it was time for Zack's December trip to Iceland. I'd given him a list of Christmas goodies to bring back, of course! The house purchase was going well, and we were still thinking about wedding options. It was hard to settle on the never-ending choices.

Zack seemed beside himself with happiness, but I still felt a little off; I couldn't put my finger on it. He wrapped me up in a tight hug near the security gates inside the airport that Sunday evening.

"I'll see you in five days; I miss you already."

I kissed him before I replied, "I miss you too. You're going to call me tonight though, aren't you?" I raised an eyebrow and smiled.

"Counting down the hours," he whispered. "Love you."

"I love you too." Our fingers slid away from each other. I blew him a kiss before he disappeared through security, then headed home to curl up with a book and a large glass of wine… possibly chocolate too.

I'd been expecting a quiet day at work on Monday as I knew mediation was taking place in a swanky hotel in the city centre, and everyone important would be there, leaving me in peace. Margaret jumped on me the minute I walked through the door though.

"Lily! I tried to call you!"

I pulled my phone out of my bag, confused; it was still on silent, and I could see three missed calls flashing on the screen.

"Sorry. What's wrong? What did you need me for?" I asked.

"The mediator's assistant has let him down; I said you'd do it instead. You need to get to The Sandhurst now. Take a cab, just give me the receipt later," she instructed.

"What? I can't, I…"

"Lily," she screeched. "How hard do you think it was to get four solicitors, a mediator, a premier league footballer, his manager, his ex-shag piece and a PR person in the same room at the same time?! Just get a cab now."

She stomped away. Zack was going to lose the plot. *Luke… fuck fuck fuck*! I wasn't even dressed for this.

I ran into the toilets as I swiped away at my phone for an Uber. I looked at myself in the mirror- could have been worse. I pulled the bobble from my ponytail and shook my head upside down as I ran my fingers through my hair to try and get a bit of volume. My eyes looked good, but I reapplied the lipstick that had rubbed off on my Starbucks cup earlier. My dress was nice; that was good. Knee length, dark blue.

I glanced down at my feet; this seriously wouldn't do. I had boring, sensible shoes on because I knew I wouldn't get a seat on the train during rush hour, and I hated sore feet for no good reason. Luke, though, totally had a thing about sexy shoes. My breaths grew deeper at the memory of a specific time in his living room, in nothing but the Gucci's. I couldn't let him see me for the first time in so long, wearing these dull flats.

I ran to Ella's desk; she always wore sexy as hell shoes. "Ella!" I puffed and panted. "I'll do whatever you want if you swap shoes with me today."

She frowned and looked at my feet; I could see her grimace. "Why? That's a bit weird."

"Oh come on, please. I've got to go in two minutes, and I *need* sexy shoes. You're my only hope. Anything Ella!" I begged.

"Cover for me on Friday afternoon so I can go meet Jake?" She smiled slyly.

"Give me the shoes, and I'll cover for you every Friday until the end of time!"

My phone pinged to say the Uber was outside as she slid her shoes across the floor to me, unable to hide her grimace at my flats.

"Thank you!" I mouthed as I ran to the Uber barefoot, clutching the precious shoes to my chest.

The hotel was a ten-minute drive away. I squeezed my feet into the too small heels; I'd be in agony later, but they were perfect. Sleek, black, tall, very Luke. *What the fuck, Lily?* Why had I regressed to this again? Desperate to be a little dress up fantasy for him. What was wrong with me?

I hoped they'd been informed; I didn't just want to walk in and surprise him. I sprayed perfume as I checked myself in my compact mirror. My hair looked a little wild, but he'd seen it wilder. My mouth curved into a smile, flashes of those wild times at the forefront of my mind. My stomach flipped over and over at the thought of being close to Luke.

My heart was on the verge of combustion as the hotel receptionist pointed me towards the conference room. Security stood outside and checked my ID before they let me in. I paused as I held the door handle; my hands trembled like crazy. *You can do this, Lily, it's just Luke. Remember when he was your honorary big brother. It's just Luke.*

I smiled widely as I opened the door and looked around all the faces... of which Luke's wasn't one. Instantly, I wanted to cry, and not only because these shoes had cut off the circulation to my toes already.

Then, an absolute chill ran from my feet, all the way to my forehead as I froze. I could feel that he was behind me. *Breathe, Lily. Just breathe.*

I walked to the empty seat next to the mediator, scared to even look at Luke. I glanced at Anna and Peter with a nod, then just focused on the paperwork in front of me while introductions were made.

I could feel Luke's eyes burn into me, but I didn't look up. I didn't dare look up. Instead, I doodled on my notepad with the fancy hotel pen, and that's when I saw my ring. It sparkled away like a bloody beacon under the conference room lights. I should've put it in my bag! *Why? For what reason? Will you get a grip woman.*

I wanted to run outside and cry. Thankfully, the meeting got started at speed. I was making notes for the mediator, looking after all his paperwork and documentation.

I'd forgotten what it was like to be in a room with Luke while he worked, his voice authoritative and strong; it actually reminded me of something else... I found myself smiling and bit my lip as I looked up, trying to quell the memory – it only flashed brighter, as my eyes met his.

Instantly. Lost.

Luke's eyes pulled the air out of me.

All the noise of the room, the talk of multi-million-pound salaries and withheld visitation rights, it all silenced for me. I could hear the fan swoosh away above me. I could hear my heart explode with emotion inside me as everything I'd kept trapped and locked up in there burst out in a flood.

I couldn't tear my eyes away from his. He was watching

me intently; I couldn't tell what he wanted to communicate. Was he mad that I was here? Was he wishing he could kiss me?

I sighed and reached for a glass of water, blinking rapidly to rip my eyes away from his as I did so.

I knew I'd missed a section of notes and started to scribble, eager to catch up. It was hard to focus; the proximity to Luke was affecting me. A little voice at the back of my mind was also nagging about how exactly I was going to tell Zack about this – was he likely to believe it had all been an accident?

Thankfully, every single person in this room was an absolute caffeine fiend. It therefore, wasn't long until a break was called. Even better – the hotel staff were in charge of refreshments; it wasn't my job for once.

I headed straight outside, cursing the throb and ache in my toes thanks to Ella's shoes. I was boiling hot and needed the fresh air. I leant against the outside of the hotel as I sucked in deep breaths; my hot exhalations caused clouds of steam in the cold December air. One of those breaths paused in my body as I realised, Luke had followed me. He grabbed me by the arm and pulled me into a side alley, away from the main street.

He stood, in silence, watching me. His eyes never left mine. His hand reached up as if to move a stray hair from my face as the wind whipped it around, but he stopped himself.

"I wasn't meant to ever see you again." His voice was soft and melodic to my ears.

"I know. I didn't know about this until ten minutes before I got here. I tried to get out of it…"

"You didn't want to see me?"

"I've been desperate to see you. Doesn't mean it's a good idea, though."

He sighed, his breath long and slow. I'd forgotten how tall he was, how much presence he had, how good he smelled. I took a deep breath in, wanting to inhale his presence into me.

"I don't know what to say," Luke sighed as he spoke.

"I get why you did what you did, but... I don't think you should've done it."

He took hold of my hand and held it up. Goosebumps popped up over my whole body. "I figure it worked for you, though?" He was looking at my ring. "That's not the ring that belongs with you."

Now that he had hold of my hand, I desperately didn't want him to let go. But he did.

We just looked at each other for the longest moment. "I better go back in," he said. "Maybe after this is done, do you want to get a drink? Could you?"

I nodded. "Zack's in Iceland again."

Luke opened his mouth as if to speak, then stopped himself and walked back inside. I stayed at the side of the building for a moment, just trying to breathe and focus.

All I had to do was get through today. Speak to Luke over a drink. Explain to Zack. Carry on as normal. Totally doable.

By two in the afternoon, I'd realised this wasn't doable. I was in absolute turmoil.

As the afternoon wore on, it became clear no further progress was going to be made, and the whole session was paused until the next day. I'd made notes about everything, yet I remembered nothing. No idea if this was working for either side's favour. There was too much information in my brain.

Luke exited the room. I remained there, pushing paper-work around. I wished Anna would leave too. I worried I was acting suspicious. "I'll message you in the morning if we need you again, Lily, thanks for stepping in," she said.

I don't know how I hid my shock at a thank you from Anna. "No problem. I'll speak to you in the morning then."

She looked me up and down before she left. "Hmm, will do."

I gave it ten torturous minutes before I headed to the bar; my nerves felt open and exposed.

I instantly spotted Luke. It was like an invisible string stretched between us, and I could always find my way back to him. I felt relieved that I hadn't driven today as I noticed he had a bottle of wine on his table. Was that a ploy to make me stay longer? I hoped so, even though I knew that it was wrong of me, and I'd never admit it to anyone.

"Hi," I said quietly as I sat down at the table next to the end of the bar. He'd chosen an out of the way spot; the only person nearby was a barman on his break, sat scrolling through his phone.

Luke smiled at me. That slow, sexy, gorgeous smile. The corners of his eyes crinkled up, the blueness of them vivid against him.

"Are you OK? You're not moving," he said, as he pushed a glass of wine towards me.

I swallowed and sat down. "I don't know."

"I'm sorry about the way I left that morning, I didn't know what else to do. You were really struggling."

"That night, before you left… It felt like we…" I ran my hands through my hair, unable to think of how to vocalise it all.

"I know, I know what you mean. I wanted to make it easy on you."

"It wasn't easy. I've learned to deal with it, Luke, but it's never been easy."

"Learned to deal with it with a big diamond?" he asked.

"What did you expect me to do? You cut me off, you told me to go be with Zack. I was in absolute bits, I could barely function. It took me weeks to even act semi normal with him. I…"

"I'm sorry. I honestly thought I was doing the best thing

for you. I always, only did everything for you, Lily." He reached for my hand as he spoke, and my body craved more of him. But I couldn't go through it again, I didn't have the strength. Our fingers grazed each other's for a moment, then I pulled back.

"I know, I know, Luke. You're too good; that's part of the problem. I miss you so much, you have no idea."

"I have every idea. Everywhere I go in my house, I just picture you there. I was thinking about selling it, just to try and get peace in my mind, but part of me can't stand to," Luke said. His whole demeanour saddened as he took a long drink.

"I saw your photo at that charity ball." I sucked on my bottom lip as I awaited his response, then pressed my teeth into it until it hurt.

"There was only one person I wanted to be there with..."

"I feel like I should leave, but I'm terrified I'll never see you again. I don't think I'm back tomorrow; it was just a favour for the mediator."

"I want every minute I can get with you," said Luke.

"I can't go through it again," I put my head into my hands. "I still can't say for sure what I would've done that morning if you hadn't left, if you hadn't sent that email, but Luke..." I looked up at him, my eyes full of tears. "I think it was going to be you. That night, that night was perfection. Nothing's ever come close, it never will."

"But you would've felt bad about Zack; I didn't want to put you through that."

"Losing you wasn't any better. I... I really need to go. I can't handle this. I can't control myself around you, and I'm getting married and..." The bar was busy now, but I couldn't stop myself from crying, utterly undignified, ridiculous heaving sobs.

"Come outside. Just breathe. You're OK, I'm with you." He took hold of my hand and wrapped his jacket around my shoulders as we got to the door. We headed to the side of the hotel where we'd spoken earlier. The winter evening was already dark, and the street was illuminated by strings of twinkling white Christmas lights. "You know everyone in there thinks I just dumped you now? Thanks for that," he laughed and elbowed me with a grin, instantly lightning the mood.

I couldn't help but join in with his laugh through my sobs. "How did we end up here again?"

"By the wall? How drunk are you?" Luke smiled; his face lit up with absolute beauty.

I continued to laugh as I wiped the tears off my cheeks. "These aren't my shoes, and I really need to take them off. I think I broke my toes."

He looked at me, bemused, as I pulled the shoes off, before a happy sigh escaped my lips as my throbbing feet touched the soothing, cold ground. "Lily... whose shoes have you got on and why?"

"Well, I wore flats for work today because I got the train. Then I found out I was coming here, and I wanted you to see me in sexy shoes, so I convinced a girl to swap."

Luke looked at the shoes. "They're not even your size, are they?"

I shook my head; I was so silly.

"You know you didn't need to do that?"

"It made sense at the time," I laughed again. "Didn't want you to see me in flats and think you had a lucky escape."

"Yeah, because I only wanted you for your shoes..." Luke laughed with me; this was nice. Friends laughing together.

"I can think of a few occasions that was actually very true!" I spluttered, but my eyes met his, and we just... stopped.

"Do you want to come back inside and finish the wine?" he asked in a quiet voice.

I shook my head.

"Do you want me to get you a taxi?"

I shook my head again.

"Do you want to stay with me?"

"Yes, but I can't," I answered with regret, honestly.

"Let me get you home safe then, hey? Like the old days?" he smiled and stroked my forehead. I could have sunk into him there and then, but I just nodded. I was an engaged woman, I needed to behave. "I'm staying here tonight anyway, should probably be working. I'll come with you in an Uber to make sure you get home safe and then just get it to bring me back."

"You don't need to. If you weren't here, I'd be on the train alone anyway."

"True, but you wouldn't be upset and two wines down. No arguments."

I booked the Uber, and we stood near the entrance in silence. I didn't know what to say to him. It took all my focus not to reach out and touch him. I actually wanted to lean in and smell him, refresh my memories. *Lily, stop it.* I twisted my engagement ring around my finger as a reminder.

Luke smiled at me as we got into the car and explained to the driver that he would be returning back to the same place. "I should've booked it on my account," he said. "Now you'll have the bill for me to come back, I'm sorry."

"It's not an issue," I watched him through the darkness of the night as we got into the car. I twisted sideways and leaned my head back on the seat, watching him, wanting to make the most of every second of being able to look at him. He did the same and gently took hold of my hand. I wished I lived hours away, but all too soon the journey was over. The ride was silent. We simply held hands and watched each other, as if to drink in every moment for it might be the last. One more ending.

The driver coughed and looked at his phone after he pulled up at my house; we both remained in the back, like statues. Luke disentangled his hand from mine, as a single, fat tear rolled down my cheek.

"Goodb—" I began to speak, but he pressed his hand to my mouth and stopped me.

"Don't say it." He ran his hands through his hair, and I could see he was near to tears too. "Go inside, so I know you're safe."

I fumbled the key in the door as I tried to see through my tears. I couldn't even look back; I couldn't look at Luke. I locked the door and ran straight upstairs. The car drove away as I threw myself onto the bed and cried with absolute devastation.

Zack had been right; I shouldn't have worked on this case. He was going to be furious. I reached into my bag for my phone but instead found a folded piece of thick paper. Just like with the others, my breath stuck in my throat; I felt lightheaded.

I loved you before I knew you
The first time my eyes
gazed upon your face
is engraved upon my heart
Round and round in aching circles
always missing the moment we needed
I would run that gauntlet forever
if it took my whole life
For one moment with you
I would forsake every other second

It was him. Had it all been him? Was this the only way he could communicate with me? Such a beautiful way. I had no idea he could write something so… so pure as if he'd drawn it from the exact place his love for me lived. It must have been agony for him.

And I'd just let him drive away from me. But what else could I do?

My phone beeped with a message, and my heart shot into overdrive. Then I realised, Luke and I didn't have each other's numbers anymore, no way it could be him.

Zack: I just got back and I'm exhausted, can I call you in the morning instead? x
Lily: Absolutely, I'm worn out too. I love you. Sleep well xx
Zack: Love you too Mrs Beaumont -well, soon at least x

Zack was going to lose the plot. I went to my wardrobe and took out the Gucci box, which hadn't been touched in so long. I knew I was completely pathetic as I put the shoes on and slid the memory card into my laptop.

Then, in the most self-indulgent act of misery I've ever known, I sobbed my way through every photograph and every message. My throat was raw and painful by the time I got to the end.

I took the poem I'd just found in my bag and placed it in the shoe box along with the one from the supermarket and the one from the granny flat. Then I thought about the birthday card… and The Metro piece… had he been leaving me these little trails, all this time and I'd been totally blind to it? I just thought I was lucky to find such words of beauty.

I fell into a restless sleep, our old favourite, The Scientist, on repeat as I slept – at least I'd always have Coldplay.

TWELVE

*Z*ack called me early the next morning, and I managed to sound completely cheery. I'd decided as soon as I woke up not to mention any of this, it would only cause tension, and it wasn't like it was anybody's fault, nor could it be changed. My mind was troubled, however, at the fact that these feelings for Luke would not fade.

I cursed myself as I got ready for work, but I knew what I was doing as I dressed in the sexiest work clothes I had. I grinned at myself as I slipped the Gucci's back onto my feet, shivering at the memories we'd made in them. I even got an Uber into the office, smiling widely as I arrived early and lurked around reception, praying that I'd be asked to go back to the mediation today.

Sadly though, I wasn't needed. Instead, I ended up sat alone with mountains of paperwork and way too much time to think. Half of my brain knew this was for the best, but half was disappointed, let down. As I packed the shoes back away later that evening, I felt pained at our brief reconnection – I missed him so much. The empty ache grew more painful, like a cavity in a tooth that got bigger and bigger, and the only thing that could fill it, I couldn't have.

I felt utterly lacklustre about everything for the rest of the week. Zack would be back on Saturday morning. I managed to get away early on Friday afternoon and meet Hannah for an impromptu Christmas shopping and birthday planning trip. She pulled me into a tight hug as we met outside the same Starbucks I'd met Zack at on that blind date; it felt like an eternity ago.

"Hey. Bloody freezing, isn't it?" Hannah exclaimed.

I smiled as I noticed the thin t-shirt she was wearing under her jacket. "You need warmer clothes." I glanced into the coffee shop window, smiling as I noticed 'our' table.

"You want coffee?" she asked.

I shook my head. "No, I was just reminiscing. This was where Zack and I had our first date."

"Aww! I didn't know. Well, if you're still looking for a wedding venue…"

"Ha! Maybe not, hey?" I laughed as she linked her arm through mine, and we set off towards the many shops that filled Manchester city centre.

"So the holiday is all booked?" she asked.

"Yes! I had to hide the credit card bill as soon as it arrived so he didn't see. The place looks unbelievable. Have you all got your flights booked? Zack and I land at about two-ish in the afternoon."

"Yep, we're all booked. We'll be there early in the morning, so we can get the place ready. I can't wait to see his face. Do you think you guys will have moved by then?"

I shook my head. "Think it will take a bit longer. I can't wait though. Have you seen the house?"

"Zack has shown me about a hundred times. Can't wait for you two to fill it up with babies. I want to be an auntie again." She winked at me.

"One step at a time. Ooo, can you imagine if we could have everyone there for Christmas next year, though? How amazing would that be?" My voice raised with excitement at the prospect. I realised I was OK again, the 'Luke' effect was subsiding.

"I'm taking that as an official invitation." She steered me towards an expensive, designer shop as she spoke. "Can you help me pick a present for Zack? He's so hard to buy for, he has perfect standards."

My eyebrows furrowed as I looked at her. "Do you think so?" I was genuinely confused; I didn't see him as a perfectionist.

"Hell yeah! He's ended up with the perfect fiancée, the perfect house, the job he always wanted, his flash car. He never settles for second best. If I get him the wrong present, it'll just be shoved in a cupboard," she shrugged nonchalantly.

"I never thought of him like that," I admitted.

"You're perfect to him, you wouldn't have noticed."

"I am far from perfect. I don't know why anybody would think that."

"I guess it's just… nothing seems like a struggle for you two. You're both gorgeous, you met in such a cute way, you fell in love instantly. Your jobs are great, you're buying a dream house that most of us could only ever wish for…" She opened the door to the shop. "Sorry, I sound like I'm all bitter. I don't mean that. You just don't see how you two look to the outside world. And that's before we get to the wedding of the century."

I didn't say a word as I took in Hannah's words. This shouldn't have been a revelation to me, but… it felt weird. This 'perfect' life didn't quite sit right with me. I laughed it off, and we had a lovely afternoon. I arrived home laden down with bags and hid all of Zack's presents. I still felt uneasy as I got into bed early that night. I reassured myself that all I needed was Zack home, and it would all feel right again. I twisted my engagement ring around on my finger as I imagined how different this bed would be in twenty-four hours. These times apart were frustrating, but the reunions were worth it.

I'd never seen a grown up as excited on Christmas eve as Zack was. I didn't think he was going to sleep a wink. We brushed our teeth together, his smile infectious as he watched me in the mirror.

"We forgot something," he said as he wiped his mouth.

"We can't have forgotten any presents, there are hundreds down there. I've never bought so many presents in my whole life as the past few weeks."

"Not presents. We haven't left the carrot and the whiskey out." He pulled such a cute, sweet face, I couldn't help but grin at him.

"Oh my God... Could you get any more adorable, Zachary?"

He wrapped his arms around me and kissed a spot of toothpaste from my lips. "I'm worried about Santa not having a drink, and you're calling me Zachary, getting me all distracted."

"Well... are you worried about *him* being thirsty or me being thirsty?" I looked up at him, all innocent eyes, then moved to his ear with a whisper. "It could be an early Christmas present for me..."

His fingers ran into my hair and pulled me tight against him as he kissed me, before he walked me backwards towards the tiled wall of the bathroom. My pyjama bottoms fell to the floor.

I bit on his bottom lip. "What about Santa?"

"He'll cope. You, on the other hand... I could never leave you thirsty." His hands reached under me and lifted me up; he pulled at my now naked legs, wrapping them around his middle.

He began to kiss my neck, and I banged my head on the hard tiles of the wall as my head fell backwards in response, wanting to open up more skin to him.

"Are you OK?" Zack looked worried as he kissed my lips and rubbed the back of my head.

"As long as you don't stop, I am."

"You know in the new house?" His hands wandered up my top and stroked at the sensitive skin under my lower ribs.

"Mmhmm…" My fingers were in his hair now, that hair was so, so sexy.

"We need a padded wall…" His voice was low as he shifted me against him. "So that I can do this to you without worrying about your beautiful head getting hurt." Quick as a flash, he put one hand behind my head to protect me as the other held me against him, then he pushed into me and the most delicious sensations exploded deep inside. My head hit his hand over and over in our joint rhythm as he moved inside me. Then he slowed, a lopsided smile on his face as he spoke.

"You know… next Christmas… we'll be married and living in our new house." His voice was deep and breathless as he spoke.

"It's going to be the best year." I kissed Zack's mouth as I shifted, encouraging him to continue.

"I don't think we should do this next Christmas eve though, sorry." He feigned a sad face.

"Aww, why not? It could be tradition. Christmas eve sex and designer shoes under the Christmas tree?"

He grinned at me, his hand still in its protective position behind my head. "I'm not telling you if I bought you shoes or not, stop! But… my point was that next Christmas, I hope we'll still be doing this," he pressed into me deeper as he said the words, and I couldn't help but moan at the sensation. "But, in a more delicate fashion because you'll be pregnant and glowing and absolutely beautiful. I honestly can't wait for us to have babies together, Lily."

"Me neither, Zack, but... you need more action and less talk or it won't happen." I bit his lip mischievously with a smile as he pressed me tighter against the wall. We were so good together. When we were like this, I didn't doubt a thing. Next year was going to be amazing, he was right. We would both be turning thirty, buying a house, getting married, and if the universe was kind to us, falling pregnant. What had I ever done to deserve a life this perfect?

Zack carried me to the bed and lay me down, smothering me in kisses. "I love you so much." He wrapped his arms around me and held me tightly.

"I love you too." I snuggled back into him, the picture of happiness. But just for a brief flicker, my mind asked me what Luke would be doing on Christmas Eve. It was a millisecond, but it invaded my thoughts and wiped out my confidence in the future, just for a moment.

THIRTEEN

The weeks after Christmas passed in a blur, even the dull January days, where everybody anxiously waits for payday, hadn't seemed to drag like they normally would. At work, the mediation sadly hadn't helped the case, it was more like a process that just had to be done before the lengthy, eye-wateringly expensive trial would begin. I may have been working for the millionaire's side, but my heart was firmly with the single mum who struggled to pay her bills. I knew Luke wouldn't be earning a penny from this unless they won, no way would he leave her struggling with more bills than she was already facing. I tried not to dwell on it, or him, too much, however.

Before I knew it, February rolled around, and it was time for Zack's birthday trip to celebrate the big thirty. Everyone had done an amazing job of keeping it secret, he didn't have a clue. The sheer volume of secret messages and sneaking around I'd been doing, though, was insane. I was surprised he wasn't more suspicious of what I was up to with the way I kept hiding my phone.

His whole family, plus Cassie and the girls, were on a morning flight together, and we would follow later in the afternoon, giving them time to decorate the villa for a surprise party. Zack was going to be shocked, in a good way, but I felt nervous that something would go wrong. I also worried I hadn't packed enough clothes for me as half my suitcase was full of cards and gifts for Zack from friends who weren't joining us.

I drummed my fingers nervously against the armrest as we waited for the plane to taxi up the runway.

"Are you OK?" asked Zack as he took hold of my hand.

"Mmhmm. Just not flown in a long time."

He smiled at me. "You'll be fine. I'm here. We'll get you a big gin as soon as we can."

I kissed him, loving the feel of his soft lips; he was so sweet. I adored that about him.

"And," he continued, "I have your undivided attention for two and a half hours, no escape. Wedding plans!"

I laughed. "It's not that I don't want to plan it, there's just too many choices. I'm struggling."

He subconsciously squeezed my hand tighter as the plane picked up speed, barrelling down the runway. My vision blurred for a moment as the front wheels left the ground. I wanted to close my eyes but kept them focused on Zack.

"I was thinking spring would be nice because it's when we met. But that means either two to three months' time or wait until next year?"

I screwed my face up as the plane left the runway; the force pushed me back in my seat. "We wouldn't get the right venue with such short notice. I agree spring is perfect, but it would have to be next year. You didn't want to wait that long, did you? Maybe we need to go with winter?"

"I thought about that too." Zack wriggled his jaw from side to side to pop his ears. He was a frequent flyer now, unlike me, and he obviously knew all the tricks. "We should be in the house by spring. The garden is beautiful, and there's loads of space. Why don't we get married there? Just picture it- marquee in the garden, band over at the back, flowers all up the staircase. Fairy lights in all the trees…"

"Wow," I smiled widely and my ears popped too. "You've really thought about this."

He shrugged; his cheeks pink with a slight blush. "I don't want to wait ages for the sake of a country hotel or manor. We're about to start our whole lives in that house, why not get married there?"

"That's ridiculously romantic, Zack."

"Is that a yes then?" he asked.

"I already said yes once." I held my hand up as I spoke, my engagement ring sparkled even under the fluorescent lights of the cabin. "But yes, it's another yes. I love that idea!"

He pulled me to him in a long, slow, seductive kiss, unfortunately interrupted by the stewardess coughing in disapproval as she checked our seat belts.

"How long until we get there?" he whispered, as he stroked my arm. "I'm having bad thoughts about you right now."

"We took off about four minutes ago. You've got a while yet! And no to any thoughts you might have about anything happening on a plane. I'm not even taking my seat belt off."

We spent the flight sipping gin and making lists of what we needed to book and choose. Even having the wedding at the house, this was going to be tight to get it all arranged. But maybe it was better than stretching it out over a year. I made a note to message my mum as soon as I landed and get dress shopping booked in urgently.

We were both super giddy, and Zack was extremely handsy in the taxi on the way to our destination. As we drove through the gates, the villa appeared, whitewashed and beautiful, also absolutely huge. The sun was beginning to lower towards the horizon, and the lights around the large pool sparkled in the glow.

"Wow, is this all ours?" Zack asked me.

"Yep! Happy birthday gorgeous." I kissed him. "Turning thirty isn't all bad."

"Turning thirty is fantastic so far," he grinned. "Everything is perfect. I love you." He looked out of the window. "I don't know if even we can christen all the rooms in a place this big in one long weekend, though."

I elbowed him. "One track mind."

He laughed. "As if you're not just as bad, Lily."

Zack grabbed the suitcases from the taxi and tipped the driver. He set them off to one side, and before I knew what was happening, he picked me up and slung me over his shoulder in a fireman's lift.

"Finally," he said. "I get you alone."

I screamed and kicked my legs, wanting to get down and open the front door to reveal his surprise. I had no chance, though, he had hold of me in a tight grip.

As he got to the front door, he lifted my skirt up and began to kiss the top of my thigh, just where it met my bottom. "Zack, stop." I tried to say in between panicked laughter as his lips tickled my skin. I was starting to panic, knowing everyone was on the other side of that door.

"Nope, never. That was a torturous plane flight, went on forever."

"Zack, listen to me, you need to put me down right now, you need to—"

He spanked me hard as he opened the door. "Shush. You are getting it, right now, right here."

The word surprise fizzled out from an enthusiastic start as everyone heard what he said. He plonked me down to the ground. "Shit, sorry."

"That's what I was trying to tell you." I was bright red. Maybe also a little sad that he hadn't been able to carry on with that plan. "Surprise! Happy Birthday," I shouted, desperate to cover up the embarrassment.

Everyone seemed to snap out of it, and we were

enveloped in hugs and kisses. Glasses of wine were passed around, and Zack's mum took us out by the pool where a veritable feast of Mediterranean delicacies awaited us.

Zack pulled me onto his knee as we cuddled on an outside lounge seat, and we all filled him in on how we'd been plotting this for months. Hannah couldn't stop laughing. "Zack, I didn't quite hear what you said when you came in, sorry, can you repeat it?"

He threw an olive at her, and I pressed my face into his neck to stifle a giggle. "That was mortifying," I whispered.

His arm was wrapped around me as he rubbed my warm skin gently. "You couldn't have planned it for them to arrive after us? I still want to carry on with that intention."

"Well, we'll be married in three months, you best enjoy yourself, it'll be all downhill from there," I teased as I stood up and drained the last dregs of wine from my glass. "I'm just going to take my bag up and get changed," I announced to anyone who was listening.

"Your room's the last one on the left, at the end of the corridor." Hannah winked as Zack followed me, grabbing our suitcases on the way.

I walked into our room and smiled, relaxed and at peace. It was beautiful, bright and airy. It looked so fresh- crisp, white bed covers, beautiful turquoise accessories. I inhaled a deep breath; even the air smelled glorious, Mediterranean and warm, hints of citrus and the ocean.

"Finally." Zack pulled me to him as he closed the door, the suitcases abandoned. His hands reached into my hair and held my face to his as he kissed me.

I relaxed into him. The heat in the room, all the wedding talk, everyone being here together like this… I wanted him so much.

He lifted me up, and my legs wrapped around him. My fingers sought out his hair as I held onto him. "What did you say I was getting? I missed it before, sorry." I bit his lip.

"Don't worry, you won't miss it this time." He slid his hand inside my skirt, teasing me as he traced his fingers softly over my skin, heading in just the direction I wanted him to.

"We need to be quiet; the doors are open." I motioned towards the open balcony doors.

"I can be quiet," he whispered. "But can you?"

At that point, his fingers found the exact spot I'd hoped they would. He pressed his lips harder against mine to muffle the noises I made. "Shh," he reminded me as he pressed me against the wall, his leg moved up under me as a balance while he drove me crazy with his hand.

"I should make the most of this," I said. "You turn thirty tomorrow; you won't be able to lift me up like this for long."

I pouted as he pulled his fingers away from me. "I can stop now if you'd prefer…" His breaths were rapid as he looked at me, those dark eyes full of love, lust and desire.

I shook my head and pulled him back into another kiss as my fingers tugged his jeans down. "Please don't stop."

"Keep kissing me, be quiet, hold on tight." He pushed against me, his tongue met mine with urgency and stilled the moans that threatened to escape my lips.

I didn't even care anymore if anyone could hear the rhythmic thuds as he pressed me into the wall over and over again. I felt on fire; the heat of the room made our skin hot and damp as we moved against each other. My mouth was full of him but desperate for more as we worked out all the frustration of the plane journey. I honestly felt as though I could never tire of having him inside me like this.

He held me against the wall, kissing me softly for a minute as our hearts returned to normal rates along with our breaths. Then, with a smile, he placed me down on the bed and cuddled up to me, continuing to press kisses to my hot skin.

"So, Lily, you know when we get married?"

I took a deep breath of him, content in this moment. "Mmhmm."

"Do you think... that maybe..." He seemed nervous. I stroked the side of his face. "Maybe you could stop the pill straight away?"

I looked into those gorgeous brown eyes. I could imagine our babies so vividly, they'd be angelic. He looked hopeful as he watched me.

"How about the day before our wedding is my last one?" I bit my lip as he pulled me even closer and took a deep breath against my skin.

"That sounds perfect. This is like heaven, you know? You and me, this beautiful place, all my family. Knowing that when we get home we have the house, the wedding and an absolute ton of baby making to look forward to."

"Not even turning thirty could bring you down then?" I asked with a smile.

"Definitely not. I can't wait, for all of it. I love you so much. I don't think you understand how deeply."

"I understand, Zack." I rubbed my nose side to side against his. "You know that your whole family knows what we're doing up here, though?"

"They'll get over it," Zack grinned at me as he spoke. "Round two while we're here?"

"Yes please..."

If anyone was suspicious about what we'd been up to, they, thankfully, didn't show it. Well, maybe just Cassie.

"I can't believe I've ended up with the bedroom next to you." She elbowed me in the side as she headed over and filled both of our wine glasses to the brim. "Hope you got it all out your systems earlier."

"Very funny," I rolled my eyes at her. "Were the girls OK on the flight?"

"They loved it," she smiled and glanced over to where they played with Zack's nephews. "Pity that Guy couldn't make it, but you know what his work is like."

I nodded. "I expect it'll be the same with Zack now, not much flexibility."

"Well, that's just a perfect excuse for us to come to places like this together without them." She winked, and we headed back to the group arm in arm.

My soul felt full to bursting as I looked around. Such beautiful surroundings and all this love and happiness. How did I end up this blessed?

Zack pulled me close to him and kissed my cheek. "Shall we tell them?"

Maisie immediately piped up, loud and shrill, "Are you pregnant?"

"No!" I said with a pout as I looked down at my flat stomach. *Why would she say that?*

Zack laughed. "No, but we can announce the wedding date and venue."

There were excited noises, and everyone focused on Zack as he spoke. "The thirtieth of May, and the wedding will be at our new house."

Lydia gasped. "That'll be beautiful! Are you going to put a marquee in the garden?"

We laughed as we nodded and shared all of our plans. The next couple of hours passed in a blissful blur of wedding and birthday talk. I'd never felt part of such a big, happy group before. It was incredible. I felt loved. So complete. For the first time, I could see that Luke had been right, this was working; the future would be beautiful.

I face-timed my mum and dad, sad that they couldn't be here to share the moment, but neither of them was keen on flying, and I knew there'd be more celebrations when we got home. As soon as the call ended, Hannah shouted over to me.

"How many bridesmaids are you having, Lily?" Her face was full of mischief as suddenly, four stunning brunettes and a beautiful blonde all watched me with intense gazes and hopeful faces.

I blushed at the attention. "Erm, I don't think I need any with it just being at the house and—"

"Lily Forshaw!" Cassie pointed her finger at me as she sternly spoke my name. "This is your chance to get revenge for that blue monstrosity I made you wear at my wedding. I demand a vile bridesmaids dress."

I smiled broadly as I looked around at all their faces. "You all want to be bridesmaids?" Lots of nodding and chorused variations of yes met me. "I guess, I'll have five bridesmaids then, and two flower girls." I glanced at Ruby and Emilia; how adorable would they be?

There were lots of whoops and cheers as we ended up in a giant, girly hug. Laughter rang out as prosecco splashed down tops and hair got tangled in earrings. Zack looked on in amusement. "I always wanted a girlfriend who liked my sisters, but this is too far."

As we all sat back down, Lydia refilled glasses, never happier than when looking after her family. Maisie looked towards Zack, "Have you chosen a best man?"

"I haven't asked him yet, but it'll be Adam." Zack took a long drink from a cold beer bottle. A drop of condensation dripped onto his arm, and I just momentarily longed to go over and lick it off. The heat was doing strange things to me.

"Please, please, please invite all those hot Icelandic guys," begged Leah with a cheeky grin. Her dad did not look impressed. The twin babies of the family were one hundred percent out of bounds to boys as far as Zack's dad, Harry, was concerned.

We stayed out by the pool until well after the sunset.

Ruby and Emilia had, as always, gravitated towards Zack, and were fast asleep, cuddled up to him on a large outdoor sofa. Everyone just seemed content together, warm, tipsy, and full of hope and happiness. I wanted life to feel like this, always.

FOURTEEN

"*H*appy birthday, beautiful," I murmured, still half asleep, as I felt Zack stir the next morning. He wrapped me in a tight hug. "I don't know how I'm ever meant to compete with your birthday ABC though."

"Are you kidding me?" He sat up and leant on his arm. "Arranging all of this? It's the best birthday. You *are* going to wander around all day in a tiny bikini, aren't you?"

I slapped him across the chest playfully. "Maybe if it was just us. I think we had enough awkward moments yesterday, didn't we?"

"If it was just us, you'd be wearing precisely nothing…" He pulled my t-shirt over my head.

"Erm, Zachary." He laughed lightly, causing me to I grin. The mischievous part of me loved the effect his name had on him. "Happy birthday," I kissed down his chest, pulling the thin covers over my head as birthday present number one began.

Lydia had arranged a delicious and extravagant birthday breakfast. A huge table was set out by the pool once again. It overflowed with pastries of every variety and fresh fruit platters. One whole section was dedicated to juices and, of course, coffee. Zack was worse than me without coffee. There were balloons, presents, and cards everywhere. I took hundreds of photographs to capture Zack's face on this happy day. His smile so wide; those dark eyes so alive as they sparkled with happiness. I loved seeing him in sexy work suits, but the difference now was striking – his whole body was relaxed, a sexy, sun-soaked sheen set on his skin. It very much suited him, we needed time out like this more often.

I sat to one side, helping the kids to colour in as Zack spent time opening gifts with his sisters. They were just such a gorgeous family; I adored each and every one of them. How lucky was I to be accepted by them the way I had been? I felt like a stuck record, but it just kept hitting me. My upbringing had been lovely, I couldn't have wished for more, but I had been lonely for company at times. I can't imagine anyone ever felt that way growing up in the Beaumont household.

Hannah came and sat next to me. "I'm glad you two set a date. It's a brilliant idea to have the wedding at the new house. What a start to your future."

"It really is. He's such a sweetheart. It was all Zack's idea, I adore it." I smiled as I looked across at him. My heart fluttered; I hoped that never wore off.

The younger and more energetic members of the family jumped in and out the pool, the sounds of their splashes and shouts echoing around the beautiful terrace. As soon as we had enough caffeine in us, Zack and I moved onto birthday champagne. He was still opening cards and gifts. There were lots I'd brought from home, so he got them on the right day. He opened a large card that was from everyone at Caddel & Boone; I knew they still missed him – he got mentioned all the time, which made me smile. There was a generous gift card for his favourite master barber shop, as well as a mysterious USB. "It's probably a daft birthday message," he said. "I'll watch it later."

Everyone spent the day lazing and playing by the pool, it was like heaven. There was also a gorgeous hot tub, which I really wanted to get Zack alone in at some point.

We'd decided to go out together on a date that night, and I'd made reservations at a beautiful restaurant in the nearest town. Taxis were booked, seductive underwear was on, we were good to go.

The heat had made my hair frizzy, and as I faffed with it in the bathroom, Zack sat on the bed with his laptop to watch the USB. I don't know what it was at the moment, but he looked incredible, the perfect mix of handsome and rugged, yet completely stylish.

Five minutes later, hair big but hopefully still cute, I walked back into the bedroom, wanting to impress Zack with my little black dress and strappy heels. I hadn't quite had the chance to get a tan yet, but there was still time.

Zack was still on the bed, but he looked as though the life had been drained out of him. His finger hovered over the laptop keyboard, his skin pale as snow, far from the tan he'd been developing.

"Zack, what's wrong? Are you OK?" I asked as I hurried over to him.

He looked at me, his eyes narrowed. "Lily… What the hell is this?" His finger hit the laptop hard as he clicked on a file.

A fuzzy, muffled sound began to play, the background noise of glasses and bottles clinked, then faded slightly as a voice began to speak. My voice.

"That night, before you left... It felt like we..."

"I know, I know what you mean. I wanted to make it easy on you."

"It wasn't easy. I've learned to deal with it, Luke, but it's never been easy."

"Zack…" I felt like my knees were about to buckle. "Please stop, I can explain this." He glared at me and turned the volume up.

"Learned to deal with it with a big diamond?"

"What do you expect me to do? You cut me off, you told me to go be with Zack. I was in absolute bits, I could barely function. It took me weeks to even act semi normal with him. I..."

"I'm sorry. I honestly thought I was doing the best thing for you. I always, only did everything for you, Lily."

"I know, I know, Luke. You're too good; that's part of the problem. I miss you so much, you have no idea."

"I have every idea. Everywhere I go in my house, I just picture you there. I was thinking about selling it, just to try and get peace in my mind, but part of me can't stand to."

"We're about to get the sweetest bit." He looked at me as though he hated me, his eyes narrow and stormy. I knew what was coming. I sank to the floor as I listened, I was powerless to stop him, to stop this.

"I can't go through it again. I still can't say for sure what I would've done that morning if you hadn't left, if you hadn't sent that email, but, Luke... I think it was going to be you. That night, that night was perfection. Nothing's ever come close, it never will."

"You want to explain this?" Zack asked, his eyes still focused on the laptop.

"Was that what was in your birthday card?"

Zack nodded, his eyes glazed with the effort of not crying. "Explain to me what the hell that was?"

"Anna must've done it, you know what she's like, she—"

Zack shouted as he cut me off. I winced involuntarily. "I don't care about who recorded it or why, I care about what you and him said to each other. I don't even get why you were with him when you promised me you wouldn't be. You promised me, Lily!"

I shuffled forwards on my knees and tried to take his hand, but he snatched it away. I gulped as I spoke, it felt as though an apple was trapped in my throat.

"When you were in Iceland, before Christmas, I got called to cover mediation at the last minute. I didn't want to go, but I honestly didn't have a choice. Everyone was there, I had to go, Margaret would have fired me if I'd said no."

He nodded briskly, then watched me, waiting for me to continue.

"We had a chat, as you've heard," I sighed. My heart beat ten to the dozen in my chest. "That was it. We didn't kiss, we didn't swap numbers, I haven't seen him since. It was a hiccup that wasn't supposed to happen."

"Then why didn't you tell me?"

"It seemed like I'd just be upsetting you over nothing. I can see now how stupid that was." I wiped a tear from my eye; I hated the fact this had just destroyed his entire birthday. *Bloody Anna!*

"What email does he mean?" Zack asked, his voice full of fury.

"It's from a long time ago, it doesn't matter. You're what matters to me, Zack." I wanted to beg him to believe me.

"Then why are you lying to me?" He barely kept his voice in check.

"I wasn't. It was an accident; I was never meant to see him. I did everything right, Zack. I spoke to him, as you've heard. Then I left. There didn't seem to be any point upsetting you over that." He continued to look down at the laptop. "I want what we've been talking about. The house, to be your wife, to have babies with you. I want that. I love you."

"Tell me about the email, the full truth."

I wiped tears away from my cheeks. To think five minutes ago, the humidity and my hair had been my biggest concern. "When I stayed at Cassie's last year, when we were on a break... Luke emailed me, and basically, told me to go be with you."

Zack's eyes flashed with hot anger. "So, you're only with me because he told you to be?"

"No, Zack, no, please, I love you."

"Let me just play this again."

"I can't go through it again. I still can't say for sure what I would've done that morning if you hadn't left, if you hadn't sent that email, but, Luke... I think it was going to be you."

"You were going to choose him, weren't you, Lily?" He spat the words at me. I'd seen him angry before, but this was different, it scared me.

"I don't know, Zack; I don't know what I was doing. That was ages ago, I *do* know what I'm doing now, I know what I want. Anna has just done this to cause trouble—"

"Don't fucking blame her!" he raged, his volume out of control. I knew everyone downstairs would be able to hear. "Yes, she's a bitch, but you were the one cosied up to *him* while I was at work." The word 'him' dripped with hatred.

"We weren't cosied up. Not at all. Please, Zack."

"Then what was that comment, Lily? That night was perfection? Fucking him was perfection, was it?"

I almost gagged, my mouth filled up with saliva as my stomach contracted into painful spasms.

"No, no, that's not what I meant. Please," I begged.

"No wonder it took so long to get you back into bed

when you came back." His face was snarled up, like I'd never seen it before. "Have you just been thinking about him every, single, time?" He enunciated each word with venom.

"Of course not. Please trust me, I—" Zack cut me off before I could finish the sentence. His voice boomed around the room.

"I don't think I can ever trust you. Every time I think this has gone away, it rears its head again. How happy have we been lately? And it was all fake for you."

"It wasn't." I gulped for air as tears rolled down my face. "It wasn't fake, I love you, I love you so much."

"Do you know… as hard as this is, in six months, when we'd be married and everything, it would be worse. I can't do this anymore, Lily."

"What? Zack… what do you mean? Please, please don't do this," I begged him as I knelt on the cold, tiled floor, in what was meant to be a dress to seduce him on his thirtieth birthday, desperate for him not to give up on us. "It was absolutely nothing. I'll find out if she has more of the tape, you'll see how it ended. It was nothing."

"You have one chance here, be one hundred per cent honest. Did you choose me, or did he make the decision for you?" Zack's eyes looked colder than I'd ever known them.

I took a deep breath; I could already feel him falling away from me. How could it be a few short hours ago we were curled up together talking about our future and now, this. "I hadn't made my decision… the email forced it."

"I want you to go. Now." He slammed the laptop shut and turned away from me.

"No, Zack, no. I love you. I want to be with you. This is stupid, over something from the past."

"No," he roared in an uncontrolled rage. Never mind his family, I think this whole region of Spain could hear him. "It's not stupid. I'm stupid for thinking you'd ever leave him behind. I said before I wouldn't play second fiddle to him.

Go screw your best friend. I give up. *I. Give. Up*. Just go. Now."

He stormed out; the door slammed behind him so hard the room shook. I crossed to the Juliette balcony, and through blurry eyes, saw people look up at me. Others headed towards him as he got into the taxi that was supposed to take us out for dinner. Leah and Maisie quickly jumped into it with him, and they were gone.

The bedroom door burst open, and Cassie rushed in. She wrapped her arms around me as I sobbed into her shoulder; my tears soaked into her thin sun top. "What the hell, Lily? What just happened? You couldn't keep your hands off each other earlier. Did I just hear him say it was over?"

I nodded as I whimpered, which spread the tears even further. She held me tight as I sobbed uncontrollably. I was hot, sticky, snotty, full of tears, crying so hard I couldn't think, never mind speak.

"What happened?" she asked in her kindest voice as she stroked my cheek and wiped my hot tears away. I gestured over towards the laptop, which Zack had left on the bed before he stormed out. Cassie sat down and opened it up. I could see her focus on the file before she pressed play.

I kept my head between my knees and pressed my legs against my ears to block out the sound of Luke and I talking; I didn't want to hear it ever again. After a couple of minutes, Cassie came back over to me and gently lifted my head up, her eyes close to mine.

"You didn't tell me you'd seen Luke. When was that?" I could sense concern in Cassie's voice but also notes of tension, hidden anger.

"Just before Christmas. We didn't plan it… I tried to get out of it. I really did try, but it was last minute, and I would've been in the worst trouble at work if I didn't go." I wiped my eyes again on my bare arm, wishing I had long sleeves. The air in the room was hot and stifling, it made me feel dizzy and nauseous.

"Why did you keep it secret? You should've said. You didn't even tell me."

"There wasn't much to tell. Honestly, that conversation, that was pretty much it. We didn't kiss, we didn't arrange to meet again, it was just one more goodbye. A horrible good-bye. I went home and cried like a banshee, and then it was done. I focused on Zack and our future. But... it's ruined everything. Anna has ruined it all; I'm going to kill her, I swear, Cassie!"

"I'm sure Zack will have calmed down when he gets back," she tried to reassure me.

I shook my head, and a multitude of fresh tears sprang from my eyes. "I don't think so. I think that was it for him."

"No, sweetheart... He adores you. You're getting married soon. He isn't going to give up that easy."

"I know him, Cass, that wasn't him... He wants me to go. I should go." I went to stand, my mind not knowing what to think. Should I pack and leave? Should I give up? She pulled me back down to her and focused her words on me, like she would when she needed to calm her children down.

"Just get what you need for tonight, and come stay with me and the girls in our room. He'll be back, he'll calm down, and you two can sort of all this out. I'll go and just vaguely explain it's a misunderstanding, and then I'll bring all the wine upstairs for us until you fall asleep. OK, lovely?"

A fresh barrage of tears assaulted me as I hugged her tight against me. What would I ever do without this girl? Of all the heartbreaks I could imagine, losing her would be the absolute worst. That brought me right back to the fact I'd denied her something she desperately wanted, denied it because Zack didn't want it.

I grabbed my pyjamas, toothbrush and phone. Who needed cleanser on a night like this?! I also grabbed the USB from the laptop, I didn't want Zack to sit and listen again when he eventually came back. If he came back.

Ruby and Emilia were asleep in bunk beds as I crept into Cassie's room and lay under the cool covers of her double bed. I watched their faces as I lay quietly, so peaceful and beautiful. Just as I wondered about if I'd ever get to lie down and look upon my own children, Cassie tiptoed in with two bottles of wine and two glasses. She grimaced and eyed the girls as the glasses clinked together, then poured the wine generously for each of us, before slipping into bed beside me.

I smiled, a hopeless, sad smile as tears leaked from my eyes again. "I'm scared to see him tomorrow, Cassie. What if he won't even talk to me?"

"He'll want to talk, of course he will," she reassured me.

"Are you sure? You know what he's like, this could last days. I'm mad at him for doing this, but at the same time heartbroken that he had to hear that, on his birthday of all days." I took a huge gulp of the wine, almost choking as it combined with my tears.

We sat in the bed, held hands, and drank the wine in silence, before Cassie took the near empty glass from me and gave me a tight hug. "Get some sleep, we'll sort it all out tomorrow."

I heard her breath settle into the slow pattern of sleep as I lay there, eyes wide open as I watched the moonlight seep in around the curtains. I couldn't sleep, there was no way. I was going to listen for Zack's return, I needed to know he was safe and not out doing something stupid again, or someone…

I shot bolt upright in bed as I heard a door slam, causing the room to shake. Immediately, I threw my arm across my eyes as bright sunshine assaulted my face. Squinting out, I saw that Cassie and the girls were gone. I felt nauseous as I realised that slamming door was the bedroom next door, mine and Zack's.

I tiptoed to the bathroom, feeling foolish as I crept around, it's not like he was going to burst in here to get me. A long, exhausted breath escaped my mouth as I saw my sorry reflection in the mirror. Eyes bloodshot and baggy, skin red from a combination of the sun and the crying. My hair was like a bird's nest. This was far removed from the sexy birthday treat I'd tried to achieve last night.

My hand shook as I brushed my teeth and forced my wild, scruffy hair into a high ponytail. I splashed water on my face and crossed to the bedroom door. It wasn't just my hand that trembled now, my whole body was in a state of alert, ready for flight or fight. I didn't know what was going to happen.

I knocked on our bedroom door, eliciting no response. I could hear the bangs of drawers and doors inside. I cautiously inched it open and peeped around.

Zack was still in his clothes from last night, his hair was still, somehow, perfect, but his face was thunderous. He had his suitcase on the bed and clothes were being tossed into it haphazardly, not at all like him, especially considering what he'd spent on the designer labels. He looked up, and our eyes met for the briefest of seconds before he looked away.

"Thought you would've run back to him by now." The words were snarled as he spoke, he was still in a total rage, and I knew it was pointless to try and communicate when he was like this.

"I don't want to be with him, I don't know how to make you see. I'm with you, we're supposed to be getting married remember?"

A mean, half laugh escaped his lips, but he didn't stop piling his belongings into the case. I stepped fully into the room, wincing as he slammed another cupboard.

"Zack, can you please stop, can we talk?"

Suddenly, he was close up to me, his face contorted in anger and rage. "There is nothing to talk about. I meant what I said. I will not play second best to him. I will not marry you and spend forever wondering if you're seeing him, missing him, fucking him. Every time I look at you, I see him all over you. We are done."

"If you just listen to that conversation again when you're a little calmer, you'll see—"

He cut me off, angrily. "Every time I see you on your phone, I'll think you're messaging him. Every time you go to Cassie's, I'll think you're secretly seeing him. I'll wonder, on our wedding day, if you wish I was him. I can't live like that." His voice wavered, and my heart cracked in mirrored sympathy. I reached my arm out to him; utterly afraid of what was happening here, he shrugged me off and turned away. "Every time we make love, I'll think you wish I was him. It's better this ends now, than I spend the rest of my life wondering if I'm just a consolation prize."

He stormed back towards the bed and continued his frenzy; clothes being bundled up and thrown into the suitcase. He tried to zip it up but it wouldn't close. He muttered angrily, swearing more than I'd known before. I backed away towards the door, just in time as he lifted the case and hurled it towards the wall. The beautiful full-length mirror that stood adjacent to the end of the bed shattered into thousands of tiny pieces of glass with the impact. I was knocked to the side as Zack barged past me without so much as a glance and slammed the door behind him, leaving me in the empty room full of smashed glass and screwed up clothes, mirroring the wreck that was our relationship right now.

Cassie bolted in a moment later. She surveyed the state of the room through anxious eyes before taking my face in her hands and looking me over. "Are you OK?" she asked.

I nodded and buried my head into her shoulder, wracked with sobs of utter despair. He wasn't going to calm down from this. I knew him. It was all over, all our dreams, our future.

I sank down to the floor, and she sat with me, her arms wrapped protectively around my shoulders. "Cassie," I asked. "Can we try and get a flight later today? I don't want to stay here, I can't be on the flight with him tomorrow."

She pulled her phone from the pocket of her shorts and began to search websites. "Of course we can, if that's what you want. Do you want me to go and talk to him?"

I shook my head. "Nobody can talk to him when he's like this."

A few hours later, after abusing Guy's credit card for four last minute flights, Cassie held my hand as our plane took off. We were on our way back to Manchester, away from Zack and into a situation that I had no idea how to handle. All I knew was that my heart was battered and bruised, and still firmly in that villa, which I had just fled from.

FIFTEEN

J found myself resident in the granny flat once more. What would we all do without Cassie's granny flat? I was completely confused about how a holiday could start with so much love and promise and yet end with absolute devastation; I still couldn't quite take it all in. A full week passed, yet another week when I rang in sick, and Margaret sounded as though she was at the end of her patience. I knew the case was at a crucial point, and I'd promised I wouldn't let her down, but I couldn't function right now, I'd be a hindrance rather than a help.

I'd messaged and called Zack over and over. I switched between begging him to speak to me, then trying to plead with his practicality that the house sale was due to go through imminently, and we needed to sort this out. He didn't reply, and he didn't answer calls. I tried to speak to his mum and his sisters, and although they were civil, it was clear they weren't prepared to get involved and were firmly on his side, which was understandable... I supposed.

The only replies I did get were late at night when I assumed he was drunk. They involved sarcastic snippets of the conversation he'd heard between Luke and I. I couldn't get through to him that it wasn't the whole story, and he was throwing us away over an incomplete anecdote somehow recorded by a devious bitch who had it in for us from the start. I remembered the barman on his break who had been sat next to us, it could only have been him. Anna must've got him to do her dirty work for her.

Cassie urged me to go back to the house and confront Zack, but I was too scared. I was petrified of how final this all was, and I didn't want that to be verified by him. I was also torn between utter rage that I was vilified here when I hadn't done anything wrong, this time at least. I couldn't eat, sleep, focus on anything properly- in a bittersweet way, it reminded me how I'd been when we fell in love, but was this the opposite?

It got to the point that we were seven days away from completion on the new house, when Zack rang me.

"Hi." I answered the phone with caution, unsure what to expect.

"I just wanted to let you know I spoke to the solicitors this morning and told them we weren't going ahead with the house purchase." His voice was cold, I'd never known him sound like this.

"Zack, why? There's no need for this."

"There's every need. I can't trust you. What do we have without that?" Zack asked. He spoke to me like I was a client to be questioned, not a person he loved.

"That night, I did everything I should've done, I walked away from Luke because I'm engaged to you, because I want you."

"You didn't tell me, though."

"Because I knew you'd get like this, and there wasn't anything to tell," I tried again to explain.

"About the engaged thing, you can keep the ring, I'm not bothered. But we're not engaged anymore, Lily."

"How can you be so cold about this?" I sobbed down the

phone. He was crushing my heart, my dreams of our future together.

"Don't you dare even say that, you have no idea the extent to which you've fucked up my life. I wish I'd never even got that coffee with you. You've destroyed me," he shouted down the phone, and I winced at the hurt his words caused.

"Zack, I know I screwed up a lot of stuff. You haven't exactly been a saint either, in case you've forgotten. But in this instance, I've done nothing wrong, and you're throwing away our whole future over that."

"I can't live our future always thinking that he's around the corner, always wondering if I was the second choice. That's the problem, and that's never going to go away," Zack said with a sigh. "I'm away all of next week, do you think you could come and take your stuff? I'll cover all the bills and rent, it's not a problem. Just leave your key when you go."

"Seriously?" I asked, choking on the sheer amount of tears that fell away from me.

"Seriously."

"You're not the person I thought you were, Zack. Not even close. You're giving up on me, again."

I ended the call, not wanting to hear his response, and threw the phone across the room. How the hell could he have taken that conversation so badly. I'd done the right thing. Yes, I'd spoken to Luke, but I hadn't kissed him; I hadn't told him I loved him; I hadn't betrayed Zack.

I'd let Cassie down for him. I'd tried everything to show him how committed I was- the house, the wedding, the baby plans. I wanted it all so much. I wanted *him* so much.

I couldn't believe it was over. His jealousy, his insecurities, that was the problem here. I sighed as the realisation dawned on me, that it was my behaviour which had sent those traits into overdrive. I really had messed him up.

I just felt cold, empty. Resigned to all this absolute bullshit. I cursed Cassie, not for the first time; she should've just left me alone. I never should have gone on that blind date. I was much better off when I was alone.

I got the train home, if it was still that, a couple of days later. The rented house was already partially packed up as we'd been almost ready to move. I'd arranged for Cassie to meet me there the following day and bring all my things back. I guess the granny flat was going to be my permanent lodging for now until I figured out what the hell I was going to do. Standing outside our house, I felt anger burn through me. There was someone who needed to answer for all of this. I opened the front door, threw my overnight bag in, then turned around and headed for the city centre.

Ella smiled at me from behind the reception desk as I walked into the lobby of Caddel and Boone. "Lily! I heard you were ill. God you look awful. Should you be here?" Her face screwed up, not entirely in concern, more like she was worried she would catch ugly from me. I hadn't worn make-up all week, no point when it all got cried off, and I guess I couldn't exactly remember the last time I'd done my hair nicely; it must have been in Spain. I was a mess, inside and out.

"I'm not that bad," I replied, my forehead screwed up tight. "I need something from upstairs, won't be a minute."

I could feel my hands fist into balls of rage as I headed up the staircase, heat surged into me, and I wiped my damp forehead nervously, not knowing what I was going to say or do. As I stepped out into the corridor from the stairwell, I heard her shrill laughter from the staff room. That's when I got a taste of how Zack felt when the anger overtook him.

In that moment, I felt as though I was looking down on myself as I marched in, right up to Anna's chair. She was concentrating on whatever tale she was sharing, and it made me smile to hear her screech as I grabbed hold of her shiny, blonde ponytail and pulled her up.

"What the hell is wrong with you?" I screamed in her face as she turned to me, her lip quivering in shock, the rest of her face not moving – I wondered how much she spent to look so plastic.

When she realised it was me, a smirk spread across her face. "Let go of me, you psycho. What are you talking about?"

I pulled her hair tighter. "You know exactly what I mean. Zack's little birthday present? I know you hate me, but it didn't occur to you what a shitty thing to do to him that was?"

"Let go of me right now, and I won't take this any further. Zack needed to know you were tarting around with that lawyer, no matter how hot he was." Her eyes narrowed as she spoke.

"I didn't do anything wrong, and you know it. This is just because Zack rejected you, how long ago now?" I let go of her hair but continued to look down at her with as menacing a face as I could muster. I was much taller than her, might as well use it to my advantage.

"As if I would want your used goods, Lily. Bet he's got that barmaid back in his bed right now—"

My palm slapped across her cheek with a deafening crack before I could stop myself, before she could finish the sentence. My hand then flew to my open mouth as I realised what I'd done. I saw the red sting appear on her cheek, then I looked across the table and saw Margaret watching, wide-eyed and open-mouthed.

I staggered back a couple of steps, horrified at myself. I'd never, ever hit anyone before. Everyone swarmed around Anna to make sure she was OK, everyone except Margaret, who marched to me and took hold of my arm, pulling me with her along the corridor to her office.

"Sit down," she commanded as she banged the door shut

behind us. I did as I was told, shaky and hot. This was definitely like I was in the headmistress's office except now my parents wouldn't be on their way.

"I don't know where to begin." Margaret paced up and down the room as she spoke. "You're not even meant to be here, I thought you were sick? Your sickness record is frankly disgraceful anyway and seems to revolve around your love life. You've let us down on this case. Then, to top it all off, I witnessed you assault a member of staff."

"I'm sorry about that, she hates me; she broke me and Zack up and—"

Margaret cut me off and held her hand up in front of my face. "We're not in high school, Lily. Can you just listen to yourself?"

I couldn't hold it in anymore; my head thumped onto the desk as I gave up; tears ran down my cheeks and dripped onto my scruffy t-shirt. I heard Margaret let out a long sigh as she sat opposite me.

"Lily, you fitted in here since day one, not just because of Zack. You're obviously going through a lot, and I don't want to add to it, but I have to act on this. It's gross misconduct. You know what that means?" Her voice had kindness in it as she spoke, but sadly, I knew exactly what she meant.

My forehead bumped on her desk as I nodded and slowly looked up at her through teary eyes. "Do you want me to clear my desk now?"

"I think it's best. Wait there five minutes, and I'll come with you, can still hear Anna screeching. I never said this – but there's been many times I wanted to slap her myself."

Margaret pulled the door closed behind her. I reached for a tissue from the box on her desk and clumsily knocked a pile of mail to the floor. It didn't even look like she'd sorted through it yet. This would normally be my job, but I'd left them in the lurch once again. I quickly picked the mail up, wanting to tidy before she came back, when one letter in particular caught my eye.

Spidery, clumsy handwriting... I knew that writing, I'd seen it all over the documentation lately. He may be amazing at scoring goals, but Kye Maloney's penmanship was dreadful. It was addressed personally to Anna, and marked as strictly private and confidential.

My decision was made in a split second as I slipped it inside my handbag and made the stack of letters look immaculate again. When Margaret walked back in the room, I was still wiping tears away.

I stood and followed her; her hand rested on my shoulder as she opened the door. This small gesture was the kindest she'd ever shown me. Maybe she wasn't as bad as I thought, but then again, she was firing me. I avoided eye contact with everyone as I emptied my desk into a cardboard file box. If we had had security, I had no doubt they would have escorted me out of the building like in some Hollywood movie.

"I'm sorry it came to this," said Margaret as we waited at the door for the taxi she had ordered. "I hope the situation resolves itself for you."

I managed a vague, sad smile as I left her there, before I climbed into the taxi and gave my address. I realised, for the last time, it wasn't my home anymore. The driver, thankfully, left me alone as I sat on the back seat and sobbed my heart out.

Twenty-nine, unemployed, living in my friend's garden, and heartbroken two times over. Fantastic. I was absolutely screwed.

My gulping sobs continued as I walked through the door and remembered every happy time we'd had in here. Zack had already taken all our photographs down. I wanted them, but for all I knew, he'd thrown them away or burned them in the garden like in a vengeful chick flick.

I wandered to the kitchen, noting he'd left dirty mugs in the sink. That drove me mad usually, but now... I loved him; I'd love to be playfully nagging him as I washed them.

I opened the fridge and found it bare. He obviously hadn't shopped since Spain. He was probably just out drinking and kissing little blonde tarts.

I didn't need food; I had zero appetite, but I did need wine. Serious amounts of wine. I still hadn't taken my jacket or shoes off so just turned around and headed straight back out through the front door in the direction of the local shop. I made sure to give my box from the office a good kick in temper as I went.

The winter weather was still cold and bleak, but I put my sunglasses on anyway, not wanting people to see how hollow and red my eyes were. What an absolute mess I was.

I bought two bottles of wine and a pack of pre-mixed gin and tonic cans. That combination probably wouldn't end well, but I was beyond caring. I was tempted to buy cigarettes, in the vague hope it would act like one of Luke's joints and chill me out, but I knew it would more likely just make me sick.

I paused outside the shop to check my phone, in the vague hope that someone other than Cassie or my mum actually wanted to speak to me right now. Nope. No messages, no calls, nothing.

I sighed as I looked up. New graffiti had appeared on the wall opposite the shop. At least it wasn't a random tag that I couldn't understand this time. It had actual words.

The endless loop of
you and I Lily
Together, anywhere
The world can see this one frozen moment
but only you and I can experience
this lack of air between us
Forevermore

My breath stopped. I read it again.

This time it had my name in it. This time I couldn't doubt.

I left my bag of precious, mind-numbing wine on the floor as I crossed over the road and walked towards the wall, oblivious to any potential danger from the traffic.

I stroked my finger over my name in the words. The paint was dry but recent. Luke wouldn't do graffiti, though, he couldn't have done this, it must be a coincidence. It must be... Had Cassie told him about me and Zack?

I read it once more and snapped multiple photographs on my phone.

If it was him... what did that mean for us?

I went back to retrieve my bag, glancing at the words on the wall continuously. Was Luke nearby, watching me? Or was I just being an absolute idiot? Lily wasn't exactly an uncommon name; this could be about anybody. This one frozen moment? That was too close to the exact words Luke had said to me as we lay in bed one morning. He took a photograph of us, said he was freezing the moment in time for the world, but nobody other than us would ever live anything so perfect. It had to be him. What did that mean for me, though?

I sloshed a generous serving of pinot grigio into my glass as soon as I got home. That word again, a home that wasn't really a home anymore. How horrible that felt. Familiar walls becoming alien. That contented happy feeling replaced by an urge to pack up and go before more of me was consumed by the negativity in here. I didn't feel like there was much of me left at this point. Every time I felt I'd got as low as I could, another depth appeared. I didn't know how much more I could take.

I spotted an envelope in the inner pocket of my handbag. The document from Margaret's office. A hot guilt flushed up my body; I shouldn't have taken it. I put it down on the coffee table and promised myself I would put it back in the post box tomorrow morning when I left.

Drunk me had crept in though, drunk me wanted to know what it was. Doing the right thing hadn't exactly got me very far in the grand scheme of life, had it? I sat and looked at the envelope as I drank another glass of wine, my eyes switched to my phone occasionally in case anyone messaged me – they didn't.

Sod this, I thought to myself as I grabbed the envelope and carefully opened the sealed edge. A few sheets of paper stapled together, and a micro sim card were inside. The papers seemed to detail text messages from around the time Holly and Kye's baby would have been born. I recognised Holly's number right away, but the number for Kye was different from what I'd seen on all our paperwork.

I tucked my feet up on the couch and began to read as I drank my precious wine.

H: It's your baby Kye, I can't believe you're questioning me
K: We were together once; you could have been with a different guy every night that week
H: But I wasn't! And I find that very offensive. I'll get a DNA test as soon as the baby is born. Will just need a cheek swab from you
K: I'm not interested. I don't believe you. I'm having trials for Man City soon, you know this, you're just seeing pound signs

H: That is not true, and I didn't know. I just want the baby to know its dad and be secure

K: Don't contact me again Holly

Wow, that was brutal of him. This proved he did know about the baby; his counter claim would be wiped out, and he'd be left with the costs. Plus, Holly would almost certainly win the maintenance aspect, so her and the little one would be secure, *and* Luke would get paid.

I let the papers drop to the floor as I blew out a long sigh and rested my head on the back of the couch. Of all the envelopes to have picked up, maybe this was fate? He must have posted this to Anna to be destroyed, something that could ruin her career if found out, it was an absolute abuse of her position, but she was exactly the type of person to cross that line, especially when a millionaire footballer was involved.

I could be in so much trouble for interfering in a legal case too. But then… what was there to link me to this? No proof at all. It hadn't been signed for, just sent in the normal post, which was pretty stupid of Kye. Plus, from reading those messages, he was not a nice man; he didn't deserve to win over Holly.

I lay on the sofa, drinking and pondering for a good hour. In all honesty, it was a relief to think about something other than Zack. Before I could change my mind, I printed out the address of Adamson Hughes on Zack's printer and stuck it onto a clean envelope – not wanting to risk my handwriting being recognised. Then after locating a couple of screwed up stamps at the bottom of my purse, I sealed the envelope up and traipsed back outside, determined to do this before I changed my mind. Holly deserved this, Luke deserved this, Kye deserved this, and most of all, bloody Anna deserved this. What I'd give to see her face when the whole case fell apart.

I walked back to the corner shop I'd been at earlier, which had a tall, red post box standing proud outside. As I faced it, I could see the graffiti again. Was Luke trying to help me, as I tried to help him? Would this connection between us never, ever end? I closed my eyes as I let the envelope drop into the post box and whispered 'I love you', as if the words would travel with it, to Luke.

SIXTEEN

*C*assie hugged me; her hands rubbed my back in circular motions as though she was comforting her children, before she headed to the car with the last bag. "Take all the time you need, sweetheart," she said fondly as she looked around, saying her own goodbye to what had been such a happy home.

I looked at the marks on the walls where our photographs had been removed. I looked down at the coffee table, bare except for my keys and my engagement ring. I felt like I should leave a note, but what would it say? What could it say?

I'd tried to explain over and over; Zack wasn't interested. He couldn't see past his jealousy and anger, and this time, it didn't seem to be fading away.

I closed the front door and stood there for a moment, assaulted by happy memories.

Zack may have been right that it was Luke's email that had chosen this life for me, but... I loved this life, I loved Zack. I wanted our future. It was gone; everything good was gone.

Cassie stroked stray tears from my cheeks as I slumped down into the leather seats of her car.

"I'm sorry, Lily."

"I wish you'd never introduced us. I can't cope with this." I was heartbroken, not only for losing Zack, but for losing his family, his friends, the life we had mapped out. I had to learn to grieve for a future that hadn't even happened yet. I guess it was similar to Cassie, grieving for babies she hadn't had the opportunity to carry. Which made me think...

"Cassie, I'm going to do the egg donation. I'll ring them on Monday," I said.

"Hey, now's not the time to make a decision like that." Cassie's eyes flicked up and down my face, trying to gauge my mood.

"It is, though, I was going to do it for you. He said no. Now he's gone, so it's a yes. At least I don't have to put up with that fifties, Stepford wife crap anymore, hey?" I went to spin my engagement ring around on my finger. The realisation that it was gone hit me harder than ever, it was one more habit to break.

"Are you going to tell Luke about you and Zack?" Cassie asked, shying away from me slightly as she did.

I shook my head. "That would just confirm what Zack thought of me, wouldn't it? Luke and I... I think that chance passed." My whole body hurt at this moment. "He's been through so much himself, and I can't set him back again now he's moved on."

"And what if he would want to know? It's not just about you; you forget that I've lived this whole drama twice, heard it from both sides."

"Cassie, I don't want him to know. Just leave him be."

She glanced at me without a reply. We drove back to the mini mansion in silence, carrying all the boxes and bags into the granny flat when we arrived.

"You can stay in the house, you know? You don't have to stay out here," Cassie said.

"I like it out here," I smiled, even though I felt sad. "Happy memories, I guess."

She opened her mouth to speak, but I glared at her. "You want eggs, you keep quiet." She laughed as she left me to my own devices.

The weekend felt torturous and long, as though I was waiting for a monumental event to happen, except it wasn't going to. I had nothing to fill the next week. No job, no partner, no plan. I knew this needed to change.

I played with Ruby and Emilia, smiled and tried to think of reasons to explain why Zack wasn't there. I helped Cassie and Guy with cooking and childcare, but I knew I had no actual purpose here. They all went to bed, happy and loved at night. I lay in the granny flat and sobbed with despair after once again consuming far too much wine.

Just as I'd got used to missing Luke, I now had a Zack-shaped hole to contend with too. The burden of the two dragged me down in ways I'd never known before.

I rang Cassie's clinic early on Monday morning. I guess it's true that money talks. With her being a private patient, they agreed to see me within a couple of days for the initial health checks to clarify I was suitable.

That part was easy; I was the right age, the right weight, had no dubious medical history. The physical examination was fine, and I knew the blood and swab tests they took would all return OK. They then told me, however, that I needed to have a counselling appointment to ensure I was ready for the emotional side of this.

And that's how I found myself seated in a comfortable armchair as I smiled at a kind looking lady with very large glasses and curly black hair. I focused on trying to stop myself from fidgeting, foot tapping, coughing, or any other little tells that may give away my stress about this situation.

"Lily, thank you for coming today. My name is Wendy. This is just an informal session to assess if you are ready for the next steps of the egg donation process. Are you happy to proceed?" she asked.

I nodded like an over enthusiastic puppy, just wanting to get to the point where I got to help Cassie already.

"Do you have a partner, Lily?"

A sharp pain flashed through my stomach again, but I ignored it. I smiled at her, forever the actress it would seem. "No, I'm single, and I have no plans to have children myself."

Wendy made notes in her book as she listened to me. "And your parents, siblings? How do they feel about the donation?"

"I'm an only child. Cassie, the friend I want to donate eggs to, is the closest to a sister I will ever have. My parents adore her. They understand this and are happy to support my decisions." *No need to mention the fact I hadn't told them, right?*

"If a child was born out of this process, they'd meet them?" she asked.

"Yes, but they wouldn't be an everyday part of their lives."

"So," she continued. "How would you feel if the egg donation led to your friend conceiving a baby?"

"I'd be absolutely over the moon. She's the best mum in the world. Her little girls are amazing. She was devastated to find out she couldn't have more children naturally. I'm moving away soon. I wouldn't impact their lives, I just want to know I helped her. If this led to her having a baby, that would be the very best outcome in the world." Why had I just said I was moving away? I didn't know where that had come from, but... it had set ideas racing in my mind.

Wendy smiled at me as she scribbled everything down in

her black notepad. "You understand that the child could contact you in the future?"

I nodded. "I have no issues at all with that. Cassie will be in my life forever. I would be there for all of her children, regardless of their origins."

The session continued. I was desperate to give the right answers, but Wendy seemed to approve of my words. As the session drew to a close, she shook me by the hand.

"A doctor will call you within a couple of days of receiving my report to discuss whether or not we are able to proceed."

"Thank you. It was lovely to meet you." I flashed my best, most confident smile. I was a single, successful woman who just wanted to help her best friend. That's all they needed to know.

That had taken it out of me, though, I needed a drink! I'd needed multiple drinks every day since Spain, but I wasn't going to worry about that right now. I'd be OK once I got through this stage, I was sure.

I jumped into a taxi and headed back to the granny flat. I knew I had no money after what was left in my account had gone, but I didn't care right now. I changed into a short, black dress and re-did my hair and make-up. It was late afternoon, that was close enough to evening to justify this. I finished the outfit with heeled, black, ankle boots and headed to a bar in the town centre. It was usually frequented by students. I knew they'd be partying at any time; that's what I needed- shots, dancing, just forget it all.

I didn't even care that I received odd glances as I walked in. So what if I was ten years older than them all and not in jeans and converse, which seemed to be uniform in here. I ordered a large sauvignon blanc and two shots of vodka, which I downed before I took a seat on a bar stool and cradled my precious wine while I surveyed the room.

There was a band setting up over in the corner; this

meant good potential for dancing. My body was restless, I just wanted to do something invigorating and fun. What I needed, in all honesty, was one of those carefree nights with Luke. I closed my eyes as if to stop the thought in its tracks before it could invade my mind any deeper. One vodka shot and a refill of wine later, the band were about to begin their set.

It reminded me of our college days when Cassie and I would watch bands and dance until late every weekend. They were a four-piece rock band, all piercings and black hair and moody guyliner... why had nobody told me eyeliner looked so sexy on guys? They were pretty good; I definitely wanted to dance to this.

I downed the wine- aware it was not wise to leave a drink unattended in a bar like this one- and headed to the small dance floor in the corner of the club, which was getting pretty crowded already. It was hot over here; I liked it. My head was fuzzy now, and it was nice having all these warm bodies around me. I closed my eyes as I threw myself into the dance, letting the lyrics about love, heartbreak and everything in between wash over me.

Just as the band announced this was their last song, I felt sweaty hands take hold of my hips from behind and a mouth press up against my ear.

"You look hot," said a mystery voice. Ugh, his lips felt slimy and much too close. I stepped forwards, trying to move out of his hands, and turned around. Hmm... he was your atypical, posh, pretty boy, blonde university student who had probably slept with half the campus in the first term. He moved closer as I stepped away, his hands back on my waist but from the front now. "You obviously wanted someone to do this, the way you've been dancing." His hands slid down and around towards my bottom.

I stepped back again and looked around me, everyone was still dancing and oblivious to this guy and his wandering hands. "Sorry, I... I think you got the wrong impression. I was just enjoying the band, that's all."

He moved forwards, and I realised I couldn't step back anymore as the wall was behind me. He smirked at me as he leaned in and ran his fingers through the ends of my hair. What was it with me and bars and creepy guys?! I shook my head, trying to get him, literally, out of my hair, but he moved in anyway and planted his mouth against mine. I turned my face to the side; his wet lips smeared over my cheek in a hideous way. "Stop," I said. "I'm not interested."

He did stop, although he still leaned over me. "Come on, nobody comes to a place like this dressed like that unless they're after exactly what I have for you." He swooped back in, and this time, got me on the mouth, wasting no time as his tongue wrapped around mine. I wanted to heave. I tried to push him away, but the way I was against the wall made it a struggle. It was as though I couldn't breathe, and I was starting to panic when suddenly, I was free.

Almost in slow motion, I saw that a guitarist had jumped down from the small stage area, grabbed Mr wandering hands and tongue off me, and was just about to punch him in the face. I winced as I heard the sound of his fist connect with the guy's nose, an even worse noise than me slapping Anna had been.

"She said no, I could hear that from up there, so what was your problem?" the guitarist shouted at him. The room seemed echoey now that the band had stopped playing.

"What the fuck have you done to my nose?" he shouted back. "You absolute idiot; she loved it. What's your problem?" His friend handed him a wad of tissue for his nose. An older guy- I guessed he was the manager- rushed around from the other side of the bar.

Band guy, as I had nicknamed him, looked at me with kind eyes. Kind eyes that looked insanely sexy rimmed by that eyeliner. "Let's ask the lady, shall we?" The question was aired to everyone watching, in an almost theatrical fashion, before he focused on me again. "Did you want this... I use the term loosely, man, to kiss you?"

I shook my head and wiped my mouth and cheek, which still felt damp and sloppy from his unwanted attentions.

"There we go then! Mark..." He looked over at the guy I assumed was the manager. "Can we kick this guy out for harassing the lovely lady, please?" I realised I'd been holding my breath as band guy took hold of my shaky hand. "Come with me, we'll get you a drink."

He led me to a small table round the side of the bar. "I'll be right back." True to his word, he returned a couple of minutes later with a large glass of wine and a tumbler of what looked like straight vodka.

"Thank you," I said with a shy smile. "For the drink and the rescue. Think it ruined your last song, didn't it?"

He grinned, and, oh my word, his face was beautiful-angular and elegant. "Don't worry about that. I'd clocked him a couple of songs back, could see what he was up to. Was obviously not a nice bloke, he'd been watching you."

"How did you manage to notice him, watching me, while you were playing?" I asked, genuinely confused.

"Because I couldn't keep my eyes off you the whole time." I felt myself blush bright red. "Sorry!" He let out a small laugh. "I didn't mean to embarrass you. You're not the average girl we see in these places."

"It's because I left my converse at home, isn't it?" I replied with a smile. I liked him. Not a hint of sleaze about him, unlike the other guy. As far as knights in shining armour went, he was pretty hot, in a different way to my usual type. "I'm Lily, by the way."

"Elijah," he replied. His dark eyes were intense with the eyeliner and the black, scruffy hair. I took a big gulp of my wine self-consciously as I found myself concentrating on his mouth. "Want to get some fresh air? Go for a walk?" He bit his bottom lip as he waited for my response; it made me want to bite it too, his lips were so full.

For a moment, my mind said no. My sensible, Lily mind. But… where had that got me? Precisely nowhere. So, before I could overthink, I put my glass down, looked Elijah in the eyes and said, "yes."

He raised a hand to the rest of the band; who were still packing up, they didn't seem too bothered. I noticed the black, swirly, inky lines of tattoos, which ran down his neck, back, and shoulders as I followed behind him. *Maybe I should have been looking for rock band guys and NOT lawyers…*

"You don't mind leaving do you?" he asked. "I always need quiet time after a show, my head gets so full."

"I don't mind at all. I could do with another drink, though." I thought for a moment; there was nowhere quiet around here. Nowhere except… "My place is only a few minutes away, if you wanted to have a drink there? As quiet as you like."

Almost imperceptibly, his smile twitched at one side. "I'd love that. As long as it's OK with you? I'm not going to be like that other guy, just in case you were worried."

"Even if I ask nicely?" I asked with an innocent face as we began to walk.

We headed towards Cassie's house; I hastily explained it wasn't mine. As if I could afford a place like that! We talked about the band and the bar on the way back. I stayed well away from any conversations about me and my situation. I turned to him as we got to the gates to the long driveway of the mini mansion.

"Can you run?" I asked as I took my boots off and held them in one hand.

His face was bemused, and cute. "Yeah… where we running to?"

"The back garden, before my friend sees me and wants to make you a cup of tea," I grinned. Elijah grabbed my hand,

and before I knew what was happening, we were running and laughing as if we were kids at a sports day, having the best time ever.

I'd left the door unlocked, so we ran straight inside, both full of laughter despite me trying to shush him to keep quiet. I was louder than him. I put one hand on my stomach, where a stitch had crept in, and pressed a finger against his lips. "Shhh." I couldn't stop laughing. "Why is this so funny?"

He ran his tongue up the finger that was pressed against his soft lips, it woke up the sleeping butterflies from my stomach. I pulled my finger away with a slight smile. "I have no idea," he said as he pulled me to him. *Guys in bands... why had nobody ever told me?* His hand pulled at the hair at the base of my skull as he kissed me. There was no slow warm up here, this was like absolute rock star kissing. His mouth felt incredible; his tongue fit perfectly against mine as I returned the kiss. I'd never done anything like this before. Maybe this was what I should've been doing. Not sitting around being lonely, followed by switching between two loves in such a painful way. I just should've been out meeting people like him, doing things like this...

His fingers were rough and coarse as he ran them down my arm- I guessed from the guitar strings- they felt good on me. I slid my hands inside his t-shirt, his skin still damp from the gig and the run. My mouth moved down his neck and across his shoulder, I loved the salty taste of him. He felt decadent and wrong and yet so, so right.

"You sure this is OK?" he asked as his hands pulled my dress higher up my legs.

"Abso-fucking-lutely." I removed my hands from him as I tugged my dress over my head and threw it to the corner of the room. He smiled as he launched his t-shirt in the same direction.

"Want me to jump in the shower while you get more

drinks? I know I'm kinda gross from the gig ," he whispered in my ear as his hands circled my lower back.

"No." I unfastened his skinny jeans. *Damn these really were skinny!* "I like you like this; you taste good. Your eyeliner is sexy, by the way."

"So is yours." He bit my neck, just a touch too hard, it caused me to suck in a deep breath, but I liked it. "Stop." He grabbed my wrist as I went to tug his jeans down, and my stomach dropped. I felt ridiculous, foolish that maybe he didn't want this.

"Sorry, I—" He cut me off with one more fiery kiss as he reached into his back pocket.

"Don't say sorry. I just wanted this." He held up his wallet and threw it onto the bed. "Might need it in a minute." He went to kiss me again, but I pulled back, confused.

"Did I… erm… you know I'm not a prostitute, right?" A hot flush crept across me, I was mortified. Why was I so bad at meeting men!?

He laughed and wrapped his arms around me in a hug, an actual lovely hug; it felt good, I missed manly hugs. "I never thought that! It has condoms in it, that's all."

"Fuck. Sorry, I look like a right idiot now, don't I?" I buried my head in his shoulder. I adored the feel of arms around me.

"Nah." He kissed along my bare neck as rushed hands unfastened my bra. "You're the sweetest, hot girl I ever met. Anyway… did you just say fuck? Shall we?" He pulled my face towards his, his mouth was back on mine in a split second. We were in those delicious moments where kisses were hot, hands were everywhere, steps were being taken towards the bed. Before I knew what was happening, I was on my back, and he was on top of me, every single glorious inch of him on top of me. His back was hot and sticky under my fingers as I pulled him closer.

With one hand, I reached out for his wallet and passed it

to him, my lips smiling against his. I'd never been naked with a total stranger before, especially a sexy rock band stranger, this was—

"Lily! What the actual!" Cassie shrieked. I sat bolt upright, and as I did so, my forehead crashed into Elijah's with a thunk.

"Ow!" I rubbed the sore spot where we'd just collided as I looked over at Cassie, stood in the doorway. Elijah was looking at her too, but hadn't moved from his position on top of me. All of a sudden, this felt as sleazy and awkward as it must have looked.

"Who's your friend, Lily?" Cassie asked, the tone behind her voice stern and full of disapproval.

"Elijah…" I replied as my face burnt red.

"Hi." In a confident move, he raised his hand in a little wave. He obviously wasn't bothered about the interruption, and he also seemed to have no intention of moving.

"Can I please speak to you in private for a moment?" Cassie asked in her best schoolteacher voice. She stepped outside and closed the door behind her.

Elijah resumed his attentions, his lips moved down the centre of my chest. "I have to go talk to her, sorry, I…" I blew out a long breath. God his lips felt nice. "Give me two minutes." I wriggled from under him, grabbed my dressing gown from the end of the bed, and pulled it on before heading outside to Cassie.

Her arms were folded tight across her chest as she leant against a large tree in the garden.

"Who the hell is Elijah?!" she hissed at me as I approached.

"I met him in a bar. What's the problem?"

"The problem is that you're staying with me, bringing random blokes back. The kids could've walked in. This isn't you… you don't do random sex, Lily."

"Well maybe I felt like trying something new," I said defiantly. "Anyway, it isn't blokes plural, it's one bloke."

"This isn't going to get you over Zack, you know? How much have you had to drink?" She leant forward and sniffed me.

"Cassie, what's your problem? If I want to get drunk and screw a guy, I will. Don't take over from Zack and tell me what I can and can't do." I'd raised my voice without realising, and she returned the pitch.

"I'm trying to stop you making a mistake. You know full well you could call Luke right now, and he'd be here declaring his undying love for you again within minutes."

"Don't!" I yelled. "Don't say his name. I am not putting him through it again, I told you that."

Before she could reply, we heard a loud cough behind us. I turned and saw Elijah buttoning up his jeans. "Erm… I'm going to head back to the band."

I stuck my bottom lip out in a sulk, annoyed at Cassie and her interference. "Sorry," I mouthed towards him, trying to portray my disappointment as he meandered out of the garden, his arse still looking incredible in the skinny jeans.

I glared at Cassie before I stalked back inside the granny flat. "Thank you SO much!" I yelled before I slammed the door as hard as I could and made sure to lock it from the inside. If only I'd thought to lock it earlier.

One more sleepless night began, my head full of heartbreak, shattered dreams, and the same names spinning around and around inside my thoughts. And to make it worse, the room now smelt like sexy rock band guy…

SEVENTEEN

assie and I made up the next morning, as we always did. I begrudgingly agreed that sleeping with Elijah wouldn't have helped anything, although it would have been a welcome distraction – of that, I was sure. She didn't mention Luke again, to my relief; my head couldn't take any more pressure.

The following Monday, I was tucked up in Cassie's kitchen with a cup of tea when my phone rang. I pounced on it. Part of me still hoped it would be Zack but I knew that day by day, that outcome grew less and less likely.

"Hello," I answered in a mopey voice, seeing the unknown number and expecting a scam or a sales pitch. Yet still glad to have someone to speak to in a pathetic way; nobody called me anymore.

"Is this Lily Forshaw?" A plummy voice spoke to me.

"It is," I confirmed.

"This is Dr Wilkinson from the Fertility Clinic Associates. Is this a good time to discuss your application to be an egg donor?"

"It's a perfect time to discuss it." I motioned Cassie, and she came to sit next to me with a nervous smile.

"I understand your application was to provide eggs for a close friend, you wouldn't be leaving eggs with us for other clients?"

"That's correct," I confirmed, hoping this wasn't going to go against us.

"Well I'm happy to say that all of your physical checks were clear and your counsellor was happy that you have the capacity to understand and proceed with the process."

"That's amazing!" I couldn't help but grin down the phone, not that Dr Wilkinson had a clue what my face was doing.

"Was the process explained to you?" she asked. "The first step is to begin you on daily injections to suppress your natural hormone production. You'll need to come in for instruction on this, and at the same time, we'll arrange to see your friend to synchronise the processes to optimum timing for you both."

She continued to talk, but it went over my head. Cassie and I grinned widely at each other like little kids. Thankfully, she ended the call saying all the information, dates, and times would be sent to me by mail, to Cassie's address.

Finally, I felt useful.

Cassie and I were like giddy schoolgirls as we sat in the clinic room a couple of weeks later and waited for the nurse to come and see us.

"What is this?" Cassie asked with a grimace as she picked up an expensive looking, framed piece of art that sat on the table next to us. I squinted at the images as she held it at different angles, but neither of us was sure.

"I think it's just modern art rubbish. Or are they eyeballs?" I shrugged as I spoke then jumped as the door opened and a nurse walked in.

Her face broke into a smile as Cassie hastily put the picture back on the table. "It's called Embryonic Development, and a previous client painted it." She held out her hand. "I'm Natalie, lovely to meet you both." Her manner put me at ease; she seemed approachable, her smile genuine. Average height, average weight, brown hair in a ponytail, she looked like an average next-door neighbour, not a mean matron or a judgemental model type.

We shook hands. I couldn't look at Cassie as I knew she'd give me the giggles again, and we needed to take this seriously. Part of me was still scared the clinic would change their mind and decide I wasn't suitable after all.

"I have your injections ready here for you to take home. All the instructions are in there, but it's one injection each a day, for twelve days. We'll do the first one together now." Natalie spoke with a kind voice, well versed in the nerves and hormones which must be abundant in this room.

My throat was parched. I'd never felt bothered about needles before, but the thought of injecting myself wasn't pleasant. Fortunately, all images of giant, spiky needles more familiar to a horror film in an old, abandoned hospital- were quashed when Natalie showed us the slim plastic cartridge which looked more like a pen. She handed us one each from our own boxes to familiarise ourselves with the feel.

"You can inject into your stomach, or the top of your thigh. Do you mind if I touch your stomach, Lily?" Natalie asked.

"Go ahead," I lifted my t-shirt up, paranoid that my skin felt clammy with nerves and anxiety.

"You need to try and pinch a little bit of skin, easier for some of us than others," she laughed and pointed at her own stomach, which was by no means big, but she obviously thought otherwise. She then pinched at the skin of my stomach and held the needle to it. "Both grab a pinch of skin like that and press the needle against it."

We did as instructed. "Great, now simply click the end of the cartridge, and the needle will inject you."

Cassie clicked it within a split second, her eyes screwed closed, then she looked at me with a giddy smile. "Easy peasy. Go on, Lily."

I held my breath and clicked the button; my whole body tensed up. A sharp sensation shot into my stomach, but then it was done. No going back now.

"Perfect," Natalie smiled. "You will likely get bruising, try and just vary the site a little each day. There's a phone number for the nurses here, in with your instructions, just call us if any problems."

Cassie held my hand as we left; I knew it was excitement, it was something she'd always done. I could see Natalie looking bemused through the window, she totally thought we were a couple now.

A couple of weeks later, more vials of blood were checked and ultrasounds were taken – transvaginally, not words I was fond of at the moment! But… it was for Cassie; it was worth it. It had been an interesting time at the mini mansion as the two of us were hormonal as hell. The consumption of chocolate and chick flicks was through the roof. Guy had been going out a lot, I suspected with Luke but I didn't ask. I was a new woman after all, well, almost.

Weirdly, Cassie and I had different symptoms. She felt all bloaty and fat from the drugs, whereas I thought I was losing weight because I was so nauseous; I couldn't eat half the time. Cassie's boobs had also grown huge overnight. I was envious that mine hadn't followed suit, although she did say they were so sore she couldn't lie on her stomach anymore.

I found myself on a procedure bed being injected with sedatives, which made me feel warm and cosy and almost,

166

almost made me forget that my legs were strapped into stir-rups- again like a weird horror movie. I found myself thinking of scary Japanese girls whose heads spun around for some random reason and had to force myself to focus on the moment. I looked at the beautiful photographs on the wall of pregnant bellies and before I knew it, tears slid down my face once more. It hadn't been my lifelong dream to have a big family but it had been Zack's, and what if he didn't get to have that dream now because of me? I felt like my heart would break in two again as I wondered how he was. Was he crying at home every night? Had he lost weight through not eating? Was he—

"Lily, are you OK? It's Natalie here," I was in a different room, and she was wrapping a warm blanket around me. "Don't worry if you feel confused, it's the sedation wearing off. The procedure is all done, everything is fine. I'm just going to check your vitals, and then you can go back to sleep."

I nodded and smiled drowsily at her. I felt, sort of, tipsy and disorientated. Sleep sounded amazing. "You got all the eggs?"

"Yes, it all went to plan. I'll ring your partner now and tell her."

I giggled at the incorrect assumption, which just struck me as hilarious. How shocked she'd be to know I'd spent so much time between two amazing, gorgeous men. Dreamy men... I wanted to dream about them right now.

A few short hours later, I was curled up on Cassie's couch with a hot water bottle and a massive bar of chocolate. Cassie and Guy were due at the clinic later in the week for the next stage of the process. She stroked my hair as she began to speak. Natalie really would think we were in love if she saw this! I did love Cassie though, she'd been there for me always, and nothing made me happier than doing this for her. It was, in fact, the only thing that made me happy at the moment.

"You need me to get you anything?"

"I'm fine, honest. It's just stomach cramps. A bath and an early night will sort me out," I replied, trying to reassure her.

"It's not that far off twenty years we've been besties now, you know? I never would've guessed we'd go through this," said Cassie.

"Me neither. You know, though, I think the timing is just right. I needed a distraction and what a distraction this is," I grinned and pointed at my stomach. "I've been thinking though, that I can't stay here."

"There's no rush at all to go; wait until you've got a job and then find a flat nearby. I don't care if that's in two weeks or two years."

"I mean this town, this area. I don't want to be near to either of them. The thought of bumping into either of them makes me feel sick, in all honesty." I sighed deeply, knowing she wouldn't be a fan of this decision. "I need a fresh start, somewhere far away. I can't think straight here."

"But you can't go somewhere you don't know, all on your own," Cassie spluttered. "You won't have any friends; I'd miss you too much. Plus, we're having a baby!"

I laughed and immediately winced as a stab of pain shot through my pelvis. "Don't make me laugh so much woman! We're not having a baby; you and Guy *might* be having a baby. Plus, I am capable of making friends, thank you." I stuck my tongue out at her before helping myself to more chocolate.

"But I don't want you to have other friends," Cassie pulled a face like she was about to burst into tears.

"You are such a drama queen. You'll always be my bestie. It won't be that different to when I was in Cheshire. We'll still talk and message all the time. It's just a vague plan at the moment anyway." I rested my head back on the cushioned couch.

Cassie scooted closer and hugged me gently. "I'm going to lock you in the house so you can't ever leave. But before that, I'll run you a bubble bath, beautiful donator of the eggs."

EIGHTEEN

$\mathcal{I}$ knew Cassie wouldn't necessarily get pregnant on the first try but they had plenty of eggs 'on ice', and I was confident it would happen for her sooner rather than later; I just had a feeling. The clinic was happy with how it had all gone so far, that was my part over; it was Cassie who had all the hard work ahead of her. Guy joked about the strain of producing 'samples' but we just rolled our eyes and ignored him. Cassie was the most impatient person I'd ever met; I didn't envy Guy putting up with her for the next few months. The poor man probably also wasn't going to see much action as she'd already made it crystal clear she was saving her vagina for the scientists and doctors now. His sample production might have to sustain him.

As for my own situation- I could still only see one solution to the pathetic existence I was stuck in.

I lived in my friend's garden.

Said best friend would soon be pregnant, all being well.

I was heartbroken over two ex's- both of whom lived too close for comfort.

I had no job.

I needed a fresh start, that much was obvious. The

thought of starting afresh petrified me. But the thought of remaining here was worse.

To go to a place where I was anonymous, where nobody knew. That wasn't all bad? I could be anyone, anything, nobody would ever know.

Cassie wanted me to stay in the granny flat forever but I knew I couldn't. It wasn't going to be easy to tell her my final decision, but I needed to. I needed to make her understand.

My mind felt as battered and bruised as my heart; I struggled to concentrate on tasks. The thing about a new start when you're alone – no need to worry about anyone else. If it didn't work, I'd just start again. Maybe I'd end up one of those eclectic old ladies who'd been everywhere, completely independent and zen.

I remembered holidaying in Devon when I was a teenager and it being beautiful- all gorgeous beaches and stunning countryside. I had an image in my head of me wandering up and down said beautiful beaches in the wind. Recovering from my heartbreak, finding my inner peace. I'd look all windswept and dramatic. I would become utterly happy to be alone, I was sure, I had been before after all. Before that bloody blind date.

Thank goodness for the internet, it made the world seem small. It was easy to research Devon and I began a daily ritual of Googling jobs and flats. I just needed to wait for the right opportunity to crop up. I never had a doubt it would. I was going to have faith in myself, stick to my decisions and not let other people sway me this time.

After just a week, it seemed that fate shared my plan. A place called 'Zoe Bakes' needed help while the owner took maternity leave. A flurry of Google later and I'd discovered it was located in a tiny village about half an hour from the seaside. It sounded perfect. I sent an email of interest and immediately planned my new life. I could imagine myself wandering around the village, serene and calm in beautiful Joules dresses, like a chilled-out countryside girl.

When my phone rang an hour later with a number I didn't recognise, I held my breath in anticipation.

"Hello, Lily speaking," I answered, trying to sound confident and professional.

"Hi, this is Zoe. You sent me an email about the job I advertised." The voice was soothing and calm as she spoke.

"Yes, I did, thank you for getting back to me so quickly."

"In all honesty, I haven't been inundated with applications, being based in the middle of nowhere doesn't help. I noticed your address is in Lancashire. Bit too far to commute," she joked, it put me at ease.

"I'm looking to relocate, just been waiting for the right opportunity and this sounds exactly what I want to be doing," I said.

"Well I'm growing to the size of a house steadily day by day. I'd need you to jump straight in, would that be a problem? I'd have to take you on as a trial to make sure we worked together OK and I know that's a big ask when you're moving so far?" Zoe asked in an inquisitive tone.

"It's not a problem. I could come down anytime. Is it only maternity cover? That's not a problem, but just so I know."

"Initially yes, it's to cover my maternity leave but afterwards I'll be keeping the person on if they've worked out. I won't be able to manage everything and spend the time I want with the baby," she paused. "I don't suppose there's any chance we could talk over Zoom could we? I can tell a lot from a face."

"Of course," I'm sure I sounded ridiculously enthusiastic but I wanted this opportunity so much. "Text me the details, I can be on in ten minutes."

I rushed through to Guy's office as soon as she ended the call. Fortunately he was away at a conference and I knew his computer password was a combination of Ruby and Emilia's names – very secure!

I was alone in the virtual meeting room as I dialled in and checked that I looked presentable on the screen before it burst into life with a face I assumed to be Zoe's. She looked to be in her mid-thirties, sporting a wide, toothy smile that reminded me of Julia Roberts. Her tanned, freckled face was framed with incredible auburn hair, which curled into wild corkscrews. Amber-brown eyes darted off to the left as she watched herself in the camera and tied the wild curls back into a ponytail.

"Lovely to put a face to the voice, that's better," she smiled at me as she continued. "Can you tell me a little more about your experience?"

"It's all amateur," I began to explain. "But I've always been told I have a natural talent. I love to bake. My brownies are famous around here, I make everyone's birthday cakes; I even did a naked wedding cake for a colleague a couple of years back. I could send pictures?"

"That would be good, I'd appreciate it," she said. "The real test would be the taste, of course. We'd need to spend time getting you up to date on all the hygiene procedures too if you were to join me."

"I did get food hygiene certificates a couple of years back because I was thinking of pursuing things more formally. I'm happy to do a refresher course?"

"You know what, Lily..." Zoe scratched at the top of her head and a stray curl fell loose over her forehead. "I get a good feeling about you. How do you feel about coming down for a trial?"

"I'd love to!" I grinned into the camera, then stopped myself and tried to look professional again, rather than desperate.

"Come down for a few days, we'll work together. You can bake me all your favourites. Be warned, I'm eating for two and I have massive sugar cravings. When could you make it? I realise it's a long way and a big ask."

I trusted this woman, it felt like I could be myself. "I'll be honest with you, Zoe, at the risk of sounding pathetic, I have no plans. I could be there on Monday."

"Monday it is then," she said. "I'll email you the details, but I need to go, baby is kicking me right in the bladder." She waved, cheerful and childlike, then the screen went blank.

I turned the computer off and spun around and around in Guy's leather office chair; imagining myself at the head of a baking empire with not a bloody lawyer in sight!

That had all progressed quickly; Zoe seemed like she didn't hang around before she made decisions. This was it then. I was off. New start, new me... Hopefully, as long as I could ace this trial, I just needed to get my head in the game.

The day before I was due to travel down to the farmhouse bed and breakfast I'd booked for the week I headed to the shops for supplies. Cassie had two cars and had been letting me use her black mini as if it were my own; I was even going to drive it down to Devon.

I was only in the shops for thirty minutes yet when I came back out it seemed the entire car park had been littered with circus advertisements. They were stuck under every windscreen wiper.

I couldn't be bothered to dislodge the colourful, flapping paper; the day was sunny- I wouldn't need windscreen wipers. Besides, Cassie might want the flyer; it said something about free tickets which might be the kind of thing the girls would want to go to. I wasn't sure; my brain was utterly worn out by this point. I was all about the easy options.

As I sat in the driver's seat I ran my hands up my face and into my hair. Constant stress didn't settle well with me. I could almost feel the wrinkles and frown lines cementing themselves on me and I didn't dare think about my poor liver. I sighed as I glanced once more at the flyer as it flapped around under the wiper blade. There was something written on the reverse. Probably only T's and C's but I reached around through the open window and grabbed it for a closer look.

It really wasn't T's and C's.

> It tore my heart apart
> to let you go that day
> Don't assume it's easy
> for the one who carries out the act
> Making us finite
> A journey that cannot flow
> All the futures that might have been
> I'd be the villain a hundred times over
> to spare you one ounce of pain

I couldn't handle this right now. If this was Luke it was bad, bad timing and I wasn't in the mood for it.

I shoved the flyer in my handbag then jumped out and grabbed a couple from neighbouring cars- they were blank on the back. This was focused. On me. It needed to stop.

If the past two years had proven anything it was that I was meant to be alone.

When I got back to Cassie's I put the flyer in the shoe box with the other poems I'd found. I couldn't bring myself to register the words; to think about their meaning or the sentiment behind them. It was just all too much and my mind needed to be on this new opportunity. Not past pains that would only be repeated.

After over six hours slumped in the mini listening to a playlist designed to not make me cry; I realised just how far away Devon felt. Perfect. It already seemed as though I could breathe easier knowing neither of them would be nearby; not having to worry every time I nipped to the shops. The village itself was beautiful with a little, quaint main road with all the usual suspects – post office, corner shop, tea rooms, hardware store and, of course, the bakery. There only seemed to be one pub but it was just gorgeous; surrounded by enormous hanging baskets full of colourful begonias and petunias.

When I'd looked for accommodation for this trial there was only one place- a farmhouse that also served as a bed and breakfast. I'd noticed that were no houses available to rent so if this worked, I may need to stay further out; hopefully the bus service was reliable.

After I checked in, if you could call it something that formal, with Sophie at the farm I lay down on the beautiful flowery bedspread in my attic room. Just breathing, enjoying the space, the quiet, the calm. A new start… I smiled at the thought, my last one until morning as the months of exhaustion overtook me, and for the first time in so long, I had a deep, satisfying, dreamless sleep.

The well needed rest, coupled with the insanely good farmhouse full English breakfast, meant I felt ready to take on the world as I headed into the village to meet Zoe.

This didn't seem to be a heels sort of place; I'd worn black ballet pumps with a long, blue, pleated skirt and cream top. Obviously I hadn't put the top on until after the fried egg and coffee spillage risks were taken care of.

A little bell dinged as I opened the door to the bakery and without meaning to I closed my eyes and took a deep breath of the amazing smell. Icing, cinnamon, and sugar, maybe melting chocolate... It smelt incredible in here. Definitely better than any man could ever smell.

"Lily?" My eyes pinged open and I saw a smiling face; vaguely familiar from our zoom call.

"Hi, yes, sorry. I was just taking a moment, smells like heaven in here," I began to explain, trying not to trip over my words. "Zoe?"

The lady in front of me nodded. She looked just like she had on Zoom only more animated; her smile shone. I also spotted an enormous baby bump barely contained behind her apron. "Zoe – almost the size of a house – Curtis. Come in, I've been so excited to meet you, Lily."

Half an hour later, ensconced in the back of the shop with cups of tea and fresh-out-of-the-oven blueberry muffins, I felt as if Zoe was an old friend. She'd had the shop here for two years; although it was only a small village she supplied a few places in the nearby seaside town and that kept her business sustainable. Her baby was due in six weeks and although she intended to still put a few hours in; she needed help with the baking, the deliveries and manning the shop.

"So, maybe tomorrow you could make me a couple of your specialities, then I can see what your work is like?" Zoe asked.

"I'd love that," I smiled as I spoke, meaning it wholeheartedly. This place felt good; I had all the right feelings going on that this was the fresh start I needed.

I lay in the soft bed at the farmhouse that night Googling recipes even though I knew my own off by heart. I was certain I would make salted caramel brownies; everyone went mad for them. Zack was obsessed with them. I sighed and rolled over; looking at the moon as it shone in through the window. This wasn't about him anymore; this was about me. Strawberry and Pimms cupcakes! The memory suddenly flashed into my mind of when I'd made them for a summer away day at Draper & Hughes, they were delicious; I'd just have to hope the local shop sold Pimms. We'd all tucked into them after we played rounders for a fun team building activity; Luke and I had, of course, been on the winning team.

There was another item I loved to bake though and I hadn't attempted it in so long. Simply because it was Luke's absolute favourite and to bake it for anyone else just brought back crazy memories and a random sense of betrayal. Red velvet cake with cream cheese frosting. I'd make it as a large cake and then she'd see my skill for the bigger projects as well as the everyday bakes.

I wished momentarily that I could take a picture of the finished product and send it to Luke; remind him of the time I'd made it at his and nearly ruined his kitchen. I wasn't used to his mixer and the cream cheese frosting had gone everywhere- splattered over every surface, including me and him. It was at a point we were just friends, but God it had been sexy. Why the hell hadn't I thought to take it further? He'd pretended to be mad and pushed me against the wall so even more of the frosting squashed into my hair; then he'd slowly lifted my arm up and licked a trail from my inner wrist to my elbow cleaning the delicious mess from me.

I sighed with a deep longing as I rolled onto my back; what I'd give for his mouth to be anywhere near me right now. I didn't even reprimand myself this time, I just smiled as I slid deeper under the covers and allowed myself to fantasise about how differently that scenario could've played out, if only I'd known, or he'd confessed.

--

By the end of Thursday I was hoping and praying that Zoe was happy with the trial; I knew this was where I wanted to be. We got along like old friends and seemed to work well together. I wanted this opportunity badly, but, given my luck lately I didn't dare hope for a good outcome.

Zoe had invited me to her house for something to eat that evening before I headed home the next day; I took that as a promising sign as I got ready. I loved the farmhouse B&B but had done the sums and knew I couldn't stay there forever; not to mention the effect all those cooked breakfasts would have on me.

"Lily, welcome," she said as she opened her front door to me. She attempted to wrap me in a hug but her bump wouldn't allow her close enough. We laughed together as she showed me through to the dining room. "It's just us I'm afraid, hubby is stuck at work."

"That's fine, don't worry. You haven't gone to too much effort, have you?" I asked, as the doorbell rang.

"Getting the takeaway from the front door and into the kitchen is as much effort as I'm putting in. I got you wine though, help yourself from the fridge."

An hour later, we were both full to bursting with sticky sweet and sour chicken, delicious noodles, and a mountain of prawn crackers. My mind also felt nicely relaxed from the beautiful wine Zoe had bought for me.

"So," she began. "As far as the trial goes, you're amazing and I think we get on like a house on fire. I'd love it if you could start as soon as possible?"

I couldn't help but break into a wide, genuine smile. "Definitely a yes!" I stopped myself from bouncing up and down on the couch like I wanted to. "I don't suppose you know of any nearby towns I could look to rent in though, do you? There doesn't seem to be anything here, I've been keeping an eye out, just in case you wanted me to stay."

"I do know of somewhere, it's a tiny place though. Edna has had to go live with family due to ill health. If you had a boyfriend, or anyone, it might be too small?" Zoe watched me closely as she asked the question, there had been a couple of times during the week she'd hinted at wanting to know why I was relocating so far.

"It's just me. I…" My fingers went straight to where my engagement ring used to be. "I was supposed to be getting married but my fiancé called it off. There's nothing to salvage. Then I lost my job… I just want to be somewhere new, a fresh start."

"If I could move, I'd hug you." Zoe looked at me, her eyes full of empathy.

"It's fine, don't worry. A place like this is just what I need."

She wrote a phone number down and handed me the slip of paper. "That's Edna's number, just tell her I told you to ring. Explain about the job. She'll be glad to not have the place empty. Basically, the sooner you can get here the better."

As I wandered back to the B&B later in the evening it felt as though my breaths were flowing easier. I looked up into the night sky; it was amazing how many more stars were visible out in the countryside. The air felt cleaner in my lungs too. For a brief moment I wished I was going home to Zack or Luke – to tell them this exciting news. But I stopped myself. No more of them. No more of that. This was all about me now, my new start. Time to focus on Lily.

Two short weeks later, all of my bags and boxes cluttered up the middle of Cassie's drive as I waited for my dad to come and pick everything up, including me. He was taking me on the one-way trip. My parents still wished I would stay closer but they were supportive of the decision, on the whole. It all had to happen fast with Zoe's baby being due within weeks and I felt like that was the best way. Rip that plaster off and move on.

Cassie reached for my hand; tears dragged her mascara

down her face. "It's not too late, you know. You could stay. You could talk to Luke. I could ring him and he'd be here in minutes. I know he would."

I shook my head. "It *is* too late, but thank you for respecting my wishes by not telling him."

"I can tell him the minute you're gone right?" She laughed as she spoke, but it didn't disguise how upset she was.

"You can tell him I moved, but not where. I wouldn't make a big deal about it though," I shrugged. "This is weird. I know it isn't, but it feels so final. Could hardly hold it together saying goodbye to the kids this morning."

"I'll keep you updated on all the news," Cassie patted her stomach. "I honestly can't thank you enough for what you've done."

I wrapped my arms around her and sobbed into her hair. "I'd do anything for you, I love you bestie. I miss you already. You're going to need to turn your phone off to get away from my non-stop messages."

"That had better be true," she sobbed back to me. "And we'll be down to visit as soon as possible."

I heard the familiar sound of dad's car as it turned into the driveway. I'd been so scared that first day of high school- I wasn't good at making friends. Cassie's beaming smile had seemed approachable and we'd hit it off instantly. I loved her so much but I couldn't stay in a painful place purely for that. I needed this new start, no matter how much it tugged at my heart.

NINETEEN

*S*ix months passed by at a different pace and my mind and body appreciated the gentler rhythm. Life was... different. Quiet, calm, stress free. It felt strange to be off the Zack and Luke rollercoaster that had been my life for so long.

Occasionally it felt a bit lonely but I just remembered the person I'd been, the person I'd become, and that I could be anything in the middle of that.

May was horrendous. My mind constantly wandered to the fact that I should've been getting married now, we should've moved now. I'd put all my memories of Zack into both a physical and mental box, just as with Luke, and I tried not to visit either often.

My job however was lovely. Zoe and I had become so close; Cassie kept telling me how jealous she was. Zoe's baby, Isla, was almost five months old and she spent many days in the bakery being cooed over- the girl would be a master baker before she started school. Even though Zoe was meant to be just doing accounts and so on from home she couldn't resist popping in for chats and to see how it was all going. I loved it when I was left in charge; I adored the happy customers in this quaint little place. The way of life was different, something the rest of the world could stand to learn from. A different life to those crazy commutes into Manchester city centre.

It was a truly beautiful corner of Dorset, about thirty minutes from the seaside, set in traditional English countryside. The kind of place where everybody knew each other, yet I wasn't made to feel like an outsider. And as nobody knew my past, the familiarity didn't bother me at all.

I rented a tiny little terraced cottage from Edna, who also loved to call for a chat. My mum and dad had helped me with the initial costs while I got settled. It simply contained a living room, kitchen/diner, one bedroom and a small bathroom. The back had a pretty little terrace to sit out in; I loved it as soon as I noticed the peonies that grew all along one side.

This life might have seemed boring to other people but I was out of the place where I felt like a failure for not 'having it all'. I had plenty of early nights and plenty of dawn starts at work. Other than the odd shared bottle of wine with Zoe; I just kept myself to myself. I read more than ever and Luke would've been proud of how healthy I was now- there wasn't even a place to order take away pizza from.

I'd got my hair cut into a wavy bob and hadn't worn heels once since I'd got here. New Lily. Country Lily. Stress free Lily. Man free Lily. That was another positive about this place- there didn't seem to be any single men. I was joyous about that fact. If Cassie thought I'd been sworn off them before, it was forged in steel now.

Summer and autumn had passed this way. I was content as long as I didn't think about the might have beens or the what ifs... no matter how pretty they were. Over that summer I also got the best news in the world – Cassie was pregnant! In a way that was unlike her she'd managed to not blurt it out and had waited until she was twelve weeks, sending me a scan photo and a million kisses. I was so, so happy for her. There were no weird feelings like Zack had implied... I flinched as I thought of him, and quickly shut him out of my head.

Cassie had planned to come down for my birthday (I didn't even want to think about thirty), but knowing she was pregnant and suffering with morning sickness I was much happier for her to stay at home and not undertake such a long drive. I promised I would travel north again soon to see her, but I honestly didn't know if I could bring myself to ever go back to that town. My mum and dad also wanted to come down for my birthday but I just felt like I was better alone, so, again told a little white lie and promised to see them at the same time I visited Cassie.

My birthday was on a Sunday and I planned to go to the beach. Even though the November weather was now distinctly chilly I still loved to walk along the shore, feel the shells crunch under my feet. Breathe in that salty air which seemed to fill my lungs up with freshness; it felt as if I could breathe deeper when I was by the sea.

Zoe baked me an amazing cake on the Saturday night and I had dinner with her and her husband Marcus. Their house was only minutes from mine and I wandered home, swaying ever so slightly with a stomach full of moussaka and pinot grigio. I drank rarely now so it really affected me when I did.

A few cards had arrived with the postman that morning but as I walked up the driveway I saw another envelope on the mat. Strange, maybe it had gone to a neighbour by mistake and they'd left it there for me?

I put the envelope down on the side with the others, locked the door and headed to bed, feeling trepidatious. My twenties had been weird; I didn't feel they were what twenties should have been. What on earth was going to happen in my thirties? I hoped just happiness and peaceful times. I was only asking for the simplest things.

As I climbed into bed, cuddled up in warm pyjamas, I worried that although I was happy to have this peaceful life, if this was how I spent the next ten years, would I just awake aged forty and feel like I had missed out on everything? Regardless, there was nothing I could do right now. I wasn't going to open myself up to those levels of pain again.

I'd made sure to get a special birthday breakfast in for myself. I could spoil myself, who needed a bloody ABC of birthday presents anyway? So flashy, so not new Lily.

Early the following morning I sat in my little courtyard garden. Even though it was cold the morning air was beautiful; crisp and clear in my lungs. I had a huge mug of Starbucks brew coffee, a warm pain au chocolat, and a stack of birthday cards to open.

The cards from my parents warmed my heart; they'd sent me one each which was gorgeous but I also worried they thought I wouldn't have many to open. There were others from aunts and uncles. A beautiful card from Cassie who had filled every tiny space with funny stories from our past; it took an age to read and made me laugh out loud multiple times. She'd also separately sent pictures that Ruby and Emilia had drawn of her with a huge tummy, which just made my heart burst open with love. How had Zack ever wanted me to not do that for Cassie? *Lily just stop it, stop thinking about it.* I put my head down into my hands, took a deep breath, and opened the last card- which I now noticed had been hand delivered. It was the one from the doormat last night and it had no post mark.

It was another beautiful illustration of a Lily plant; my mind wandered back to my last birthday, it was a similar card. My heartbeat tripped over itself as I opened it up.

You are the best of me
and I, the best of you
We meet in the middle
like a brilliant burst of stars
so bright, that love itself would be blinded

I put the card down on the table in front of me, gulping back emotions as my hand trembled. There was only one way that had been delivered. I wasn't ready, I would never be ready for that.

I gathered all the cards together and hurried back inside, locking the back door and retreating to the safety that was my duvet.

I didn't want to look at it, but I needed to read it again. I read it over and over. Was it Luke? It couldn't be coincidence after the other occurrences, and the card so similar to last years. But how the hell would he know where to find me? How... Cassie!

Lily: Have you told anyone where I live?!?!?!?!
Cassie: I'm pregnant, you aren't allowed to be mean to me x
Lily: I'm serious, I need to know
Cassie: Nothing specific, but if people figure things out based on some vague clues, that isn't my fault x
Lily: FFS!!!!!!!!!!!!!!!
Cassie: Happy thirtieth birthday gorgeous! xx

I threw the phone down on my bedside table and took a deep breath to stop myself from sending something offensive. If the doorbell went I just wouldn't answer it. It wasn't necessarily him anyway, and if it was... he'd take the hint.

I spent extra time in the shower... that way I wouldn't hear the door if it did go.

I spent ages blow drying my hair… that would also drown out the noise of the door.

Purely because it was my birthday, no other reason, I felt like I should look pretty. I wore a brand new, beautiful floral dress which made my boobs look amazing, paired with suede boots I hadn't worn in ages and a warm jacket. Thirty-year-old Lily was ready to head to the beach. Being out of the house was a good idea, it also meant I couldn't hear the door should anyone knock on it. I had never in my life spent so much energy thinking about a front door.

I meandered up the road and waited at the bus stop. The buses weren't that regular on Sundays. I left the village so rarely there wasn't much point in changing the habits of a lifetime and buying a car. I was quite happy with the slower journey and the chance to daydream out of the window.

Paranoia had set in, though, which was stupid; this was all in my head. Luke wasn't going to charge down here and try to rescue me on my birthday. Even if he did I wasn't interested. I was completely not interested. I didn't need rescuing.

Convinced of these facts I stepped up onto the bus and smiled at the driver as I paid my fare. Still nothing untoward had happened, and nor would it. It had definitely all been in my head. It was probably just a local customer who saw the card and thought of me… and wrote romantic poems… like my ex. I sat down with a dramatic sigh, trying to chase the thoughts out of my head. Scared to admit to myself that there was a slight tremor of excitement alongside my fear.

The feeling of stepping off the bus and being at the seaside never got old. I smiled at the sensation as the cold, salty air hit my lungs. There wasn't a cloud in the sky today, it was bitter, but bright and clear; perfect weather for how I wanted my birthday to be.

I headed straight for the sea front, smiling as I saw the beach on the horizon. Something about it just calmed me. I'd love to have a place by the sea one day. Maybe my own bakery; it would be chaotic in summer with the tourists, but, during the winter I could just take my time- stroll like this, enjoy the moments. What was life without these moments, after all? Slowing down had made me realise for certain; it was the little things that made life worth living.

I passed by a large coffee shop and looked longingly inside, but I was trying to support smaller, local businesses, so decided to continue and find my favourite. A small café we'd supplied cakes to over the summer. A cosy spot on the beach with a large coffee and my thoughts to myself was what I needed. I had a book and, of course, chocolate in my bag. There was pretty much always a book and chocolate in my bag.

It soon became apparent though, that on a quiet, out-of-season Sunday, my favourite local businesses were closed. No caffeine for me. I'd given up a lot of vices, including wine and designer shoes, but coffee and I would never be torn apart.

Stepping down onto the sand I sat on the long sea wall and tucked my legs up under my chin; holding onto my dress so as not to expose myself to the seagulls, should a gust of wind catch it.

As I watched the waves roll in and out my breath slowed to their rhythm. So, this was thirty? It could be better but it could be a whole lot worse. There was not a soul about; I loved the peacefulness of this place. How different to where I'd been a year ago, and a year before that. I didn't want to feel glum as I looked back; best just to focus on this birthday.

I closed my eyes and held my head up to the sky, letting the weak, winter sun rest on my face. I was in shadow all of a sudden; where had dark clouds appeared from? I held a hand up to my face to block out any glare as I opened my eyes.

But I didn't see any clouds, or any sun. I saw him…

TWENTY

*M*y eyes met Luke's for the briefest second and I tore them away in shock; I couldn't get drawn into his eyes, into him, into another situation. I cursed Cassie for getting me into this.

"Happy birthday," said Luke.

I swallowed, trembling, as I kept my eyes focused on the waves. In and out, in and out; just like my breath. Just keep breathing. I had missed that voice though.

"Thanks. You came a long way to say that. A WhatsApp would've done it."

"No, it wouldn't." He sat down next to me and held out a coffee cup. "Besides, I don't have your number, Cassie wouldn't give it to me, said you would kill her. Caramel Macchiato for the birthday girl?"

My lips betrayed me with a smile which I tried to stop before he noticed. Luke held the cup out towards me and as I reached for it our fingertips touched for the briefest instant.

"Thank you," I snatched my hand away and lifted the lid, enjoying the smell of my old favourite. I took a long drink, the warm feeling flowed down my chest, against the coldness of the air in my lungs. I needed to just concentrate on that, and not the proximity of him, because there was no way I was turning my favourite coffee down.

"Are you going to look at me?" Luke asked.

I shook my head and took another long sip, my eyes rooted on the horizon.

He wriggled closer, his arm against mine. I tried not to react, not to move, just kept my eyes ahead; but that touch was sucking the air out of me.

"Your hair suits you like that."

"Thank you." My face was on fire now as a blush overtook me. I was worried I sounded like an idiot who just kept saying thank you, but I was scared to get drawn into more.

"Why didn't you tell me you were leaving?"

"It's not normal to contact your ex's and pass on new address details," I replied, almost in a whisper.

"Is that all I am to you? An ex?"

I shrugged and tried to wipe a tear from my cheek without him noticing. *When did I start crying?*

"I tried to do the right thing. I thought you and Zack would be OK," he sighed and ran his fingers through his hair. I glanced my eyes to the side as he did so, noticing how beautiful his face still was; my memories had been perfect. That chiselled jawline, even the tiny chicken pox scar underneath his right eyebrow. "What went wrong? Cassie said it wasn't her place to tell me. She's extraordinarily loyal to you, that girl."

"When we were at that mediation, Anna somehow recorded our conversation and sent it to Zack on his birthday. I think she paid the barman to record us." I didn't want to think about this, especially not on my own birthday.

"But nothing happened that night, or any night." Luke sounded confused.

"No, but we discussed the fact that it was you made the decision for me. Zack lost the plot that I hadn't exactly chosen him. We were on holiday with all his family, it was awful."

"I'm sorry." Luke said.

"Not your fault, Anna's always been a bitch. Slapping her silly at work didn't help because then I got fired. But… it's all worked out, I guess. I'm happy here."

Luke reached for my left hand and lifted it up, he traced his fingertip over the place where my engagement ring used to sit, there wasn't even a slight indentation there now. "I told you it wasn't the ring for you."

I pulled my hand away and shivered. His touch set off ridiculous sensations in me.

"When I heard about you and Zack I wanted to rush straight to you, but I knew it wouldn't have been the right time. Us and timing, hey?" Luke's voice shook as he spoke. "I've been trying, and wanting, to find you ever since I found out you moved. Cassie was adamant she couldn't betray your wishes but gave her own little clues. What you did for her is amazing by the way, you should see how happy they all are."

"Why did you want to find me, Luke? It just makes this harder. Three people got horribly hurt, we don't need to revisit that." I took another drink, sad that it was almost all gone, was this moment over when the coffee was gone? The cup was almost empty, like I needed to keep my heart.

"Two of those people have the chance to get this right. It really would help if you'd look at me, Lily."

"I can't look at you. If I look at you, I'll get all lost in us again," I admitted.

"And that's a bad thing because?"

"Because I can't go through it all again. I'm fine here. I don't want to ruin the life I've managed to build."

Luke sighed. "There's much more to life than being fine. I thought you'd be aware of that by now."

"I've put you through so much, I don't want to be the person who keeps doing that."

"What if I want you to be that person? Because for every bad moment I went through for you, I also went through a hundred good moments." He put his hand on my knee as he spoke and I felt his touch throughout my entire body. "I know you. I know you need time to deal with this. How about I come to yours later this evening? See if you can stand to look at my face by then? I think I should have a say in this, Lily."

I knew he smiled as he spoke, and, like a beautiful contagion, the smile spread to my own mouth.

"Maybe I'm just worried you've aged horribly and you aren't pretty anymore. I'm a very shallow girl."

"Only one way to find out. Do you want a lift back home?" Luke asked.

"No," I shook my head. "How do you know where I live anyway?"

"Wasn't hard in a place that tiny with just one bakery," Luke said as I felt him tense up beside me. "I'm sorry, I didn't mean I was following you or anything like that. I…"

"Shh, I know. I know that's not you." I turned towards him with a smile; I wanted to reassure him that it was OK, but my face just froze as I looked at him for the first time in so long. Truly looked at him. Luke reached for my hand again and this time I didn't try to stop him. The moment stretched on, the intensity was too much; I couldn't let myself crack. I pulled my hand away and looked back towards the beach. "I might see you later then? I guess… If you happen to be nearby."

Luke kissed the top of my head as he stood and I melted underneath his lips; it felt as if my hair was rising to try and stay in contact with him. "If it's up to me, that's a definite yes. Hope the birthday coffee was perfect for you," He took a step away, then stopped. "Hey, did you hear we won the Maloney case?"

My cheeks burned crimson. "No, I hadn't heard."

"Yeah, some anonymous evidence turned up. Holly bought a lovely little house, her and the boy are doing so well. I wonder if I'll ever find out where it came from?" His voice teased, but I wasn't going to admit a thing.

"I doubt it but that sounds like the best outcome. For Holly, and for your firm."

I didn't look up as I heard his feet crunch across the shell strewn sand. I took a deep breath in, savouring the scent of him mingled in with the ocean. My eyes closed again of their own accord. Between the kiss and the scent, I didn't think I could move.

I was petrified to think about this but at the same time my entire body was going berserk, having had him close, but not quite close enough; it wanted more.

I wandered up and down the beach for a short time but I was too restless. I thought more about the beautiful words, poems and clues he'd left me over the last year. A year of not being able to see him. A year of unknowingly reading his feelings for me. And now, he was here, on my birthday. Although he hadn't quite said it outright, he seemed as if he still wanted me. It terrified me. Yet it also excited me; my stomach fizzed with anticipation.

Right now, though, I just wanted to get back to the cottage. I wanted to read his words again. And this time I wanted to be prepared for seeing him; this time I wanted to be able to look him the eyes.

I made haste to the bus stop as the various parts of me assaulted my mind with different emotions and intents.

My heart bounced around as though it had been injected with happiness.

My head was gloomy- warning me of more heartbreak to come.

My body told me… I really needed to shave my legs.

TWENTY ONE

I raced into the cottage and pulled the front door closed behind me. I had no idea how long I had to get prepared; this was stressful. Thankfully the place was immaculate, I always seemed to have time for cleaning now. It was just myself I needed to fix up.

I ran a hot bath with my best bubbles, and as the hot water tumbled into the tub, I surveyed myself in the mirror. He'd said he liked my hair; I smiled as I pulled at the ends of it, still not used to it sitting up above my shoulders. Thanks to the early nights and lack of alcohol my skin looked better than it ever had. What kind of image did I need to portray here, though?

I mulled it over as I lay back in the bath, my razor had worked harder than it had ever known. It would be weird if he turned up and I was dressed up to the nines. I also couldn't do pyjamas and no make-up Lily. I didn't even think I had eyeliner in, however, which would have been unheard of in the past.

I daren't stay in the bath too long in case I missed a knock at the door. After smothering myself in expensive body cream, I dressed in tight black jeans and a soft, dusky pink jumper that I'd bought online a couple of weeks ago. I knew he was a sucker for cuddling up to soft material. I convinced myself that it was for no particular reason that my best matching underwear was underneath, after all, I wasn't planning on anything happening. Nothing at all was going to happen.

Lily, what are you even doing? I wished I had wine in the fridge. I felt weak and silly; all this time I'd insisted I was fine alone, then fifteen minutes sat next to Luke and I was like a giddy teenager. It would be better to not let him in. What was the point of getting his hopes up when this could never be? *We* could never be? I was back to that feeling of being torn; I couldn't stand it.

Apart from mascara I left my face bare, my hair had settled into lovely waves which suited the bob. My whole body was on tenterhooks in case the door went, but so far, I hadn't heard a peep. I misted myself in a cloud of my favourite perfume before I took the Gucci box downstairs and settled at my small dining table. It seemed a fitting time to put our playlist on again, of course, beginning with The Scientist- it felt as though Coldplay had written it just for me and Luke.

I always smiled at the shoes as soon as I opened this box; they were beautiful and none of the heart ache was their fault, shoes this beautiful would never cause pain like that! I noted that the memory card was still safely stashed away too.

I wondered how long Luke had worked on this. Had it been a plan to get me back? Had it been therapeutic? I didn't know but I adored everything about it. What a story it would be to tell our grandchildren. *Lily... get a grip. You are NOT getting back together, there will not be grandchildren.*

I shifted the papers round and round on the table, opening up the photograph on my phone of the graffiti and adding it into the mix.

I read through the message in The Metro again.

The scent of you close
So near, yet so far
A simple memory, almost a ghost
I envy the darkness of the coffee
As it passes by your lips
The memory of your kisses
still burning at my skin

Thinking back, there had been that feeling a couple of weeks earlier, when this exact song had played. When I'd felt on edge, like he was close. Had he been close? Was this message in relation to that? I had no idea if this was definitely him, but I felt that it was. His words resonated with me.

Then I looked at the paper I'd found by the granny flat; such a special place for us.

Our smiles, merged into a kiss
Eyes dark to the world
You pulled me close
Not knowing I was already
A fragment of your soul
Our double heartbeat
That tandem beating
Is it any wonder I lost myself?

Some things I was certain were from Luke, others I just didn't know about. Like the supermarket one – that was only a couple of weeks after he sent me the email, that could have just been random. Yet the style seemed to fit, and, every time I read it, I felt something shift inside of me. It reminded me of the night in the tepee in Luke's garden for some reason, such an incredible night.

It was almost beautiful fate
but we were in the wrong place,
the wrong time, the wrong state
Nevertheless
My soul knows yours
on this, I'm steadfast
Our connection wasn't forced
My heart misses yours
I need belief
that next time around
We... can be us...

It was like the most romantic puzzle in the world. I continued shifting the pieces around for a moment until I froze, hearing the sound of feet on the driveway. Who was I kidding? I would never be able to say no to Luke. Me and him... we were something else entirely.

TWENTY TWO

*T*heard a gentle tapping on the front door and my stomach plummeted to the floor as a rush of heat shot up to my face. I was going to have to talk to him; I was going to have to look at him. I was going to have to figure out what the hell I was doing – because if nothing was happening here I needed to make sure I didn't get his hopes up. I couldn't cause one more ounce of pain to him.

I checked myself in the mirror one more time and opened the door with a shy smile. For someone who'd been my best friend for so long, who I'd shared so much with, he really set off the nerves in me.

I decided it was better to meet this head on; I looked straight into Luke's eyes. You know how they warn you to not look directly at the sun? Yeah… Luke needed a similar style of warning.

He was even sexier than before if that was possible. Maybe I'd just managed to forget how inviting he was but he was drawing me in right now. Was it possible that his eyes had grown bluer over the course of a year? My gaze drifted down his face to his full lips, his happy smile, his soft, smooth neck.

"Lily," his voice was soft. My eyes bounced back to his and I couldn't stop my heart going insane; it was why I hadn't looked at him earlier. Before I knew what was happening I was in his arms, breathing him in, feeling the strength of him enveloping me into his safety. I felt his breath against my face and realised it was hot against the stray tears that had begun to run down my cheeks. "Lily," Luke repeated. "I love this, but it's freezing out here. Are you going to let me in?"

I laughed, and, for an instant I felt lost as his arms left me. I motioned him inside and closed the door.

"Do you want a drink?" I asked, trying to sound casual, as if this wasn't the most important conversation I could've imagined. As if I wasn't wiping tears off my face that his touch had caused. "I don't bother having wine in anymore,but I can make coffee?"

He pressed his hand to my forehead and frowned. "Is this really my Lily?" I laughed and batted his hand away but my heart had doubled in size as he called me 'his Lily'. "Coffee's good but I brought your favourite gin, you know from that shop at home?"

"From the deli?" I squealed. "I miss that place. I don't have tonic though," I said, as disappointment washed over me. I'd missed gin, not as much as I'd missed him but still…

Luke held two bags out to me. "As if I wouldn't bring tonic, you think I'm an amateur?"

"Take a seat," I motioned towards the small couch that took over most of my living room as I grinned at him. "Won't be a minute."

I watched him, biting my lip, as I sliced up the lemons and limes he had also brought along- so well prepared. He looked way too big to be in this little cottage but also perfect at the same time; I could picture him lounging around on lazy Sunday mornings… *Lily, stop!*

I placed a gin and tonic down in front of him a couple of

minutes later, alongside my own, before I sat on the opposite end of the couch and turned towards him expectantly.

"You look good."

"So do you," I replied, my nerves creating chaos within me. "This feels weird."

"Things between us, they don't have to be weird. I've been fearful to come here, to talk about this. But, knowing what happened last time when I put it off and everything that led to… I need to just say it." His Adams apple bobbed deeply as he swallowed his nerves. "Lily, I love you, nothing has changed for me. Every part of me wants you. I'd go anywhere for you. Be anyone for you. We've been to hell and back, I know we have. But now, now we're both in a position that we could make this real."

I reclined my head onto the soft material of the couch; his fingers had inched closer to mine and I couldn't help but reach out to touch them. "I don't feel sure about anything anymore, Luke. Except for the fact that I still love you, I've never stopped. All those amazing words you sent me, I only fully realised as I put them all together today, how incredible they are."

"It nearly killed me to not be able to tell you what I felt. It was a poor consolation prize, but, if something made you smile, it was worth it."

"I thought you had a girlfriend though?" I dreaded his answer.

"No! Cassie set me up on a random date for a ball and then it ended up in a magazine. Everyone thought it was something, but it was nothing. I didn't even kiss her. I was devastated at the thought of you being engaged, even though I'd pushed you in that direction."

"But, I live down here now and you have the partnership and—"

He pressed a finger to my lips. "I'm sure I said this before but we could go anywhere in the world together. I'm not going to let something like distance, or a job stop me from being with the girl I'm supposed to be with. I spent too long sitting in the side lines, putting other people first. I'm not doing that anymore. I want you. I'm not giving up on you. We are supposed to be together and I will fight every single day until we are."

I felt tears run down my cheeks at his words. How incredible was this man?

"Was The Metro you?" I asked.

Luke nodded his head softly.

"The Graffiti?"

"Well, I paid a gang of kids to do that one, I just supervised," he admitted, with a sweet blush and a soft laugh. "I was a bit scared of them, to be honest."

"All the poetry pieces scattered around over the last year?"

"I just needed you to know."

I shuffled closer to him on the couch and saw a faint smile flash on his face as I did so. "You want to be together? Like a couple?"

He stroked his hand up my arm and I saw him soften at the touch of the jumper, so delicate. "Yes. I want what we should have been all along. I want forever, Lily."

I bit my lip as I looked at him, scared, but so sure this was inevitable, again. As it had been before; as it always would be. Did it even matter what anyone thought? All the past hurt was there anyway, nothing would change it, but did it need to affect forever?

Neither of our drinks had been touched as I moved my face closer to his. My eyes danced across his features, remembering the familiar and beautiful shape of him.

Then... his lips touched mine and the rest of the world faded to nothing. His hands ran up into my hair and held my face close as I pulled myself towards him. Our mouths moved together, my legs wrapped around him instinctively as I straddled his knees.

He took hold of my face with both of his hands and kissed the tears away that fell from my eyes. "You don't ever have to cry for us again, Lily. This can be it. This can finally be it. I love you." Then his tongue pressed against mine, his hands slid inside my jumper and up my back, pulling me closer still. "I dreamt about this every single night I was without you," he spoke against my lips as my hands pulled his shirt from his jeans, desperate to feel the soft skin of his back under my fingers once again.

"I love you too. I switched myself off from how much I missed you, I shouldn't have done. Is it pushing things if I ask you to come upstairs with me?" I asked as my lips placed kisses along his neck, along that super smooth neck, breathing him wholly into me as I did so.

"Nope," he grinned as he lifted me up and my legs wrapped around him tighter.

"This is why I couldn't look at you earlier."

"Yeah, we'd get arrested for this on the beach."

I laughed at his words, the happiest laugh I could recall in a long time. I'd missed him so much it felt as if my heart scorched through my chest right now; like a sun about to collapse in on itself, the burn was so bright.

Our mouths locked together again as Luke stood. We moved towards the stairs and he placed me down, his touch gentle yet so needing. I took his hand and led him up the steep, narrow steps towards my room. "Mind your head, this place wasn't designed for tall people."

As soon as we were through the door to my bedroom, he lifted the soft jumper over my head. Our hands couldn't leave each other alone, desperate for each piece of skin to be reunited with the other.

I kissed his neck again; I loved his soft neck. That insanely sexy point where neck turned to shoulder, I could sink my teeth into that point all day, breathe in his smell, taste the softness there...

"Lily..." Luke's voice distracted me from my focus as he spoke. "You know last time, when we didn't use anything? Is that still a thing or..." The rest of the sentence was lost as I slid back to his mouth.

"That last time is burned into my mind. I know I'm fine, I had to have loads of tests for the egg donation. You?"

He tugged my jeans down as he responded. "I haven't been with anyone since that night."

I paused, moving to look him in the eyes. "Really?" I asked with genuine surprise.

He nodded, looking embarrassed. "I couldn't stand to be with anyone but you, it sounds silly but—"

Now it was my turn to stop him, I pressed my finger to his lips. "You don't need to explain. I know what you mean. Knowing you were the last person who touched me was... everything. It's not silly."

He lay me down onto the bed and I almost lost myself there and then. I couldn't stop smiling. Luke was here, and kissing me, and he loved me, and oh my God, we were about to— "Crap!" I exclaimed.

He pulled back from me, alarmed. "What's wrong? Please don't let there be something wrong?"

"No, I just realised. It hasn't mattered so I hadn't thought about it, but I had to stop the pill to do the egg donation and there wasn't any reason to start it again."

"That I can cope with," he blew out a sigh of relief. "I thought it was going to be a secret boyfriend or weird trauma."

I smiled as I kissed him again, how lucky was I that I got to kiss Luke again? I'd never get bored of it.

"Nothing like that. You know me, sworn off men."

He stroked his finger down the side of my face as he looked down at me. "Except me, I hope?"

"Except you. I'm sorry about the sex though."

He looked momentarily confused before he grinned and reached into his back pocket. "Oh, that's not a problem. I mean, I wasn't being presumptuous, but I have to be honest, I was hoping." He placed the condom at the side of us and threw my bra and knickers to the side of the bed.

"Thank fuck for that," I pulled him down onto me as we met in a frenzy of love, lust, passion, lost time, relief, excitement... every emotion and feeling I could imagine. I just wanted to absorb him into me. It was as though all that love that I'd kept at bay for so long, through fear and regret, just rushed out and into him, flowed through us, around us, into us. It was almost too much, almost...

We headed back downstairs a couple of hours later, holding hands and grinning at each other like love struck idiots. Luke smiled as he saw all the bits of paper and poetry spread out on the dining table.

"You kept them, even from that first one?" he asked.

"Yeah, they were all beautiful. How could I not?"

He looked bashful as his eyes glanced over the messy stack of paper.

"There was actually one I never got around to sending," he said. "It was my favourite, but there never seemed to be the right opportunity."

"I think you should read it to me right now in that case." I smirked at him as I tugged the t-shirt I'd hastily thrown on down over my knees and sat on the couch.

He looked flustered as he pulled his phone from his discarded jacket before sitting next to me. The room was dark now, only a spotlight from the kitchen illuminated the downstairs. The beautiful blue of his eyes was magnified by the light of the phone screen. I also spotted the delicate trace of pink that blushed across his cheeks as he began to speak. I got the impression he knew the words well and didn't need the phone, it was more of a focus for him. If my heart swelled any bigger I was going to have serious issues. He his fingers delicately up and down my arm as he began to speak.

"You have simply
unwritten
everyone else who ever touched me
Your kiss became my first
completely new, and thrilling
So now I need
those lips to touch
every single cell of my being
So that you are the only one
to have ever known me this way
You have become
my past
my present
my future
No other hand will graze this skin
No other kiss will land upon me
Enraptured by your touch
Unwrite me, over and over."

I heard him swallow deeply, his eyes never left my own. "I didn't even know you wrote words like that." I said quietly, my heart threatened to leap out of my chest at any moment. "Unbelievably beautiful."

"I didn't until… well, you know."

I saw sadness pass over his face, and I just wanted to kiss every little piece of it away. I hated he'd ever felt the heartbreak of us and I wanted to remove every trace of it. Simply spend forever loving him, making sure he felt it to the bottom of his heart for every single second of our lives together.

"I don't think we ever need to worry about that again Luke."

"You have to stop this switching off and hiding away on your own though. You have to talk to me, involve me in your decisions."

"I know," I agreed. "I just don't handle things well, I'm sorry."

"You don't have to ever apologise for being you." He kissed me softly, it was almost as though we didn't physically touch, our souls just reached out for each other in delicate, smoky wisps.

"Remember when we said it just wasn't the right time for us?" he asked.

I nodded, adoring the warmth of his breath on my face as he spoke.

"Now is the right time, isn't it? I couldn't stand to leave here tonight without you." His eyes were wide, I knew he was scared.

I took both of his hands in mine and rubbed my lips against his as I spoke. "This is absolutely the right time. This is forever. I'd say I love you again, but we both know it's more than that. I don't ever want you to leave."

Then, all that poetry, all the papers, all the words, were pushed to the floor. Luke lifted me onto the table, his mouth desperate against mine; his hands gripped me tightly, as if petrified I would slip away from him.

This was rough, hard, frantic… but I needed it as much as he did. There'd been so much pain between us and we needed to express it somehow; expel it. Luke drove into me deeper and harder each time; the lip of the table cut into the backs of my thighs, but I didn't want him to stop. I never wanted him to stop. He bit at my shoulder as my nails sank deeply into his flesh. The room felt as though it was on fire as our breaths came faster and faster and then he was pushing me deeper down. My back ached with the unnatural bend as he pressed me into the hard table; his whole body stiff against mine as he peaked once again, spasming deep inside of me.

His face sank against my shoulder as he pulled me down to the floor. "I'm sorry, I didn't mean to…" he began to say.

"Shhh," I pressed kisses against his hot skin and wrapped my arms around him. "It doesn't matter. Everything is OK now. We found each other again."

"But I didn't use a condom and…" his breath shuddered and a shiver ran through his body.

"It's one time, don't worry. I'm going to get straight back on the pill, because I want you every single day from now on. Is that acceptable?" I tried to look serious as he lifted his face to look at me, then our lips met with the softest of kisses. I could taste his stray tears which had fallen in the emotion of the moment. "What's meant to be, will be. You taught me that."

Luke pulled me against him. We were a tangled-up mess of tears and laughter, kissing and love, hope and trust. It had taken a lifetime to get here, but here we were.

Before my eyes had even opened on Monday morning, I took a long, deep breath and instantly I remembered. The scent of Luke, his proximity, it slid over me like melting chocolate – smooth, silky and utterly delicious. My entire body was warm and relaxed, wrapped in his arms; we could have been floating in the clouds. I felt weightless and light, utterly content, and that didn't just apply to my body. It was as though my mind had been soaked in hot caramel, my thoughts were slow and sultry. I felt delirious with love and desire.

A slither of fear still remained, this was a big step and I knew the heartache that awaited me if it should all go wrong. Yet, I also knew I'd take any risk for this man, I trusted him implicitly. I was his entirely and I wouldn't let anything, any emotion, any person, come between us.

Luke's fingers slid gently into my hair and I blinked slowly as my eyes opened, meeting his. The world could have ended and I wouldn't have noticed; there was nothing except him in that moment. Sunshine hadn't been in abundance lately yet I could still see the vaguest hint of freckles smattered across Luke's nose and cheeks. His skin so soft, broken only by the stubble that had grown overnight. His hair, that gleaming dark caramel blonde, flopped over his forehead and I couldn't help but smile as he softly blew it out of his eyes. His eyes… The blueness entranced me, they always made me think of the beach; a beautiful azure ocean under a clear, blue, sunny sky. It was as though nothing in the world could ever hurt while I had those eyes watching over me.

The room was silent as his lips brushed against mine, barely touching as his hand gently stroked through my hair.

"Is this real?" I whispered.

"Completely," he replied, his breath tickling my lips. "I never want to wake up without you again."

"Do you know it's Monday?" I sighed sadly at the thought this fairy-tale twenty-four hours might be ending. "Don't you have work?"

I squealed as Luke pushed me from his chest, pinning my arms down on the bed as he moved over me. "Are you trying to get rid of me, Lily?" he asked, as he pressed his lips in a trail of kisses along my neck and down my collarbone.

"I never want you to go. What are we going to do, though?"

"I have two weeks off, we can figure it all out. As long as we're together, I don't care where." His kisses worked up my other collarbone as he headed back towards my mouth. "Have you got work today?"

"No, the bakery doesn't open on a Monday," I replied, purposefully lifting my hips slightly and pressing against him. The way he had my arms pinned down was driving me insane. "I should probably book that doctors appointment though if you're going to keep putting me in positions like this."

Luke reached over to grab his phone, frowning at the glare. "It's only just seven."

I wriggled out from under him while he was distracted. "Plenty of time then, I'll get an appointment for later today, and, in the meantime I have a plan." I pushed Luke down onto the bed and clambered over him, my legs either side of his hips. His body felt perfect against mine, warm and firm, positively oozing sexual tension.

I wanted to taste every single bit of him as I began a journey down his body, covering him with kisses, licks and soft bites. He'd always been fit but had obviously worked out a lot over the last year. I rubbed at his defined shoulders as my mouth grazed over the muscles in his chest. His stomach was so sexy, I had to stop myself from just biting down; I wanted to devour him completely. As I sucked softly on the skin just below his belly button, his breath shuddered and I grinned to myself as I wriggled down lower, purposefully letting out a long breath, knowing he'd feel the hot air upon him.

He twitched as I glanced featherlight kisses up and down his length; a memory flashed into my mind of the night we'd laughed about micro penises and how much it had turned me on when he'd been pressed against my back. I was almost drooling I wanted him so badly as I moved lower, his hands in my hair and my mouth full of him.

There wasn't anything sexier than this, knowing he was mine again. In this moment I had him completely enraptured, under a spell as I moved up and down, running my tongue over that soft skin, feeling the throb of lust that ran up him in response to me. With a delightful shiver I remembered last night, the feeling of him inside me, how perfect we were together.

His breath was ragged as he gripped my hair, I shifted so his knee was between my legs and as he felt me rub myself against him, he pressed deeper into my mouth. We moved faster and hotter, until he clenched his fingers into my hair, holding me down as my mouth flooded with the taste of him. Mine. That's all I could think, he was all mine.

I placed gentle kisses along him and back up his stomach as he took a moment to regain his breath. Nuzzled into his neck, I felt as if love was overflowing out of me. It was too much and tears began to drip down my cheeks and splash upon his shoulders.

"Luke, I'm so sorry," I spoke quietly through sobs. "I hurt you so much. I don't know what I've done to deserve this second chance with you, but I will spend forever making up for everything, I promise."

He pulled me up, looking into my eyes as he replied. "You don't have a thing to apologise for, stop," he gently kissed my forehead and wiped stray tears from my face. "Everything that happened brought us here. This is where we're meant to be, and if all that other stuff hadn't happened, this wouldn't be happening. Let the past go."

I kissed his neck as I snuggled back into him sleepily.

"Fucking good wake-up call though, Lily. Same time tomorrow?"

I laughed at his joke, knowing I'd happily wake him up that way as many mornings as possible, before slipping into a blissful snooze, in the arms of my man.

I hated leaving Luke in bed the next morning to open up the bakery, but, as he kept reminding me, we had forever together. I knew in my heart that I wanted to go home, back to Luke's house, and be there with him. How could I let Zoe down though? Especially whilst Isla was so young. The bell above the door rang out with its tinkling sound just before eleven, interrupting my thoughts. I looked up to see Zoe stroll in, her eyes narrowed, that beaming smile of hers was obviously missing.

"Morning," I said. "You OK? Bad night with Isla?"

Zoe shrugged and paused a moment, open mouthed, before she began. "I'm rubbish at bad news and I should lead up to this somehow. But I don't know how, and I just need to tell you, but I feel like the worst person in the world and... I'm so sorry, Lily—"

"Take a breath," I came out from behind the cake display and stood beside Zoe. "What's wrong, what bad news?"

"Marcus got a promotion, which is brilliant, but it's in the French office. We're moving to France," she said, looking down at the ground.

"That's not bad news, that will be an incredible adventure for you. How exciting."

"It means I'll need to close this place down. Which means no job, and you've been so amazing. I feel like crap."

I stroked her arm absentmindedly as I thought, remembering some of Luke's wisdom. The universe gives you what you need, when you need it. This job had happened at a time I needed to get away, and now... now I had Luke and a whole world of options. This job wasn't for me anymore, the universe had already given me the best thing in the world.

"Zoe," I couldn't help but grin as I spoke; her eyes widened with surprise at my reaction. "Don't worry, everything is perfect, don't worry," I laughed, giddy with love and excitement as I took her arm and twirled her around in a little dance.

She joined in with my laughter, looking me up and down. "Is this anything to do with that sexy as hell Lexus outside the cottage?"

I nodded, biting my lip in anticipation as I thought of going home with Luke. Home. Luke. Words I'd never thought I'd get to put back together again.

"Coffee, now," she ordered, a smile on her face as she headed through to the back. I spent the next hour filling her in on the saga that was me and Luke. Every time I said his name, I couldn't help but smile. The heat in my heart was bursting out of me; like I was swirling around in love-drenched delirium. I adored the feeling!

When Zoe met Luke her eyes nearly popped out of her head; I couldn't help but laugh. We agreed I could leave in a weeks time as she wanted to wind the business up quickly and get on with her French house hunting. Luke asked if I was interested in taking the business over, but the same thought was central in my mind- I wanted to go home. Maybe I'd start a business there, I wasn't decided. What was meant to be, would be, of that I was sure now.

I smiled across at Luke as he drove out of the village and headed north. We were going home… Together.

TWENTY THREE

I glanced at Luke as we wandered along the beach, our fingers laced together as always. I was barefoot; I loved feeling small next to him. When he hugged me like this my head slotted perfectly under his chin and he always left kisses in my hair.

Another birthday had just passed; it amazed me how life changed in a single year, and it had to be said that my thirties were beyond belief, I'd adored every day. To celebrate that, and the first anniversary of when we finally got together, Luke had booked a trip to Lastovo. We were holidaying on the Croatian island in a beautiful house that overlooked the shimmering Adriatic Sea. The island was off the beaten track, sparse of tourists, and absolutely stunning.

It had become a new, captivating habit to walk along the beach and watch the sun ether rise or set each day; cuddled up on the sand together as if we were the only people in the world. This place was remote and peaceful, it was easy to imagine that we were, in fact, the only people in the world.

Tonight we were watching the sunset and planned to stay out here well into the darkness. The other amazing thing about this place was the night sky. It was renowned for having one of the most beautiful starry skies in the whole of Europe. Luke knew I loved the stars and had thought of every detail for me when choosing this place for our holiday, he put so much thought into everything.

Luke sat down in the sand and I followed, sitting in front of him and taking a deep, happy breath in the warm, salty, evening air as his arms wrapped around me like a protective cloak.

I laughed as his fingers tickled my neck, he scooped all of my hair to one side and kissed around the now bare skin.

"I love you," I said, leaning back against him. "This feels like heaven."

"Definitely does. Considering a year ago we were on a beach and you refused to look at me."

I dug my elbow back into him in a playful gesture. "It all worked out in the end, didn't it?"

"It did, and that's all that matters."

We were both quiet, contemplative, as we watched the sun set over the horizon, its reflection cast brilliant hues of pink and amber along the ocean. We'd given up trying to take photographs of it after the first time as there was no way we could do justice to just how beautiful it was to the naked eye.

We had one more night after this before it was time to head home, but I didn't feel sad. Our new home was waiting for us, a place we would be together always; close to Luke's office and with a huge kitchen extension for my new baking business. How could anyone be sad when returning to that? Plus, I had auntie duties to help with at Cassie's. I hadn't got to spend anywhere near enough time with baby Arlo yet.

I could see a man strolling along the beach towards us which was unusual, we usually had this section to ourselves. I smiled as I noticed his thick jacket, we thought the temperature was lovely and warm, but the locals were in full on winter mode.

Luke kissed the top of my head and jumped up. "Give me

one minute," he said, before heading to meet the stranger on the beach. I watched lazily from the corner of my eye, too invested in the beautiful sleeping dance of the sun over the water. I heard Luke say, "Hvala," and the man handed him a bag, nodded his head to me with a smile, and turned back in the direction he had come from.

I raised an eyebrow at Luke as he carried the bag back to me. "What have you got there?"

He sat back down in the sand. "You're so impatient!"

"I know. Thought you loved that about me?" I teased.

"I love everything about you." He tapped the end of my nose with his finger and pulled a bottle from the bag. "This is homemade wine from the vineyard just up the hill from us. I was worried about glasses breaking and I didn't want to have plastic, so, these are wooden wine goblets that we get to take home, and, I hope, drink wine out of together many more times."

"Aww, that's lovely. What did I do to deserve you?" I asked.

"I don't know but… you need to stand up so I can pour this. Sun's going to be gone in a minute." Luke stood and held his hand out to me, pulling me up from the soft sand. He poured the wine and we stood together, my head rested on him as his hand stroked my arm and, together, we watched the sun dip below the horizon in a slow, exquisite journey.

"You remember when I went backpacking?" Luke asked, his voice tickled me as his mouth rested close to my ear.

I turned to him, holding his hand. "Feels like forever ago, but yes. Why?"

"I know we weren't great then, but, I had the vaguest hope that we would be one day. So, while I was gone, I bought you a present."

I grinned. "I already think you're adorable and perfect and now I find out about surprise presents from the past?"

He blew out a long breath. "I saw this while I was in

Malaysia. I just… when I saw it, I just felt it belonged to you. That's why when I saw your other one, I knew it wasn't the one for you." He blew out a long breath as he reached into his pocket, and pulled out a delicate ring.

I could feel Luke tremble as he stretched out the fingers of my left hand. "You know I don't get the deal with traditional weddings, but, Lily, I want nothing more in the world than for you to be my wife. But on our terms," he smiled and pressed a kiss to my lips. I blinked, not wanting to forget a moment of this. "If you would have me, if you would say yes. Let's get married, under these stars tonight. You and me and the beautiful universe above us, the grains of sand below us. We don't need anything more than that, do we? Just our promise to each other."

My mouth had stretched into the widest smile as I looked into his beautiful eyes, all the stars above us that he had just mentioned seemed to be reflected in them. "We don't need anything else, Luke. Of course I want to marry you, I'm yours, forever." He placed one soft kiss on my forehead.

"You haven't looked at the ring, do you like it?" he asked, his face utterly alight with a radiant smile.

I looked down as he slid the delicate band down my ring finger. It was if it had been made for me. A brilliant blue sapphire sat in the middle of the platinum band, a blue that would always remind me of the ocean, and of Luke's beautiful eyes. On either side of it sat tiny, sparkling diamonds which twisted off to complement the band of the ring.

"It's incredible," I said, my voice caught in my throat as my mind struggled to comprehend the enormity of this moment.

"I just knew it was meant for you."

"You're meant for me," I said as I stroked his cheek with my left hand, watching the ring shimmer, like the reflection of a star in the moonlit sky.

"I know we don't have traditional vows to say. This time

last year you loved my poetry, I seem to recall. So, I thought..." He took a deep breath. "Maybe we could just say what felt right, say the words that flow through your mind right now."

I nodded. "I want to hear every word that passes your lips, especially these ones."

He took a drink of his wine and blew his hair out of his eyes nervously. I couldn't help but laugh softly, I loved how he got nervous still. Who was I kidding? I loved every single, tiny thing about him, a fact that had only become more apparent over this last year.

"I'll go first," I volunteered, taking a sip of the crisp wine. "This isn't my specialty but... I've thought a lot of senti-mental ideas about you recently."

"Luke... you are the reason I exist
The love that draws each breath
You keep my blood flowing
You drive my dreams
You make life what it is
Magical and heartfelt
Sometimes, raw and painful
But I don't care
Because we are written in eternity
This moment has been destined
Here, under these stars
There's a reason I shiver at the very thought of you
We've been falling in love
Over and over
Since the beginning of time
In every existence
Through every reincarnation
And we'll never, ever stop
Our love will outlast everything."

Luke wiped the tears from my cheekbones with a soft smile, taking a deep breath before he began his own pledge.

"I was lost before you
As I stand here now
Know that you are more than my soulmate
You're my equal half
We are remnants of the same star
A star that burst into beautiful shards
So very long ago
But now, Lily, that stardust has pulled us back together
Completing the perfect puzzle that is us
We found each other
And nothing in the universe can pull us apart again
I want to get drunk
And chase storms together
Not know where we wake up
Be best friends and lovers
Fall over in the snow
Cook food, make a home
I want to laugh until we cry
And cry until we laugh
I just want everything to be you
You and I are one, eternally
The very definition of love."

I buried my head in his chest, embarrassed by how much I was crying. He stroked my back and kissed my head until I was in control. The same amazing way he always had, not in a rush, letting me deal with every emotion the exact way I needed to, for as long as I needed to.

"Please say you know that off by heart, because I need it in a frame." I bit my lip as I looked up at him.

"We'll both remember every word," he reassured me before he placed a finger over my lips. "I don't need you to say anything else, I just need you to answer this next question."

I took a tiny step back from him, the warm sand settled between my toes. I wanted to focus on his face, to live in this moment.

"What's your name?" he asked, with utter sincerity. I was confused for the briefest of moments before I burst into happy laughter and jumped up into his arms. We twirled around in the sand, our arms holding each other, my legs wrapped around him, our lips pressed together, before I answered.

"Lily Adamson."

"Good answer, wife." He grinned, pure joy on his face, before laying me down in the sand. The deserted beach became our bed for the night. We lay there, still smiling as the sun rose the next morning. The first morning of the rest of forever.

EPILOGUE

Team Zack – Don't worry, I wouldn't leave him in a bad place!

I sat at the bar and sighed in frustration as I glanced at my phone. Today was Lily's thirtieth birthday, I couldn't help but wonder what she was doing, who she was with. It had been nine months now since we split up, despite everything, I hoped she was having a better birthday than mine had been. She could be anywhere, with anyone, it wasn't even worth thinking about. The past was the past, at least that's what I told myself.

I sipped at the expensive whiskey, watching the snow fall in heavy drifts outside the window. I was going to be in Iceland for three months now. It was easier than travelling backwards and forwards in the winter weather, and I preferred being here, away from the memories and with work to keep me busy.

At times I hated my stubbornness; it would have been so easy in those first few weeks after Spain to try and fix things, to work through the problems. That nagging thought at the back of my head wouldn't stop though, and, I knew I'd never fully quieten it; I'd always wonder about her and him. It didn't stop me missing her though.

Work had saved me. I'd thrown myself into this job, learning the language, travelling anywhere and everywhere they wanted me. Which is what found me back in this hotel, the hotel I promised I wouldn't come back to, not that it mattered anymore.

I was staying in an apartment that had been arranged for me for the three months; I didn't even care that I'd be here alone over Christmas. Tonight, though, I'd just felt like being around other miserable company, and this place was always full of people travelling alone for business, propping up the bar. I laughed to myself as I downed the whiskey; I'd been miserable about Lily last time I was here too. Sometimes I wished I'd never met her, just sometimes.

I looked up, ready to order another drink, and saw the barman walk away, his replacement headed behind the bar with a smile. His replacement who I had vague memories of entering my hotel room, but I couldn't for the life of me remember her name. A pity because I'd stand a chance of being able to pronounce it by now! I was just wondering if it would be easier to sneak to another bar, when she locked eyes with me and her face flashed with recognition.

"Zack?" she asked as she headed towards me, her eyes wide, taking me in.

I nodded, clearing my throat awkwardly. "Yes, I'm sorry, I remember you, obviously, but I don't remember your name."

She laughed. "You couldn't say it, I wouldn't expect you to. It's Arnkatla. Just call me Kat."

"I'm sorry about… last time I was here, I wasn't in a good place, and it's not fair, that I took advantage of you."

"You didn't, it was me doing the chasing, if you recall." She filled my glass up as she watched me, quizzically. "You still don't look like you're in a good place? Not the same girl is it?"

I shook my head. "No, we split up months ago. I work for a company based in Reykjavík, I'm here for three months."

"Hmm," she pursed her lips before she continued. "So, you're here for three months and you're single? I hoped you'd come back, you know."

Her confidence suddenly seemed sexy and appealing, no shyness or blushes here.

"You didn't want it to just be a one-night stand?" I asked.

"No, but I knew I wasn't likely to see you again. I looked at your room details, but it was all booked under the company name."

I raised an eyebrow at her, hoping this wasn't going to turn into a weird stalker moment. She just laughed however, a sweet playful laugh that lit her whole face up.

"Sorry," she replied. "I didn't mean that in a weird way, I just had a great time that night. I was hoping I would get to see you again."

"Are you only just starting your shift?" I asked, wondering what I was going to do with the answer.

"Yes, I'm working until the bar closes, will be late. But, it's my day off tomorrow..." She let the end of the sentence tail off as she smiled at me mischievously.

Kat was stunning, I hadn't taken it in that last time I saw her. Her eyes were a pale blue, set perfectly amongst her pale skin and pointed lips. Her long hair was ice-blonde and wavy. As she smiled, I noticed a gap between her two front teeth, which was actually the cutest thing I'd ever seen.

"Well, I'm working until five but it would be lovely if you wanted to do something after that?" I felt surprised as I heard myself ask. I'd been one hundred percent sure I wasn't ready to see anyone after what had happened, but, this felt different. Maybe because I already knew her, sort of, maybe because I was so far from home. Whatever it was, I hoped she was going to say yes.

"One condition," she said, tilting her head to the side. "No bars, I'm fed up with being in a bar."

"Deal," I smiled back at her. "I don't know what there is to do around here though. I've only seen the office and a couple of hotels."

"Meet me in the lobby, here, tomorrow at six," she said, that confidence on display again. "I'll plan something touristy but fun for you."

"I look forward to it." She walked away with a smile to serve customers whose patience grew thin as she'd spent so long with me. I finished my drink and gave her a wave goodbye. Suddenly, tomorrow seemed a lot brighter.

———————

I spotted Kat straight away as I entered the lobby; I could hear her laughter as she chatted with the girls on the reception desk. Her laugh was warm, vibrant and lovely. It was beautiful and cosy in here; a huge fire dominated the entrance to the hotel, outside it was only 2° and the wind stung any exposed skin.

Kat wore dark, fleecy jeggings and thick soled, black boots that laced halfway up her calves. The girls here dressed differently to Cheshire, no wobbling around these unforgiving icy streets in heels and a strappy dress. Her beautiful, pale blue jumper caught my eye as it matched her own eyes. She looked amazing. Understated perfection.

She said goodbye to her friends and headed toward me with a smile, a padded coat and large handbag slung over one arm. Raised up on her tiptoes she kissed my cheek, she seemed tinier than I remembered, and I ducked down as I returned the gesture, kissing the warm skin of her cheek.

"Glad to see you dressed for the weather," she grinned as

she took in my warm clothes and coat. "So many tourists underestimate the temperatures here."

"Hey, I'm more than a tourist," I replied. "I'm learning the language and everything."

Kat reached for my hand, I loved how confident she was to make moves like that. "Well, maybe I'll give you special tuition. First of all though, I'm taking you to one of my favourite places."

She drove for about twenty minutes, it felt natural as we talked about how I ended up working over in Iceland. I learned that she was studying to be a teacher, the bar work was just to top her student loans up. She would be leaving the bar in the new year, it seemed serendipitous that I'd met her now, just in time.

"Here we are," she said as she pulled into a large car park. "I'm worried now that this was silly. I love this place; I adore animals and the ocean. I thought it would be different, for a date."

Well, that answered the little doubt in my head about if this was a proper date or not. I glanced across the car park to the large building and saw giant posters of whales everywhere, there was even a whale themed climbing frame outside, although it was way too cold for anyone to play out now.

"I love whales!" I grinned with real, actual enthusiasm; I hadn't felt that in a long time. "This is like a perfect date place for me."

We hurried over to the entrance, eager to feel the warmth inside. Kat had already booked tickets and driven us here, I felt guilty that she'd paid, but she didn't seem concerned and refused any money.

We held hands as we strolled around; her delicate fingers felt lovely in mine. I was awe struck by the life size models of the whales, all the different species and their relationships with the Icelandic coast. This was an amazing country, suddenly the thought of three months here seemed exciting and full of possibility.

We seemed to have so much in common and maybe the fact that the ice had literally been broken when we first met made this less stressful. I wasn't worried about what I said or did, or what she thought. This just felt natural and every time I looked at her she seemed more beautiful.

Two hours later as we climbed into her car and hastily switched the heater on, I wondered whether I should suggest a drink at mine. Kat beat me to it.

"So, Zack, are you going to invite me to this apartment of yours for a drink? Just because I don't want to hang around bars, doesn't mean I don't like a drink."

"I'd love that," I replied. "Maybe you can teach me how to say your name at the same time?"

"I'll have you saying my name by the end of the night, don't worry." She winked before driving out of the car park, and I think, for the first time ever, a girl had left me speechless.

January rolled around too fast and the thought of going back to Cheshire whilst Kat remained in Iceland was horrible. We'd become inseparable; she stayed at the apartment most nights with me. She was just… everything. I knew I'd said that before about someone else, but I'd been mistaken, because what Kat and I had was special, different. She was my best friend, my partner in mischief, my lover, my future, all rolled into one, and I'd become sure of that fact very quickly.

Kat held onto me in the airport lounge; her face pressed into my chest. I looked down on that icy blonde hair that took my breath away, she was pure beauty, inside and out.

"I'll be back next month. I'm going to speak to them and

see if I can be in the office here more, just like we discussed. You can come visit me in England too, it's only a short flight. We'll get you booked on, OK? Please don't cry." I stroked her hair, not wanting her to feel this sad, even though I felt that way myself.

"I love you," she sniffled into my chest as she spoke.

"Ég elska þig," I whispered as I stroked her hair. She looked up at me, a laugh brewing at the corners of her mouth. I knew I hadn't pronounced it correctly, yet again.

As the plane lifted off into the sky, taking me back home, I felt sadness. It wasn't home anymore, it just wasn't. Home was wherever Kat was.

———

Twelve months had passed and I remembered that plane journey as I ran through the hospital corridor. The realisation of what I wanted, and, where I wanted to be, had struck me so hard as I headed back to England. As soon as I'd got into work the next day I'd asked to be moved permanently to Iceland. The situation ended up the reverse of my original contract, but it worked for everyone, three weeks in Iceland and one week in England.

Kat and I bought a house together just outside of Reykjavík, and, on the day we moved in, she nervously told me she was pregnant. It hadn't been planned but within minutes the two of us danced around the house, dodging cardboard boxes, filled with happiness.

I burst through the door into room four on the delivery suite, Kat still managed to smile at me as she focused on what the midwife was saying to her. I placed a kiss on her forehead and took hold of her hand, just in time for her to scream, and squeeze the life out of my bones. I don't know what these words were she was saying but I don't think they covered them in the language classes I'd been attending.

Time passed in a blur but this tiny little blonde warrior woman was awe inspiring, her strength and perseverance through labour, her stubbornness as she refused all the drugs. I adored her more each second if that were possible. We weren't a couple anymore; we were a family.

I cuddled Kat close to me on the bed as she held our baby boy to her chest. The only sound in the room- his soft murmurs. Every single thing that had happened, had brought me to where I was supposed to be. I'd never imagined love like this existed, but, here I was, surrounded by it.

AFTERWORD

When I wrote The Missed Kiss, I wasn't sure anyone would even read it, and now here you are, at the end of the sequel. I'm going to miss writing about this bunch of lovely characters, but there are new stories to tell, I promise!

I never imagined I'd meet so many lovely readers, and amazing authors whilst on this journey. The support and encouragement I've had from you all is incredible, thank you, I adore the new friends I've made.

If you could spare five minutes on Amazon / Goodreads to leave reviews for To Kiss You Again and The Missed Kiss, it would mean the world to me. Every single review and star rating means so much, and is the best way to help me grow my audience, and write more books.

I often write short stories and poetry for my website and social media. I have included one of my favourites at the end of this book - Anemoia - I hope you enjoy it. I loved the addition of poetry in To Kiss You Again, and have added the poems separately at the end of this book, in case you would like to read them individually.

As always, I love to hear from readers, so please do feel free to reach out to me via social media, email or my website.

I hope to see you all soon with the next book!

Nicola xxx

ANEMOIA STORY

Anemoia Definition -
Nostalgia for a time you've never known

Another Wednesday rolled around; it didn't, in all honesty, matter to me what day it was. They were all much the same. Work, home, television, with the occasional visit to the gym or a coffee shop. I felt disassociated from my own life and I still couldn't decide if I blamed myself or him, the most.

Don't fall in love young, that's what I'd advise. I was too naïve and he was too calculating. Nobody teaches you, at that age, what a healthy relationship should be, so I had to learn the hard way. Unfortunately for me that involved getting home early one night to see my friend (I use the term loosely), Violet, on her knees in front of him. I think the lack of remorse and shame from either of them in the following weeks was worse than that moment. It was the last straw, on top of three years of making me feel less than him, somehow not quite enough, but also too much, all at once. It had got to the point I didn't even try to speak up anymore, it wasn't worth it. I think Violet and her gobby mouth had actually done me a favour, but I wasn't sure if I'd ever feel like me again. I felt a bit broken and a lot less confident than before; trust would not come easily to me in the future, of this I was certain.

This particular Wednesday however was slightly different. I'd reluctantly agreed to join everyone from the office for a game of bowling and some beers after work. At least I didn't have to try and make much conversation if we were bowling. Hearing them all talk about their dating, their plans, their holidays, just got a little jarring when I never had news of my own to share. They always tried to involve me, but I just preferred to be left alone, quiet, live up to the introvert label that had been planted on me early in my teenage years. Nobody had understood it was perhaps just awkward shyness that would have passed had it not been made into such a big deal.

Halfway through the first game, in which I'd managed to stay firmly unremarkable in the middle of the scoreboard, my manager, Laura called me over.

"Ella," she smiled at me kindly as I took a seat in the booth. "This is Alex. He's starting in the office on Monday and I thought as you were the last newbie you could help him learn the ropes? He's come along tonight to quickly meet everyone, break the ice before his first day."

I nodded obediently and returned Laura's smile, before glancing across the small table to Alex…

That was the exact moment every ounce of breath was sucked wholly out of my being. I couldn't even describe to you what he looked like; I was just lost. I was not in the bowling alley anymore.

My eyes had closed and I had no wish to open them again. I wondered briefly if I'd died, had some freak accident occurred as I sat at that table with my boss? It would be an embarrassing place to die, but it wouldn't matter, because surely, this had to be heaven. I was complete.

My entire body felt cushioned as if I was nestled in blankets of angel feather and cashmere, so soft against me. I ran my fingers down my arms and felt the balmy warmness of my skin, as though it had been under a hot Mediterranean sun for most of the day. God, I felt so good but… I was also very, very naked I realised as my fingers pressed against the bare skin of my thighs.

With my next, deep, satisfied breath a familiar scent flooded my mind. Alex… He'd been working outside again, that pine smell always lingered in his hair, and, come to think of it, I could feel his fingers were slightly sticky with tree sap as they rubbed lazily up and down my back. Wait…

Too late. My taste buds were accumulating around his mouth as it met mine, dividing and multiplying, desperate to taste more of… him. He was everything, how had I lived before him? His kiss, the sensation of it. I'd kissed him a million times before and I'd kiss him a million times again. I tried to speak his name into his lips but I was lost, so lost.

Time shifted quickly and I could feel in my body that we'd made love and it meant everything to me. It wasn't the first time but still a tear ran down my cheek. My body shivered as clouds of goosebumps washed over me at the sound of his voice in my ear. I'd missed that voice so much. The words were jumbled, a different language, but I knew they were full of love. I'd never felt as cherished and adored. He had me on the highest pedestal, but we were equal. I placed him beside me and we were inseparable, nothing would, or could, ever come between us. His words, whatever they meant, were making me want him all over again. I slowly turned, in the soft cocoon we were embedded within, and opened my eyes to look at him…

An endless vision of possibilities flashed by in a blur. Life after life after life of me and him. I saw children, I saw car crashes, I saw so many graves, weddings, christenings, adventures, boredom, a myriad of countries. Every parallel universe that ever could have existed was right there, and, in each of them, we were together in some form. None of this made sense, yet at the same time *all* of it made sense. Alex, how had I forgotten his name?

"Ella! Ella, are you alright?" Laura's high-pitched voice broke through the trance. "Are you having some sort of seizure, are you sick?" Her hands were gripping my arms and shaking me, the skin sore where her fingers pinched.

"I'm... I'm fine," I stammered, shaking my head, and trying to control my breath; I was hyperventilating. I looked at Laura, too scared to glance across the table to Alex again. Alex... for God's sake I hadn't even known who he was ten minutes ago and now I couldn't think his name without shivering. What the hell was going on? "Could you please just get me some water, think I must be getting a virus or something."

Laura let go, leaving white marks on my arm where she'd gripped me, and scurried over to the bar in search of water. I frowned as I looked at her empty seat, too scared to turn to him in case it happened again.

"Ella?" His voice was exactly as I remembered. But how could I be remembering someone I'd never met. This was insane. I ran my hands through my hair as I slowly, cautiously, cast my eyes in his direction. "Are you OK? Your eyes were rolling around so fast, your breathing..."

Now that I coerced myself to look at him, I couldn't help but smile. That familiar face, younger than I'd just seen it, he was maybe twenty-two. His hair all floppy and messy, by his mid-twenties he'd like it shorter, but, for now, it fell over his right eye, the dark, dirty blonde that I adored. His eyes, brown and deep, like open books to his soul showing his kindness and humour. His nose was a bit big and he didn't like his double chin, but I adored every single part of him; I could never find him anything except beautiful.

"I missed you." The words left my lips too quickly, and I

felt a stab of pain as his head tilted to the side with confusion.

He sucked in a breath before he spoke, his jaw tense. "Laura will be back in a minute, don't worry, I'm sure you'll feel better soon."

"You don't remember me?" I asked, hearing the needy edge to my voice, the panic at the thought he would walk out of here and never be seen again.

Then, Laura was back with the water and I was ushered into a taxi, told to go home and rest, take the remainder of the week off and come in on Monday. Never getting chance to hear his response or further the conversation.

Monday... Alex would be starting on Monday. My mouth set into a satisfied grin as I sank into my soft bed, recalling the feelings I'd had earlier, reliving every moment of them. It would come back to him too, I knew it.

Yet he didn't remember, or, if he did, he deserved an award for his acting skills. Six months passed and I turned from over exuberant puppy, positively panting with excitement every time he came near me, back to that girl whose light had been dulled, whose hope had been lost. I was grieving for something that I didn't even know was real, what was wrong with me? Maybe I was just losing my mind; maybe I needed help.

It could have been a virus after all; maybe I imagined everything. But somehow, I couldn't quite convince myself of it. It was so real; how else did I know his voice, his taste, his touch, his smell? Every time he walked by me I inhaled as deeply as I could and the memories flooded through me. In every lifetime, he always smelled the same.

The universe had its plans, though. I guess patience was needed, although it had never been my strong point. One

Friday, not long after, I was dawdling, not in a rush to leave the office for the weekend. The others had all fled as soon as possible, for their drinks, their partners, their plans. There was nothing for me to rush home for; I was always the last here. I heard a voice coming from the staff room- his voice.

"So, I can't go back there? Until they've checked its safe tomorrow? Great, thanks for nothing." The voice was exasperated, defeated, and tired. I knew those emotions in him. He'd be trying to appear brave now, but, in reality he'd just desperately want a long hug.

"What's wrong?" I asked as I poked my head around the door. "Sorry I couldn't help but overhear, sounded like a problem?"

He jumped ever so slightly as he looked up. Was there a slight hint of a blush or was it just this awful strip lighting? "There's a gas leak in the building I live in. Not even allowed to go back in to get anything until it's signed off as safe, which won't be until tomorrow. I'll never find a room around here on a Friday night, not at this time of year."

His eyes darted to the window quickly, mine followed. The Christmas market outside was in full swing. Colourful fairy lights were strung between the buildings, including ours, lighting up beautiful stalls selling gifts, wine and candy canes. Also, predictably, giant bratwurst which seemed to dominate every Christmas market I'd ever been to for some random reason. The market was a massive tourist attraction, and, he was right, the few hotels and B&B's that serviced the picturesque town we lived in would be fully booked up.

"Come and stay at mine," I offered, probably too quickly. Something flashed behind his eyes and I sadly thought it was reluctance.

"I don't want to put you out," he said as he began to Google places to stay; the tension in his shoulders told me he was having no luck.

"You wouldn't be. I haven't got any plans," I winced

immediately, realising I was making myself sound pathetic. "The sofa's really comfortable, I was going to order Chinese anyway tonight. You're more than welcome."

I took a small step back, giving him space to decide. "Thank you," his eyes met mine and I couldn't help but smile. "That would be great."

Two hours later following a stop at a supermarket for urgent supplies such as a toothbrush, razor and a couple of bottles of wine, we sat on the colourful rug that dominated my living room floor. The large coffee table in front of us was full of the cute little boxes my local Chinese used for their deliveries.

"I'm sorry I don't have a proper dining table. I like eating down here, and, living alone there isn't much point using all the space," I began to explain.

"I like sitting on the floor to eat. Feels rustic," he replied as he refilled our large glasses with deep, red wine. Bless him, trying to put me at ease. We'd already had a large glass each while we waited for the food; the last thing I needed was to get drunk and try and kiss him or confess my undying love.

With the food devoured and the second bottle of wine opened, we slumped onto the couch. Seemed as good a time as any to try and dig a little deeper into this version of Alex I didn't yet know.

"So your accent doesn't sound local, where are you from?" I asked, wanting to make the most of this opportunity.

"Bristol," he replied. "I should've been getting married soon, but it all went horribly, horribly wrong. I wanted a fresh start."

"She obviously wasn't the right girl." As soon as I said it, I realised it sounded callous. "I mean, erm… I think people are sometimes meant to be together, and, maybe she wasn't meant for you. Maybe someone else is."

He watched me closely for a moment, and the silence felt deafening. "Anyone specific?"

I shrugged, hoping to not look so obvious. "Did you ever meet someone and just feel... instant connection?"

He rested his head back against the deep cushion of the couch. "Even if I did, I'd run a mile. What she put me through... I'm not going there again."

"I got my heart broken too," I replied. "I know what you mean, but... what if the right person, who'd never do that to you, was so close?"

"That night in the bowling alley. Something weird happened, didn't it?" Alex put the wine down on the table as he spoke.

"I don't want to sound crazy, you'll never speak to me again. But, yeah... it was like I could remember us being together, like I was remembering another time and place," I covered my face with a cushion and the rest came out muffled. "I can't believe I just said that out loud."

"I felt... something but... Ella. It's not you, I just..." He sighed deeply before he continued. "You're lovely and sweet, so beautiful even though you don't know it but... I just don't want to go through it all again."

I wanted to cry, but I knew I couldn't. He'd already think I was insane based on this conversation. I went to top our wine glasses up again as a distraction, but the second bottle was already empty.

I don't know why I'd let my mind conjure up all these potential outcomes for the night. Like he was going to realise he loved me as I offered him the last spring roll. I was pitiful, no wonder he didn't want me. This was never going to end with us tumbling into bed and living happily ever after.

"I'm going to head to bed, I left blankets and pillows behind the couch for you." I stood up slowly, the wine suddenly making me feel nauseous. Was it the wine, or his words?

"I didn't mean to upset you. I'm just trying to be honest.

It's why I avoid you at work, I don't want to get close, and I feel like to you... I would."

"Don't worry, you don't have to explain," I tried to sound breezy and bright, but my heart was aching, I could feel hope slowly dissolving within me. "Night, Alex."

"Night, Ella." I heard him say quietly as I closed my bedroom door and leaned back against it with a sigh.

My entire body felt restless and agitated as I tossed and turned in the bed, trying to force sleep that was impossible. Why had I got my hopes up? Why had I ever thought things would work out for me? All those images and feelings, it was just my stupid mind playing painful tricks and I was sick of it. So, so sick of it. Eventually I drifted into a jerky, angular sleep, not the softness that brings rest and healing.

Even whilst in slumber though, I couldn't escape him. I was remembering *that* life again, as ridiculous as it sounds to remember a life that wasn't even mine. But the happiness of it was just forcing a different reaction from me now. My fingers clenched into fists during my sleep as the anger hit me at the unfairness of everything, fury how I was stuck in this weak, pointless existence watching other people be happy. Always other people, and now to rub further salt into the wound, I'd been shown the happiest me imaginable and then had it snatched away. And he was right through that fucking wall.

I awoke with my face pressed hard into my pillow as I silently screamed, furious tears burning down my cheeks. But I didn't want him to know. I didn't ever want him to know what he was doing to me. He already thought me deranged from what I could gather, this would just be the icing on the cake. Sobbing like a heartbroken teenager over a memory that wasn't even mine.

The next few weeks were like a torture for me. A constant, spinning cycle. A sickening ride that I couldn't get off, it wouldn't stop, it wouldn't let me rest.

The first Ella was convinced that this had to be fought for, that we were meant to be together. It wouldn't matter how long it took or how hard it was to get him to trust me and realise that I wasn't like the others, I wouldn't hurt him. That Ella would spend her whole life working to achieve the goal of that happy place she'd seen. She was however completely eclipsed by the second Ella.

The second Ella felt as though her heart and soul had been cracked in two. I couldn't handle seeing him at work, it hurt so badly. Plus as much as he said he was too hurt for anybody, it didn't seem to stop him flirting with the sandwich girl every, single, lunchtime. I'd taken to walking around the park at that time to try and avoid the spectacle; it made the acid in my stomach bubble up and add to the poisonous thoughts that were brewing inside of me.

I hated him so much at times. Hot, angry tears ran down my face as I spent more time hidden in the toilets than at my desk. I began taking more and more days off sick. I hadn't exactly been enthusiastic about life to begin with but now, every day felt like a heavy drag, my thoughts were black and pulled me to the floor. I struggled to see an outcome where I'd be in the light again. I didn't want to see people, people made me feel worse. I didn't like being awake, but I was scared to sleep because those feelings – I can't even call them dreams because they weren't made up, they were real – those feelings flooded my mind and my senses. His touch, his smell, his very being.

In the end, I lost my job. I thought he might come to see me, check on me. For days I sat in my flat, all tidy, hair done, fake smile ready and waiting for him. But he never did show.

An infinite array of alternate realities, parallel universes, dreamscapes. An endless mingle of he and I together, in love, in some form or another. Why did I have to be living the one where he didn't want me? The one where I was rejected. The one that had the saddest ending imaginable.

ANEMOIA POEM

We met, in the wrong place and time
Distant, hurt, misaligned
I know there's meant to be more
Yet it can't exist in this current form
It's as though, when I look into your eyes
every parallel universe opens wide
just waiting for me to approach
and there's one I would run to
every single time -
It calls to me, like a soft lullaby

It's a time I've never lived through
A place I've never been
But I feel the warmth of it through my body
Your love buried deep within my bones
Instead of meeting those wrong people
the people who hurt us
taught us shame, regret and doubt
We simply met each other
Ignored everyone who said
we were too young, it wouldn't last

For we never needed the rest of the world
Not once we'd found each other
We lived had a life of perfect imperfectness
together
I grieve that I missed out on it all
By being in this space, this time
Because the me and you who exist there
are the luckiest creatures
Creation ever saw

The Anemoia I feel
Rages through me like a passion
I know, if we tried, we could feel it here
It would be harder,
so much harder
We both have pain and pasts
issues and scars
and half healed hearts
But you know …
maybe if we worked through all of that
The feeling at the end
when we were just us
Would dwarf every other feeling
from every other universe
Nobody would sense it but us
Like silent shockwaves
Taking our breath, leaving us speechless
but divinely blissful

So maybe…
this Anemoia hit me for a reason
To push me on
To not give up
Because the very best thing that could ever be
The place where my life was destined to lead -

It's worth every struggle
And if it ever gets too hard
I stop and close my eyes
Let that nostalgia fill my senses wide
And carry on, to you
To where our stars align

The Supermarket

It was almost beautiful fate
but we were in the wrong place,
the wrong time, the wrong state
Nevertheless
My soul knows yours
on this, I'm steadfast
Our connection wasn't forced
My heart misses yours
I need belief
that next time around
We... can be us...

Birthday Card Number One

If this precise moment
Was frozen in time
I'd love the world to see
How I made you mine

The Metro

The scent of you close
So near, yet so far
A simple memory, almost a ghost
I envy the darkness of the coffee
As it passes by your lips
The memory of your kisses
still burning at my skin

The Granny Flat

Our smiles, merged into a kiss
Eyes dark to the world
You pulled me close
Not knowing I was already
A fragment of your soul
Our double heartbeat
That tandem beating
Is it any wonder I lost myself?

Mediation

I loved you before I knew you
The first time my eyes
gazed upon your face
is engraved upon my heart
Round and round in aching circles
always missing the moment we needed
I would run that gauntlet forever
if it took my whole life
For one moment with you
I would forsake every other second

Graffiti

The endless loop of
you and I Lily
Together, anywhere
The world can see this one frozen moment
but only you and I can experience
this lack of air between us
Forevermore

Birthday Card Number Two

You are the best of me
and I, the best of you
We meet in the middle
like a brilliant burst of stars
so bright, that love itself would be blinded

The Cottage

You have simply
unwritten
everyone else who ever touched me
Your kiss became my first
completely new, and thrilling
So now I need
those lips to touch
every single cell of my being
So that you are the only one
to have ever known me this way
You have become
my past
my present
my future
No other hand will graze this skin
No other kiss will land upon me
Enraptured by your touch
Unwrite me, over and over

Croatia

Luke… you are the reason I exist
The love that draws each breath
You keep my blood flowing
You drive my dreams
You make life what it is
Magical and heartfelt
Sometimes, raw and painful
But I don't care
Because we are written in eternity
This moment has been destined
Here, under these stars
There's a reason I shiver at the very thought of you
We've been falling in love
Over and over
Since the beginning of time
In every existence
Through every reincarnation
And we'll never, ever stop
Our love will outlast everything

I was lost before you
As I stand here now
Know that you are more than my soulmate
You're my equal half
We are remnants of the same star
A star that burst into beautiful shards
So very long ago
But now, Lily, that stardust has pulled us back together
Completing the perfect puzzle that is us
We found each other
And nothing in the universe can pull us apart again
I want to get drunk

And chase storms together
Not know where we wake up
Be best friends and lovers
Fall over in the snow
Cook food, make a home
I want to laugh until we cry
And cry until we laugh
I just want everything to be you
You and I are one, eternally
The very definition of love

ABOUT THE AUTHOR

Nicola lives in North West England with her family. She has three daughters, and therefore will never be rich or sane, but does have a house full of hormones and hair bobbles!

Turning forty during lockdown spurred her to pursue her dream of writing. Once she began, she realised she couldn't stop!

Like her characters, she loves a glass of wine with her best friends, but sadly cannot walk in gorgeous, designer heels!

ALSO BY NICOLA LOWE

The Missed Kiss

To Kiss You Again

Romance, friendship, conflict, loyalty, lies and love were all part of an engaging, sentimental, and evocative read with the understanding of dilemmas of the heart we can all face.

The writing was exceptional with characters, descriptions, scenarios and emotions I could visualise in my head. This romance book demonstrates love isn't always easy, that sometimes we have to make difficult decisions and that love and loss can go hand in hand.

— AMAZON REVIEW

I loved this book and it's dramatic twists. The emotions run high and you're in those pages along for the ride with the totally relatable story and the characters. Get your feet up and get ready for a day of reading because you won't be able to put this book down!

— AMAZON REVIEW

The storyline was captivating, compelling and an emotional rollercoaster. I laughed and cried with Lily in equal parts. There were real tears because the way the story is written it was hard not to be swept away with the characters and all the emotion expressed.

— AMAZON REVIEW